THE LAST AUTUMN

The
Last
Autumn

by
Herbert Gutterson

WILLIAM MORROW
AND COMPANY
New York • 1958

C.2

© 1958 by Herbert Gutterson

Library of Congress Catalog Card No. 58–8004

For my mother

THE LAST AUTUMN

When young Tommy Conway leaped to his death on a school field trip, the masters knew it was his father's fault. Some of them wanted to tell Conway, but Kendrick refused—and time proved his wisdom.

1

FOLLENSBEE had no presentiment of disaster on this October morning. He was climbing "the Rock" with his Third Form science class as he had done annually for the past forty years. There was nothing different about this time, except that it was the last time for Follensbee, the last autumn of his teaching life. And in knowledge of this, perhaps, he looked a little longer at the New England hills today. In their flaming mantles of scarlet and gold they were striding nobly along the horizon beneath the agate blue of an Indian summer sky.

The boys were strung out all along the trail which began in the forest floor and ended abruptly on a pinnacle of granite beyond which the empty air eddied over a stony brook hundreds of feet below. Follensbee had lectured his class severely about the dangers inherent in the upper reaches of the Rock and had pointed out that the only reason for undertaking so potentially hazardous an expedition was to observe the remarkable changes that took place between the mossy, verdant base of this freakish little mountain and its bald stone summit. Grouped in a kicking, elbowing, whispering semicircle, the fourteen-year-old boys stared up at their teacher. Although he was a squat little man with white hair and a pink complexion, he reminded them somehow of a kindly-faced chipmunk as he chattered away in the nasal accents of his native New Hampshire. They listened and thought not, and when at last the interminable voice gave the signal, they stampeded for the trail with shouts of derision. Follensbee had always been grateful for the speed of their leave-taking. It was one of the things he liked most about teaching the Third Form. Some of the things that he didn't like but had learned to expect floated back to him from the thrashing in the underbrush on either side of the trail.

"Look out, boys. Here comes the Stinger."

"Don't let the Stinger get you."

"Hey, Stinger, kiss my butt."

Follensbee trudged along, taking his time and ignoring the voices although it flashed through his mind that the last one belonged to Jim Boucher, a fat, vulgar oaf who almost single-mouthedly had lowered the morals of the entire Form in his first month at boarding school. It had been another fat boy, Follensbee recalled, who had given him the nickname years ago when Carver had twenty-five students and four masters. As the newest member of the faculty and a bachelor besides, he had occupied the least desirable quarters in the school, a miserable little hole in the wall at one end of a noisy dormitory corridor. One night he had been correcting papers after lights and had removed one of his shoes to ease the pressure on an ingrown toenail when all at once he had heard the familiar thumping, bedspring squeaking of a wrestling match. Tired and exasperated beyond words, he had stormed out of his room and raced down the hall, wearing only one shoe and completely oblivious to the fact that in the tiny cubicles behind the closed doors alert ears followed his progress and small minds assumed from the sound that he was merely strolling by, unhurried and unaware. When he had burst in upon the sweating combatants on the mangled bed, they had stared at him, first with shocked surprise, then with dismay, and finally, noticing his feet, with angry disbelief. Johnson (or was it Johns-*ton*?), yes—Tim Johnston from Tulsa, Oklahoma had sat on the edge of the bed with his fat belly pinched into thick rolls over his straining pajama pants. He had cupped a hand over his mouth and turned to his roommate.

"Stung," he said.

"You fellows cut out this wrestling," Follensbee ordered.

"Yes, *sir*," Johnston said with an insolence that Follensbee had chosen to ignore. Then a slow smile spread across his face and once again his hand went up to his mouth.

"Stung by a Follens*bee*," he said in a choking whisper. Doubled up with laughter, both boys tumbled over backward on the bed.

"That will be two hours, Johnston!"

"But sir!"

Follensbee had closed the door firmly and without another word. Then, feeling both foolish and angry, he had removed the other shoe before hurrying back to his room, convinced that the punishment was just and the incident closed. The next day he had seen it with variations on every blackboard in school.

"Stinger teaches here."

"The Stinger stings again."

"That's no ringer, that's the Stinger!"

Follensbee stopped to wipe the moisture from the shiny pinkness of his forehead. Tim Johnston had died a few years after that in the forest of the Argonne, but the seed of his wit had produced a hardy perennial which had survived over the years at Carver. Follensbee had long since accepted the nickname as one of the certainties of the school year along with poison ivy and term reports.

Stooping to pick up a chunk of fluorescent mineral that had flashed for an instant beside the trail, he turned it slowly between his fingers, inspecting it with loving care. His thoughts, so rambling and reminiscent this morning, returned to the old days before it was necessary for schools to campaign for swimming pools and artificial ice rinks and the imposing buildings that sprang from the granite hearts of the hills and the plump pocketbooks of the alumni. Back in the old days, amid the stimulation of material deficiencies, there had been no well-stocked labs, and a good science man had been required to invent many of the tools of his trade and to visualize for his students beyond the limits of the paraphernalia at hand. And the boys in those days, it seemed to Follensbee, had been much more appreciative. When he had shown them an ancient tree or a dinosaur print in a slab of limestone, they had looked at these wonders of God's creation with proper reverence and respect. Not so today.

The boys of the second half of the twentieth century were not humbled by the grandeur of the design or the immensity of the concept that had envisioned the physical world. The majority of the class scrambling up the trail ahead of him now would look at a majestic tree and begin at once to figure how many feet of lumber it contained, how many houses, how many motel rooms. And when they first gazed upon a dinosaur print, they thought of comic-book monsters and they would argue fiercely among themselves as to how many machine-gun slugs would have been required to kill the beast. These kids of today were all problem solvers; they worshiped slide rules and automatic computers. They looked toward the heavens, seeking not to wonder and to praise but to conquer and to harness. To Follensbee there was something fundamentally wrong with this modern approach. In his heart he considered it sacrilegious.

But then he would remind himself that he must avoid the

pitfalls of generalities. Every now and then a boy would come along and upset his gloomy equation—a boy such as Tommy Conway, for example. There was a strange little fellow, very sensitive, very polite and gentle, very intelligent and very unhappy. Follensbee had been aware of the boy's unhappiness from the very first day, and one of the reasons for it had been obvious: the Rooming Committee with its gift for pairing strange bedfellows had placed Conway in a small double room with Boucher, his very antithesis. They had hoped, perhaps, that Conway's presence might dull the edges of his roommate's vulgarity; they might as well have expected a piece of pulp wood to discourage an ax. The two boys had simply ignored each other and looked elsewhere for more congenial spirits. Boucher had soon attracted a veritable entourage who followed him about and listened respectfully while he discoursed at length on the facts of life. Although many of his descriptions were fantastically inaccurate, Boucher did know certain specific things that little boys of his age were not supposed to know, and as a result his social success at Carver was assured.

Conway, on the other hand, appeared to have no friends and worse than that he didn't seem to want any. He was a slender, wiry child with enormous brown eyes in whose depths Follensbee had often seen a look which he didn't like and didn't understand. It would be there sometimes during class, a brilliant, glittering stare as though the boy were looking right through the blackboard at some distant treasure which was invisible to everyone else. His classmates had observed that unnerving stare, and being at a loss to account for his unfriendly aloofness, they had written him off as "that little queer" and made him an island in an unfriendly sea. Follensbee was worried about the boy. He had been intending to mention the matter to the headmaster and he should probably talk also with Alan Richards, Tommy's housemaster. Richards was young, impulsive, and in some ways too serious, the way the new men often were. He certainly hadn't learned to keep his mouth shut at faculty meetings. On the other hand, he was an extremely able teacher and the boys respected him. It was doubtful that Richards had managed to get close to Tommy Conway, but sometimes, of course, a boy came along whom none of them could reach.

Follensbee dropped the chunk of mineral into his shirt pocket and pushed along the trail which was steeper now as it wound up toward the timber line. The warm fingers of sunlight poking through the shriveled leaves were beginning to make him sweat inside his flannel shirt. He slowed his pace a little. They had waited for him up there in other years and they could wait again. When he arrived, they would be sprawled about in various attitudes of temporary exhaustion, and he would be able to direct their attention for a little while to the physical geography of the terrain spread out below them. He would not have to search for the words nor prepare them in advance. They would come to him with professional ease when he wanted them and after forty-two years of teaching they should come that way. He knew that they would just as easily leave his students' memories shortly after the next examination period. It was a measure of his professional qualifications that he could accept this fact now with none of the anger and the sense of futility that had once possessed him whenever he had come upon the crumpled notes of his classroom lectures, sealed with bubble gum and reposing in the wastebasket.

There were bits of paper scattered along the trail now. Candy wrappings mostly. Follensbee detested people who flung away their garbage. He straightened grimly and squinted ahead, making a mental note to have every one of those little outrages picked up on the return trip. Up where the trail left the thinning woods and crossed the first of the steep ledges that crowned the summit, he could see the Conway boy walking alone, head down, his hands thrust deep into the pockets of his windbreaker. An expensive camera with a genuine pigskin case and strap was dangling unheeded from his shoulder. The camera was a gift from his father. Mr. Conway had given his son a lot of things. He was good at giving things. They had come through the mail with monotonous regularity—the bicycle, the phonograph, the gold pen-and-pencil set, and now the camera. It wasn't a good idea to give a boy so many things and especially before he wanted them, but Tommy's father did not understand that. He should be told a few truths about youngsters, but from what Follensbee had heard, nobody could tell Roger Conway anything. And nobody would be inclined to, now that word had leaked out that the long-wished-for dormitory would soon become a reality, thanks to the generosity of Roger Conway, '27.

When Follensbee reached the ledge where he had seen the Conway boy, the sun hit him flush on the back of the neck and he felt suddenly tired and out of breath. Nearby there was a scooped-out place in the rock where the wind had eroded a natural seat. Follensbee hesitated and then sat down, pressing his back against the timeless rock, feeling some of the stiffness go out of his weary muscles. He was going to be late for class this morning, but he would be sixty-five two months from now and since he had been obliged to climb nearly half a mile to reach his classroom, perhaps his tardiness could be forgiven. He turned his face to the sun, and feeling relaxed and contented in its warmth, he let the past come flooding back and all at once he was thinking of the day he had met his wife.

His marriage to Emmy Southwaite had been the most wonderful event of his life. So many marriages these days, it seemed to him, ran out of delight in a few years. The lovers came down off the heights and trudged along the endless plains of habit or went their different ways. He and Emmy had never left the heights.

They had met as the result of a fantastic set of coincidences which their friends refused to believe. In the spring of his fourth year at Carver, Follensbee had attended a teachers' convention in Boston. He hadn't wanted to go at all, having planned a field trip along the Connecticut River for that week end, but he and Guy Evans, the junior members of the department, had flipped a coin to see who would have to go, and Follensbee had lost. All the way up in the hot, poky train he had sat restlessly, yearning to be out in the fresh air away from the soft coal dust which seemed to be oozing right through the grimy windows. At one point, unable to bear the stuffiness of the ancient day coach another minute, he had flung open a window, stuck his head out, and promptly caught a stinging cinder in his left eye. He had poked at it with a handkerchief for awhile and then tried futilely to dislodge it by pulling down his upper lid and rolling his eye in a bath of tears. Nothing had worked and he had arrived at the gloomy old South Station with a badly inflamed eye and a strong inclination to chuck the whole convention and escape into Connecticut.

Fate, he decided later, had then intervened in the form of a cabdriver who wore bifocals and who had hustled him knowingly across town to the eye clinic of the Massachusetts General Hospital. It was nearly noon by this time and the temperature had soared into the nineties. Follensbee, holding his handkerchief to his eye and perspiring uncomfortably, had been sitting in the waiting room about five minutes when the girl came in. He had noticed at once and with restrained amusement that she, too, was holding a handkerchief to her eye, but he had been more aware of her diminutive good looks and the assured, decisive way in which she had crossed the room to take the seat beside him. The fact that it was the only unoccupied seat in the room had not occurred to him at the time. He had felt that the girl welcomed his presence and wanted to talk to him. Under the circumstances, conversation had seemed quite proper and introductions had followed easily. Incredulously, Follensbee heard her say that she was heading for the same teachers' convention and that coming down from her home in Vermont on the train she had gotten a cinder in her eye.

"I don't believe it," he said.

The girl laughed. "No one ever will."

"Do you teach science?"

"No, English."

"That's better," Follensbee said. "Makes all this seem more real." He looked directly into her eyes and reddened.

Actually there had been nothing unreal about it nor about their departure a little while later, wearing dark glasses and laughing as they walked close together down the sidewalk. For Follensbee the day was no longer a chore to be accomplished; the Connecticut River had temporarily become a remote and uninteresting stream. He and Emmy were in love, they agreed later, before they even arrived at the convention.

From the beginning Emmy had shared many of his deepest convictions. When he had told her that he believed the average tree to be a nobler object than the average man, she had smilingly directed his attention to the poetry of the young Wordsworth. They both agreed that modern art was often confusion in the guise of profundity, and sitting on the beach one summer afternoon after their engagement had been announced, they came to the conclusion that broiled lobster in melted butter was the ultimate in food. That was the afternoon when in spite of their mutual New England reserve, they had talked about their desire for children. They were to have only one child, a son, and he was conceived on their honeymoon in September. A few weeks later Follensbee had proudly introduced his bride to the Carver faculty and to Dr. Parsons, who had registered unqualified astonishment and some disapproval when Follensbee had explained to him on the first day of school exactly why he would require larger quarters in June.

They had christened their son Peter Geoffrey Follensbee, and very early in his life they had known that they were unusually blessed. The boy had given their lives a new dimension and a new joy and when at length he had entered Carver and won almost every honor an undergraduate could attain, they had tried unsuccessfully to stifle their pride. His career at Harvard had been one of equal distinction and on the day after his graduation in 1942, he had gone off to join the navy with a bright smile and a casual parting wave of his hand. They had almost believed in his bland assurances that he would surely be stationed somewhere within the continental limits of the United States. But four months later two Japanese torpedoes sank a U.S. cruiser in the Coral Sea with the loss of nearly every life on board. The telegram about Ensign Follensbee had come a few days later, but it was months before the medal came.

They hated it at first because it insisted that they remember, but gradually Follensbee had wanted to teach again and there came a day when Emmy was able to take the medal and the photograph out of the bureau drawer and place them in the open. That had been fifteen years ago, but even now in the sunshine of another autumn day long afterwards Follensbee could recall the awful heaviness that had weighed upon his heart. Nothing, he knew, would ever completely dispel that feeling.

After that he had been more grateful than ever for Emmy.

As his retirement approached, she had kept him from becoming entirely disenchanted with his work. She understood his despair at times when confronted with the overwhelming indifference of young men, and she had taught him from her own experience that one good seed taking root in a youngster's mind was worth the hundred that he must sow in barren soil. But he was weary of it now; the routine of the years had become a yoke that no longer fitted easily and he yearned for June with all the pent-up anticipation of a Third Former.

The school would give him and Emmy a farewell dinner, of course. The occasion would begin with sherry at the headmaster's house and proceed to filet mignon and asparagus, followed by ice cream, coffee, and speeches. There would be a parting gift from the school, most likely a silver tray suitably engraved: *To Hugh Geoffrey Follensbee, Master of Science, 1916-1958*—Follensbee didn't know what the rest of it would say, but after all that time he wished they would give a man something he could eat, trade, or exchange for groceries. There would be something for Emmy, too, a "small token" equally well intentioned and equally inappropriate. The school wasn't to blame; nobody was to blame. It was part of the inherent absurdity of trying to say good-by to someone after forty-two years. And how could they be expected to know that Emmy wanted an overnight bag and he a leather case for his contour maps?

Follensbee smiled, blinking sleepily in the sunshine. One more minute of this was all he could allow himself. The shouts racketing down from above sounded perfectly normal, but it wouldn't do to leave those kids alone for very long. Well—a few hundred more papers and tests and reprimands and he would be done. It had been a good life, for the most part, and he wouldn't have really wanted to do anything else. He would tell them that at the dinner in June, and because he was no good at public speaking, he would be brief and unsentimental. He wasn't feeling sentimental, anyway. There was too much ahead for him and Emmy. They had planned their future together in exciting detail. Having lived most of their lives in a secluded and controlled environment, they wanted now to be as wandering and migratory as a couple of unfettered birds. They had already bought the trailer, tested it happily during the past summer, and parked it for the winter in the barn on his family's old homestead in New Hampshire. With the income from his annuity plus the social security checks and the sale of an occasional article, they could manage, cruising south in the winter and coming north with the spring. They would see all the trees of the land and the lakes and the mountains. They would take their time and go where they pleased and stay as long as they liked.

Follensbee sighed gently. No, it wasn't going to be difficult to say good-by. Carver could carry on very nicely without the services of Hugh Geoffrey Follensbee. There would still be plenty of others to carry on, men like Justin Kendrick who held more of the reins in his hands than anyone else at school. To the alumni, looking back over the years, Kendrick more or less *was* Carver. He had been there nearly as long as Follensbee, and when he left, he would have no wife to accompany him and no dream to seek beyond the campus gates. Carver was everything to Kendrick. Follensbee's chin dropped down on his chest and as he sat there in the warm sunshine, propped against the ledge and surrounded by memories, he fell fast asleep.

He was never sure what woke him up. It might have been some inner, automatic response to the strange and deathly quiet that suddenly prevailed at the summit of the Rock. More likely, it was the urgent pressure of Boucher's fingers prodding his shoulder.

"Mr. Follensbee—*Mr. Follensbee!*"

Follensbee opened his eyes and sat up. The sunburned cords in his neck tightened. "What is it?" he said. "What's the matter?"

Boucher's small, pig eyes were glazed; he was gasping for breath and as Follensbee stared up at him, the whole, unlovely face seemed to dissolve as the fat flesh wept. Boucher's voice was as hollow and toneless as a robot's.

"Tommy Conway jumped, sir."

2

JUSTIN KENDRICK'S office was in a small, ivy-smothered building that had once been the gatekeeper's cottage on a private estate. The boys had long since christened the cottage "The Powerhouse" because the headmaster and the dean also had their offices within the cold, stone walls. The latter had their titles stenciled on their doors, but as no one had been able to think of an all-inclusive title for Kendrick, his door was simply marked "Mr. Kendrick."

It would have been impossible to measure Kendrick's authority at Carver. There were only one or two men ahead of him in seniority, members of the original faculty, but Kendrick had been around so long and knew so much about everybody and everything connected with the school that he had a grip like an octopus on the place. His job was also without dimensions. Originally hired by Dr. Parsons to teach Latin, Kendrick had gradually worked his way out of the classroom and into a web of administrative duties that were inextricably tangled. Thus, in a normal hour at his desk, he might grant a week-end permission to a boy, arrange for a dance, write a letter to a worried parent, and tactfully suggest to the chef that there had been a little too much pepper in the mashed potatoes recently.

As far as the boys were concerned, Kendrick's office was like no other at Carver. It was both a court and a kind of church, a prisoner's dock and a beggar's stand, a place of laughter and a place of tears. Unholy confessions were made here and strange secrets were whispered to the man behind the desk. All manner of pacts, deals, arrangements and promises were made here. Only Kendrick knew the extent of this personal trust fund that had been bequeathed to him over the years by generations of Carver men, and except for an occasional slip after a few highballs, he had kept their secrets well. During the times that the headmaster was away on business, Kendrick held the reins officially; at all times he was the most feared and the most respected master on the campus. Kendrick's faculty colleagues and their wives treated him with a kind of wary cordiality. Some had for him a genuine affection; others had been trying for years to cut him down. Kendrick knew which were which.

Physically Kendrick was rather disappointing and his appearance belied his reputation. He was a large man whose heavy legs and thighs supported a pudgy frame. Kendrick was big all over, but it was the soft bigness of a muskmelon topped with thinning, sandy hair and having a small, uncertain mouth. His eyes had a greenish cast and his pale skin was peppered with tiny colonies of freckles. The effect of a soft body and a face that seemed to sag from its moorings was deceptive; on the inside Kendrick was neither flabby nor vulnerable. Now in his fifty-ninth year he could move with surprising, elephantine speed and his eyes had lost none of their shrewdness. Only a handful of men had looked into those eyes in moments when they were unguarded and too revealing. Kendrick always saw to it later that these intruders had reason to keep their mouths shut.

On this Saturday morning Kendrick as usual had his finger squarely on Carver's pulse. All around him like a smoothly integrated machine the school was functioning under the implacable domination of the master clock, an IBM electrical wizard which rang bells all over the campus at precisely the same instant. On Kendrick's desk his secretary had placed a schedule of the week end's activities, headed by the Harland football game. Harland was for Carver a major rival as Andover was for Exeter, Choate for Deerfield, Taft for Hotchkiss. The boys were always excited before the Harland game which was to be at home this year. All week long the tension had been mounting and last night it had culminated in a gigantic rally and torchlight parade that had almost literally set the campus aflame. As Kendrick was making a note now to have a parking space roped off for the cars of Harland rooters, his telephone rang. When he picked up the receiver, the school operator informed him that she had a collect call from Mr. Follensbee. Kendrick's eyes narrowed. He glanced through the doorway, knowing already that something was wrong, wondering how bad it would be.

"Put him on," he said into the telephone. And then in a low voice, "Go ahead, Hugh."

Kendrick listened for several minutes, issued some quick, incisive instructions, and then hung up. After glancing into the hall again, he closed and locked his office door. His lower lip was trembling as it always did when he was under stress, but his eyes were alert and resourceful. He picked up the telephone.

"Get me the headmaster, Mrs. Henry."

"Mr. Pettengill is addressing a PTA group in Boston this morning, Mr. Kendrick."

"I know," Kendrick said. "I don't care where he is. Get a message to him. Ask him to call me right away."

"I'll try, sir, but I don't think they will let me disturb him unless this is an emergency—"

"This *is* an emergency," Kendrick cut in sharply. It occurred to him that Mrs. Henry was up to her old tricks again. As usual, she had probably eavesdropped on his conversation and she knew exactly what had happened. She was simply using this pretense of innocence to convince him of her integrity as a telephone operator. Mrs. Henry was an old fraud, but she would try to raise the dead if she had a connection to make.

"Before you try Boston," Kendrick said, "will you get me Dr. Whelden at the infirmary?"

"Whelden," said a laconic voice a moment later.

"Sam, are you in the middle of something?"

"To tell the truth, Justin, I was about to attack one of the nurses."

Ordinarily Kendrick would have laughed but he didn't now. "Sam," he said, bending close to the phone, "Tommy Conway was killed about an hour ago."

There was a long silence at the other end of the wire before the doctor said, "What happened?"

"I don't know much yet," Kendrick said. "He was on Follensbee's field trip. You know—they climb the Rock. Apparently Tommy lost his footing at the summit. It's a sheer drop from there."

Another silence ensued, and Kendrick could picture Sam Whelden glowering at the telephone. The school doctor was a heavy-set man whose bulldog scowl was on the outside only. Underneath his rough exterior the boys were quick to recognize one of the softest hearts on the faculty.

"I've been worried about that boy, Justin. He came in here several times recently. We gave him a basal metabolism test the other day which didn't show anything, but he was very depressed. It passed through my mind that I ought to order a psychiatric evaluation on him. I wish to hell I had now."

"Well, accidents—"

"I'm not so sure it was an accident. That boy was in a very unhealthy state of mind."

A slight flush had crept into Kendrick's face. "Now look, Sam," he said. "Follensbee told me something about the boy having jumped, but we have no proof of that and I'm sure you'll agree that we've got to be careful about any statements like that. You know his father, of course?"

"Can't say I do."

"Roger Conway, Class of '27."

"Oh, *that* Conway."

"Exactly."

Whelden whistled softly. "I see your point. I guess I'd better get on out there."

"I wish you would," Kendrick said. "I told Follensbee not to move the body until you got there. You may have a few hysterical little boys to treat and you'd better make sure that Hugh is in good enough shape to drive home. I've got a call in for Mr. Conway, but I want to get in touch with the Head first. What shall we do with—?"

"Well, I can't do anything until the medical examiner arrives."

"Do you have to notify him?"

"It's the law."

"I wish you didn't."

"Can't be avoided, Justin."

"Then what?"

"I'd better get in touch with Mosher. We aren't set up properly to keep him at the infirmary. There can be no criticism if we use the funeral home."

"Will there have to be an inquest or anything?"

"Not if the medical examiner reports it as due to natural causes."

"Well, I guess you'd better go ahead then, Sam."

"Where is Hugh now?"

"He called from a farmhouse. It's near the junction where you leave the main highway beyond the quarry. You'll probably see the school station wagon parked there."

"Right."

"And, Sam?"

"Yes?"

"Will you check his clothing carefully? Pockets and everything. I want to know if there is any evidence that he—"

"So do I, Justin. You just leave it to me."

"I'll call you later," Kendrick said and hung up.

For several minutes after that he sat back in his chair and stared thoughtfully at the cat's-eye ring on the little finger of his left hand. Someone would have to contact Roger Conway very soon. There wouldn't be any excuse for waiting much longer. Kendrick knew what was going to happen after that and he needed a little more time to prepare for it. Mrs. Henry interrupted his deliberations.

"They said they'd give your message to Mr. Pettengill right away, sir."

"All right," Kendrick said brusquely. Then he added in a kindlier tone, "Good work, Mrs. Henry." He could almost see the complacent smile on her homely face.

He stood up and moved to the window. All over the campus the small, unmilitary phalanxes were forming and marching off to the next class. There were several buildings out there now, but Kendrick could remember when there had been nothing but a patch of woods and a small carriage trail winding off between the trees to the private mansion which had become Carver's main building. The boys still lived and worked and played for the most part in converted structures of one sort or another. Carver was a small school, struggling for a place in the academic sun, working to cut into the reputation of the big boys like Andover and Exeter and Lawrenceville which had endowments to keep tuitions down and the cash to put new buildings up. Carver had managed to add a few new buildings to its modest plant, and wherever Kendrick surveyed them from his office window, he was like a man counting his treasure.

They were to a large extent *his* buildings. He had fought for them over the years in one way or another as he had dreamed, worried, pushed and manipulated much of Carver into existence. He still walked with a dream in his head. It was a dream of more buildings, more scholarships, more endowment, more of everything that would help make Carver the top boarding school in the country. Kendrick considered himself an idealist, but his idealism had a very practical core. He believed that the mind had to be nurtured but so did the body that housed the mind. A school was an institution dedicated to higher learning and the search for understanding; it was also a corporation with a budget to meet. "We need ideals," Kendrick had said on more than one occasion, "and we need cash. About fifty-fifty."

He knew that some of the old-guard trustees had been shocked by this mundane view of the task ahead, but they were a bunch of old ostriches with their heads in the sands of the past when Mark Hopkins sat on one end of a log and his student on the other. You had to provide a little more equipment than that nowadays. Dr. Parsons, who had preceded Ken Pettengill as headmaster, had gone on to the end accusing Kendrick of being a rank materialist and had loudly proclaimed that great schools resulted from great teaching. Nobody, Kendrick included, was going to argue that, but Kendrick also believed that great teachers by and large did rather better on a full stomach and with a few of the material comforts.

The old man hadn't wanted to bother with such things. He had liked to keep his masters teaching in the morning, coaching in the afternoon, and counseling in the evening in their modest cubbyholes from which, after a few hours of rest, they hurried forth into the Spartan dawn to labor in their chalky vineyards once again. A master had sold himself body and mind in those days, and Dr. Parsons had not been loath to take an extra hour or so in faculty meetings to discourse upon the importance of getting to know the boys. At the drop of a mortarboard he would talk on his favorite topics: "The Dedicated Master," "Motivating Boys," "The Spirit of Carver," and anything else that might pop into his large and roomy head.

Over the years people who didn't know claimed that Dr. Parsons had acquired new buildings and equipment in the effortless way a dog acquires fleas. They were only partly right. Dr. Parsons had remained at ease in his windy, pedantic tower while Kendrick, climbing rapidly through the faculty ranks, had badgered alumni, sought out philanthropists and never missed a chance to pursue a likely donor. All the successful schools had their Tafts, their Fords, their Mellons, but Kendrick had never run into anyone who might give on that scale until Roger Conway had come back to Carver. Kendrick had had his eye on him almost from the first time they had met and for years he had regarded Conway as a kind of long-term investment, one that until this morning had seemed almost certain to pay off handsomely.

He had last seen Conway about a month ago during the opening days of school. Towing his son in his explosive wake, Conway had kept an appointment with the dean and afterwards charged into Kendrick's office like an angry steer.

"What's the matter with those people in the dean's office?" he had shouted. He was red-faced and scowling.

"Sit down, Roger," Kendrick had said. Then he had smiled at the boy who had looked a bit peaked. "How are you, Tommy?"

"Fine, sir."

"They want him to take Spanish!" Conway had brought his big fist down on the edge of the desk. "I want him to take French."

"They probably have their reasons, Roger."

"Sure they do. They gave me a lot of crap about language aptitudes. They aren't too strong, according to them, and Spanish would be easier for him. What do they mean 'not too strong'? I never had any trouble with French."

"We aren't all the same," Kendrick had said gently. "Even fathers and sons." He had looked at the boy again. "Which would you—?"

"Never mind about that," Conway had cut in harshly. "I know what's best for him. He can do French just as well as the next guy. There's nothing a man can't do if he sets his mind to it. I learned *that* from experience."

Kendrick was thinking that Conway hadn't really learned anything. He was just the same as he had been thirty years ago, bullnecked, assertive, stubborn, and filled with that blind, terrible pride which could not for a moment admit defeat of any sort. Kendrick had felt sorry for the boy with his big eyes and sensitive, almost delicate face. Strange flower from so tough a weed, he thought, and put his arm around the thin shoulders.

"We'll work things out," he said. He smiled at the boy again and tightened the pressure of his fingers until he felt the sudden, instinctive resistance. Pretending not to have noticed, he withdrew his hand and glanced up at Roger Conway. "I'm sure we can."

There was an odd look in Conway's eyes. "You haven't changed a bit, Justin." Kendrick stiffened and then abruptly Conway had laughed. "Same old God-damned diplomat, aren't you?"

"I have to be," Kendrick said.

And in the end his diplomacy had won, although there was an ironical twist to it. Almost from the start Tommy had done badly in Spanish as he had in most of his subjects. No doubt Conway would hold that against the school, too.

Kendrick rose and began to pace up and down again, his small mouth pursed in concentration. Conway wasn't going to be so easy to handle this time. His rage would be terrible and for reasons that no one except Kendrick would understand. Certainly the headmaster wouldn't understand it. He had never liked Conway anyway, his roughness, his lack of breeding, his driving, aggressive, uncontemplative approach to everything. Ken Pettengill was a sensitive, scholarly man, a little too aware of his impeccable background; Conway was of a tougher breed and he drew much of his power from a basic fear that he had never acknowledged. He would not for a moment entertain the possibility that his son had committed suicide. Any explanation like that would be intolerable for him.

Kendrick shook his head. Where had Follensbee been this morning when it happened? What had he been doing? Conway would insist, of course, that it had been an accident. There was no telling what he was going to demand. He might charge them with criminal negligence; he might even withdraw his support of Carver. Kendrick's lip quivered and his pudgy bulk seemed to sway from an invisible blow. From his window he could see the very spot where the new dormitory would begin to rise any day now and beyond it the Carver School of the future of which he had never ceased to dream. It could stand out there in reality, all of it someday, unless they lost it now because they could not handle a man like Roger Conway.

Kendrick swung into action. He had better have a talk with Alan Richards, preferably before Follensbee returned. Then there were the boys in Follensbee's class; he could pretty well make sure that they didn't talk. He would see them, too, before lunch. Matter of fact, he had better make an announcement to the whole school at lunchtime. Tell them it was an accident, of course, an unavoidable accident. Try to get them back into stride again. Remind them of the big game with Harland this afternoon. Then—

The knock on the door startled Kendrick. When he opened it, a red-haired boy said, "Sorry to bother you, sir, but where's the doctor going?"

"Where are *you* going, Mahoney?"

Mahoney grinned. "To the library, sir. I was just down at the infirmary and I saw the Doc driving off in the ambulance. I thought maybe somebody had appendicitis."

"Somebody does," Kendrick said, "but not around here. Suppose you just let Dr. Whelden go about his business and you go about yours."

"Okay, sir," Mahoney said and started off. Then he looked back over his shoulder. "But you can't tell me he was just going out for a ride, sir."

"I'll have something else to tell you," Kendrick said, "if you're not in the library in ten seconds."

Observing Mahoney's hasty departure, Kendrick thought to himself that the boys never missed anything at Carver but their lessons. His secretary came in a moment later.

"Something's come up," he told her. "I'll have to go out in a little while. If anybody calls, just ask them to leave a message."

"Yes, Mr. Kendrick."

"And would you get a note right off to Mr. Richards. Have

a boy take it to him. Tell him I'd like to see him here after his last class."

Grateful for her competence, he smiled at her and locked his office door again. He had better call Conway himself. He was approaching the telephone when its sudden ringing startled him. Picking up the receiver, he heard Mrs. Henry say with a note of triumph,

"I have the headmaster for you, Mr. Kendrick."

3

FROM the moment she had seen the blue and gold sky outside her window Nancy Richards had been unable to face the thought of housework. Right after breakfast she had bundled the baby into his pram and set out for a walk along the well-clipped paths of the Carver campus. She planned to skirt the football and soccer fields and climb the hill on one of the pine-needled trails that led into the woods and the open country beyond. It would be warm and sunny up there.

The baby was lying back against his pillows, staring with wonder at the passing world. Nancy smiled down at him, the wide, lovely smile that the boys admired, and seeing how much he resembled his father already, she felt a sudden, sharp delight. Then she straightened and her gaze swung toward the ancient classroom building where Alan was teaching in one of the chem labs. She could faintly discern the venerable stone gargoyles which guarded the entrance to the hideous old mansion. She stared at it for a moment, thinking of her tall, handsome husband and of how much she loved him. Now, with the birth of their son, their contentment should have been complete, but one nagging, uneasy doubt persisted to flaw their happiness.

The trouble was not in their personal relationship which from the beginning had been gay and passionate and mutually rewarding, but rather in Alan's attitude toward his job. He was twenty-seven and he had been teaching nearly four years now at Carver without the certain conviction that this was the work he wanted to do. A part of him was still intrigued by the opportunities and inducements of the business world. Even before he had graduated from Cornell with highest honors in chemistry, he had received astonishing offers from the big industrial concerns who beat the campus underbrush every spring in search of young, ambitious talent. Tucked underneath a pile of chemistry outlines in his desk drawer, Alan had right now a proposition from a firm of chemical consultants whose terms were fantastically generous. Five or ten years with them, as he had pointed out to her, would give him the experience and the contacts to set up an office of his own. Meanwhile, they would have their own home with a genuine privacy where discretion would no longer have to be the order of the day and of the night, too. They could see their friends on a year-round basis and not be limited so much of the time to a small faculty circle. And Alan would be free to accept the challenge of a competitive society where his professional talents would reap the financial rewards they deserved.

And yet she had been growing more and more convinced lately that Alan did't really care so much about financial rewards and would quite happily give them up if he could have something else. That something, as nearly as she could tell, was a certain basic satisfaction which other teachers derived from the profession but which Alan had somehow missed. This fact was the more surprising because on the surface there appeared to be no reason for it. Alan's love for science was almost poetic in its intensity, and his persistent, uncompromising search for truth in all its manifestations was in the nature of a religious act for him. She knew that he taught with great thoroughness and with the highest standards, demanding, she often thought, far too much of his students. He was deeply concerned over the welfare of the boys in his charge; he could worry in the morning about a boy's chemistry grades and be just as anxious about his progress as a fullback in the afternoon. In his spare time he liked to tinker in the lab for the fun of it and he usually had some intriguing project under way in which some of his more serious students were delighted to join.

All that was fine. The boys were impressed by his industry and they had an enormous respect for his skill. They did not, however, quite trust him with their friendship. More accurately, she suspected that they despaired of achieving his approval. And it was true that in his towering standards for himself as well as for others, in his absolute refusal to tolerate anything that was undertaken halfheartedly, Alan often made too little allowance for human weakness. Sometimes he smothered an incipient friendship by rushing too eagerly into a boy's life instead of sitting back and letting the boy come to him, the way some of the older masters did. Once or twice she had thought that he was aware of his failure here and of what was missing in their life at Carver. At other times he had seemed merely to be exasperated with the boys and their unconcern with the things he cared most about. She could remember how his body had suddenly tensed when they had been lying in bed together a few nights ago.

"I don't know, honey," he had said wearily, "maybe I'm just wasting my time around here. I'm talking every day to a bunch of kids who don't care enough. What am I doing it for?"

She had not been able to answer him then or since. Other men had faced this indifference and found a justification for their efforts, men like Hugh Follensbee whom Alan admired so much. She was still hoping that Alan would learn something from Hugh and that he would find the work that was right for him and know that he had found it. Meanwhile, last night when she had brought him a cup of coffee at his cluttered desk, he had been reading the letter again from that New York firm. Seeing the troubled look in his eyes, she had felt her uneasiness stirring once more.

She turned away from the classroom building now and resumed her walk, pushing the pram along slowly in the sunshine and looking up every now and then into the serene blue depths of the sky. It was impossible not to be thankful on such a morning as this. Her attention was abruptly distracted by the ambulance which was just coming out of the infirmary driveway. Dr. Whelden was riding in the front seat beside the driver. He waved to her in his casual way as they passed. To her surprise, the ambulance was not heading toward the hospital but out into the country. She watched in astonishment until it disappeared over the hill. Instinctively she glanced down at the baby, but he was chewing happily on his new mittens.

She was still wondering where Dr. Whelden could be going at this hour of the morning when she caught sight of Emmy Follensbee walking along one of the paths in her brisk, energetic way. Nancy waved and hurried to catch up, deciding on the spur of the moment to invite Emmy and Hugh to dinner. This was the Follensbees' last year at Carver and people weren't paying much attention to them any more.

"Take your time, my dear," Emmy called out, "or that poor child is going to be sick."

Nancy smiled, thinking how much she was going to miss

Emmy Follensbee. As everyone knew, she was one of the few wives at Carver who were completely devoid of malice, a dark-eyed, gray-haired little lady who was sweet, gentle, and kind to everyone. For Nancy, especially during her first year at the school, Emmy had often been a source of advice and comfort with her special blend of humor and wisdom.

"Hello," Nancy said warmly. "Am I keeping you from something?"

"Only my housework," Emmy said with a smile. "I've just been to the post office to mail a letter that Hugh was anxious to get off. He didn't have time to mail it himself this morning."

"I've been intending to call you," Nancy said. "We want you and Hugh to come to dinner next week."

Emmy was surprised and obviously pleased. "That's very sweet of you, dear, but are you sure you want to spend the evening with a couple of fogeys like us?"

"Of course we do," Nancy said. Then she caught herself and blushed. "I mean, we don't think of you that way."

Emmy's eyes were twinkling. She reached out and patted Nancy's arm. "I'm sure you do, but you're too nice to say so. I'd love to come but I'll have to ask Hugh. Make him think he's being consulted anyway."

"Would Tuesday be all right for you?"

"That would be fine. I don't think Hugh's on duty that night. By the way, he's a great admirer of yours, you know. He's always saying to me, 'Now there's a girl with *manners.*'"

Nancy made a disparaging gesture, but she knew the compliment was sincere. "And I think he's wonderful," she said.

Emmy was looking toward the distant hills. "He's out there this morning with a dozen little boys climbing that terribly steep mountain because he says it's very 'interesting.' I can imagine how interested the boys are in mesozoic formations."

"So that's where—" Nancy began and then stopped, grateful that Emmy was absorbed in her admiration of the baby. Where else could the ambulance have been going? Hugh Follensbee or one of the boys must be in some sort of trouble. Hugh was too old to be trudging up a mountain with a pack of yelling kids to worry about. She remembered all of a sudden that two of the boys in the house, Jim Boucher and Tommy Conway, had been talking to Alan last night about the field trip today. Tommy certainly wasn't the type to cause any trouble, but she wouldn't trust that bold little Boucher boy around the corner.

"Such a healthy-looking baby," Emmy said.

"Thank you." Nancy smiled. "He eats everything, including his mittens."

Emmy continued to look down at the child and for a moment the longing in her eyes was plain to see. "How wonderful," she said, "to have a strong, healthy baby who will grow up to be a fine young man someday."

Nancy felt her heart go out to the older woman, who could so easily have spoken of another young man destined to lie forever in the depths of the South Pacific. She wondered if she shouldn't try to prepare Emmy to some extent for the shock that might come with the returning ambulance, but then it occurred to her that she might only provoke several hours of needless anxiety. She freed the pram's brake with her toe.

"I thought I'd take a short walk," she said. "Would you like to come?"

"Yes," Emmy said. She gave a little laugh. "Even if I haven't made the beds this morning." She lifted her face to the sunshine. "It's such a lovely day. And what a beautiful spot this is!"

Nancy looked down at the village crouching in the heart of the New England hills. Everything sparkled today with the swept-clean look of autumn. It was one of the times when the campus was at its best and she loved it most. And there were other times when the familiar buildings, so brightly lit on snowy evenings, so quiet in the summertime, gave her such a feeling of warmth and permanence that she had no desire ever to leave this place.

"I guess I'm looking at things a little more carefully this fall," Emmy said with her slow, sweet smile as they began to walk along together. "Hugh and I can't quite believe we won't be seeing them again."

"But of course you will."

"I mean as faculty undergraduates, you might say. But we have much to look forward to in retirement and much to be thankful for."

They crossed the main road and as they passed the varsity football field, they saw two of the school's workmen putting fresh lime on the yard lines. The team manager, a skinny boy with a sallow complexion, was staggering out from the gym under a load of blankets which he would drape ceremoniously over the back of the benches. In a little while the visiting team would arrive in its formidable bus, the stands would fill, and the Carver band would come swinging down the field as autumn leaves scampered on the wind and footballs went spiraling through the dusk. Autumn was the best time, the time when the lush stupor of summer departed and the blood tingled again; birds winged south and fat pumpkins smiled in the amber fields. Autumn was the artist's time of melancholy and fulfillment; it was everybody's time for the counting of blessings, for thanksgiving and stuffed turkey delight. Even William Eliot, staring round-eyed from his pram, had a sudden, inexplicable urge to rejoice. He threw back his head and laughed at the sunshine.

From a distance the woods were a blanket of reds and yellows stitched with the white threads of slender birches and the dark beauty of the ubiquitous evergreens. The pine-needled trail was soft underfoot, and through the dry, crackling leaves that had drifted together they could glimpse a squirrel every now and then, hustling to stock his winter larder. Emmy took a deep breath of the mountain air and when she spoke there was nostalgia in her voice again.

"I envy you and Alan just starting in, having it all before you."

Nancy hesitated. She had already learned from unhappy experience that she could not safely confide in some of the wives at Carver, the ones who sat over their coffee cups each morning, endlessly brewing the latest campus gossip. Let a secret decision be reached in the headmaster's office and they would hear about it; let a wife conceive and they would be the first to know. They kept their ferocious little daggers always handy to stab the unwary and cut down the secure. It was different with Emmy who was somehow delightfully free of the petty need to compete. And so after a moment to find the right words, Nancy spoke freely of her misgivings and of her husband's uncertainty about his future. "Was Hugh," she concluded, "always sure that he wanted to teach?"

Emmy glanced over at the pretty brown-eyed girl beside her and for a moment she looked rather startled. "I don't know, my dear. I guess he was. But there were times, I remember well, when we were both discouraged. Some of the boys made things awfully difficult for Hugh. I could have wrung their dirty little necks. And during our first two years we lived in that stuffy old apartment on the top floor of Baxter."

"Where the Caswells are now?"

"That's right, but it didn't even have a kitchenette in those days. I had to put a board over the bathtub and cook on a hot plate if we wanted to entertain anyone. The youngest boys in school were rooming up there and they made a dreadful racket, sometimes just to annoy us, I'm sure. Our son was a baby then and you know he slept right through it all. I don't think we could have stood it if he hadn't."

"We're lucky," Nancy said, "to have one of the better apartments. I'm certainly not complaining about that. I asked you about Hugh because, frankly, Alan isn't at all sure that he wants to stay in teaching. I wouldn't want anyone else to know that."

"Of course not, dear. You can trust me."

"I know," Nancy said. She gave Emmy a grateful smile. "Alan can have a good business job immediately if he wants to take it, but I have a feeling he would wish he were back here." She frowned, trying to form the words that would state her thoughts exactly. "I wouldn't say that Alan was a popular teacher; he's respected by the boys, but there is some reward from the profession that he needs but doesn't get. It's as though he expects too much or wants to do too much. The boys won't let him, if you know what I mean, and that makes him feel defeated."

Emmy nodded. "I know so well what you mean, dear. It's been very much like that for Hugh. All his life he has wanted to give of his learning and his experience, and the boys have not appreciated the extent of the gift he had for them. Not at the time, anyway. Many of them do later."

"Later?"

"Yes. It's a wonderful thing, really. Hugh has never quite been able to communicate with the boys, you know. I mean, on a personal basis, away from the classroom. He's shy and the boys mistake it for aloofness because he doesn't know how to put them at their ease. But later they begin to understand what he is really like and they come back. I'm sure this happens to lots of teachers. You return to your house one afternoon and find one of your former students sitting in your living room. There isn't any reason for his coming back to see you; he just turns up one day and finds out where you are living now and you discover him sitting there waiting for you, looking sort of ridiculous somehow with a cigarette in his hand. They always have that cigarette. He's older, a little more poised but essentially the same, and while you struggle in a little panic to recall his name, you find to your amazement that he seems to regard you as an old friend. I've seen them talk to Hugh by the hour as though they had never given him a bit of trouble in class, as though all those marks, the punishments and all the rest of it had really happened to somebody else whom they can laugh about now. They smoke their cigarettes and sometimes they even have a drink with us, but in spite of it all, the teacher-student relationship persists in some ways. I've heard men in their forties sit there in our living room and call Hugh "sir" just as they did when they were here. But the main thing, of course, the good thing is that they do come back. It is both their apology and their thanks and although they don't realize it, of course, it means an awful lot to us." She shook her head. "Goodness, I didn't mean to rattle on so much."

"It helps to hear things like that," Nancy said. "I just hope that some of the boys come back to see Alan."

"They will," Emmy said. "Tell Alan not to give up teaching too quickly. Perhaps he hasn't quite settled in yet. Tell him not to be discouraged."

"Settled in," Nancy said. "That's it. He's always threatening to leave."

Emmy smiled. "Don't be fooled by that, dear. It's one of the marks of the profession. Teachers all have their islands somewhere."

"Islands?"

"Yes, figuratively speaking. The islands are the places to which they are going to escape next year. They've all got some place in mind. It may actually be an island or it may be a cabin in the mountains or a shack by the sea. It's always a place where they are going to live on nothing. They plan to become writers or bartenders or go into vague, attractive partnerships with kindred rebellious spirits. You hear them talk most about it just before vacations when they are most fed up." She smiled. "Go along with them, dear. Figuratively speaking, of course. Nine out of ten of them never really go to those islands. They'd be bored to death inside of a month."

Nancy laughed and then she leaned down to tuck the blanket around the baby. She was feeling better now, more certain in her own mind that Alan should resist the temptation to look for greener fields elsewhere, at least for the time being. She glanced ahead and saw that the trail had gradually come full circle so that they were once again on the ridge above the football field. The white lime stripes made vivid patterns in the sunlight and over behind the Harland bleachers several of the school workmen were roping off a parking space.

"How busy they all are down there," Emmy said. "I remember the first time I came up here. I guess we had only been at school two or three days. Hugh brought me up here so that I could 'see the school' as he put it. I have to laugh now because there was almost nothing down there to see but more woods. Just the main building and the headmaster's cottage which is the office now. We went down there and had tea with Dr. Parsons. I don't think he approved of me. I had only been married a month and I already knew that I was going to have a baby. Dr. Parsons couldn't tell, of course, at that point, but I think he sensed that I was secretly proud of myself and perhaps he guessed. Hugh felt that it was his duty to tell him before anyone else knew about it. I'm sure Dr.

Parsons was rather put out because it meant giving us a bigger apartment."

Nancy laughed. "Oh Emmy," she said, "how delightful. Did he really feel that way?"

"I'm sure he did."

"He must have been quite a 'character' as the boys say."

"He certainly was. And he knew everything there was to know about the school, too, and all the people in it."

"You mean the way Justin Kendrick does?"

"Yes, but in a different way. Justin is cool, shrewd, amazingly effective and sometimes I think just a tiny bit unscrupulous, although I don't for a minute question his loyalty to Carver. Dr. Parsons just sort of bumbled along in a hearty way. He always reminded me a little of Scrooge on the morning after."

"Somebody told me he carried around a big bunch of keys."

"That's right. And he used them, too. He was always poking into storerooms and locker rooms and basements and sometimes, Hugh told me, he would walk right into a class without warning and more or less take it over."

"Weren't the masters furious with him?"

"Yes, at times, but many of them thought he was the greatest man in the world. Of course, as he grew older he couldn't do much and had to delegate a lot of his work. Mostly to Justin."

Nancy paused for a moment, observing that Emmy was a little out of breath. The baby was stirring and soon he would demand his lunch in no uncertain terms.

"You know," she said, "from all I've heard about Justin, it seems strange that he didn't become headmaster after Dr. Parsons retired."

"I know," Emmy agreed. "A lot of us wondered about that

but there were probably many reasons. I don't think that Dr. Parsons really wanted him."

"But hadn't he more or less trained him?"

"That's true, but you see Dr. Parsons never wanted to retire and when he finally had to, between you and me, I think he was determined to keep his finger in the pie as much as possible. Under the circumstances, he didn't want his successor to know as much about the school as Justin did. He preferred someone who would be inclined to seek his help and he knew that Justin wouldn't need it and wouldn't want it."

"But didn't the trustees have anything to say about it?"

"Yes, but as most of them had been hand-picked by Dr. Parsons, they naturally went along with his choice. Also I have an idea they were a little afraid of Justin."

"I wouldn't have thought that," Nancy said. "In what way?"

"Well, this is just my opinion, dear, you understand, but I have always felt that Dr. Parsons was afraid that Justin would outmaneuver him in some way. And then, of course, we are often afraid of what we don't understand. Justin is a very complex man. There has always been gossip about him."

"I know," Nancy said.

"Hugh and I have kept out of it. It's not our business." With a wave of her hand she seemed to brush the whole conversation aside. "I really must go home now, dear, and make those beds before Hugh gets back. He'll be tired and I'll try to make him take a nap." She smiled. "It's his last trip up that precious mountain of his, thank goodness."

"Thank you for the walk," Nancy said. "I enjoyed it."

"So did I, my dear. I'll call you about Tuesday night but I'm sure Hugh will love to come."

Nancy lingered for a little while in the sunshine on the

edge of the hill. It was good to have had that chat with Emmy Follensbee and she was grateful all over again for their friendship. Little Bill was grimacing and as he gave the first of his clarion calls for food, she saw off in the distance one of the boys running across the campus. He looked as though he might be carrying a message and she wondered where he was going.

4

THE COLUMNS of symbols marching across the blackboard had been added up, the equation solved, the work done. Ten minutes remained in the period, and Alan Richards knew that the class was hoping to sidetrack him before he gave them another problem.

He sat on the edge of the desk, dangling his legs comfortably, scanning the fourteen faces turned up to him. The fifteenth face belonged to Larry Connors and he was busily engaged in scratching a girl's initials into his desk top. Alan wasn't getting anywhere with Connors and he knew it. The boy had a good mind but for some mysterious reason he chose to use it as little as possible. Connors had excellent aptitudes, but he coasted along with average grades. Nobody knew why, and several faculty members had done their best to find out with no success. The headmaster wrote his parents that Larry was "not properly motivated" and that he "lacked determination." Alan's own exasperation with the boy was only a shade less keen than his desire to see behind the mask which Connors presented to the world. Alan looked straight at him now.

"What are you doing, Larry?"

Larry looked up blankly. "Nothing, sir."

"Carving her initials there won't make her like you any better."

The class burst into laughter. Once in a while Mr. Richards broke down and cracked a joke. Nothing so became a master.

"I suggest you write her a letter," Alan continued. "It's easier to mail than a desk top."

There was more laughter. Mr. Richards certainly was in a good mood. Most of the time you couldn't get him off the subject, even for a minute.

"I don't know what will become of you, Connors," Alan said. "I suppose you'll be able to get a job someday and hold it, but I can't imagine what."

"He ought to be a broker, sir," a boy named Harding spoke up. He was moonfaced and very solemn. "My father is a broker and he likes it a lot. But of course he has to work very hard."

"Connors wouldn't like that," Alan said.

"Every night—"

"Skip it, Harding, for Pete's sake," came a voice from the back row. "Who cares what your old man does?"

"Every night," Harding persisted, "he brings home a whole briefcase full of work. Sometimes he has to work all night."

"The poor guy," Alan said.

"Oh, he's not poor, sir."

Alan laughed along with the class. Unlike Connors, Harding made the most of his abilities and led a blameless life. He was the type who died at eighty-five while reading a market analysis in the lounge of the Harvard Club.

Alan glanced around the room, his smile slowly fading. "There's nothing wrong in not wanting to be poor, gentlemen, but we must always bear in mind that money and the

power that often goes with it are not worthy goals in themselves."

"Why not, sir?"

It was Larry Connors again. His face was guileless, too
much so, and Alan was certain that the boy had asked the
question primarily to needle him. Connors was an enigma, all
right. There were times when Alan felt that he was really getting across to the boy and there were other times when it
seemed that Larry felt almost obliged to waste his talents and
lower himself in the estimation of the masters.

"I'll tell you why," Alan said, trying not to take the bait
too eagerly. "Let's take a very recent example. The Russians
have launched an earth satellite. Scientists everywhere applaud that considerable achievement for its own sake. As
long as the satellite is up there in the interests of science,
men of good will in every land can profit from its discoveries.
But should any group of men pervert this marvel in order to
attain domination over other men, then I think it is obvious
that something which began nobly in a search for knowledge
has ended evilly in a quest for power."

Alan stopped, aware that the faces had taken on a frozen,
impassive look. Gone was the animation which had bright-
ened them a few moments ago. They were quite plainly
bored now. Damn it, Alan thought, they want me to crack
jokes all the time; they don't really care about the tremendous implications of that thing up in the sky; they just
want to be entertained. And they are the ones who will have
to push on now beyond "Sputnik," on toward the new fron-
tiers or on to oblivion. Looking at the faces again, he felt a
kind of anger and despair and remembered all at once one
of the masters remarking the other day that in the years immediately following puberty only the glands wished to learn
anything.

He was as glad as the rest of them when the bell rang a

moment later. The class filed out quickly except for Connors who had purposely lagged behind. He stopped beside Alan's desk.

"Why do you want to be a teacher, sir?"

Alan was caught off guard. This was the other side of Connors, quite sincere and friendly. "I don't know, Larry," he said and smiled. "I don't think I can answer that one off-hand."

Connors continued to stand there, shifting his books from one arm to the other and poking his toe vaguely at a lumpy, pink eraser which had dropped under one of the seats. "Well," he said, "well, good-by, sir."

"See you Monday," Alan said. He glimpsed the embarrassed smile before the boy turned and hurried after his classmates. Connors had obviously wanted to say more. Perhaps he would try again.

Alan crossed the room and threw open one of the windows. Looking out at the autumn sky where the thin, white traceries of some high-flying clouds streaked the blue above the chapel spire, he wondered if this might be the last autumn that he would stand in a classroom and hear the pencils scratching. He could see a boy running down the broad steps of Carver Hall and off to the left the slender figure of his wife came into view. She was wearing the brown tweed suit that looked so well on her and she reminded him of the proud young matrons pictured in *Vogue* and *Harper's Bazaar*, only Nancy couldn't afford the clothes they wore in those magazines. She was bending forward now and pushing hard against the pram. Little Bill was probably howling for his lunch. Alan smiled and as he turned to gather up his books, a boy, clutching a note, came running into the room.

"For you, sir."

Alan tore it open, glanced at the signature, and then read the brief message carefully. Kendrick wished to see him immediately. What the devil could be so urgent? He thought at once of his house and mentally checked the rooms in rapid succession. No trouble there, so far as he knew. He hadn't missed any of his regular appointments recently or departed from his normal routine. His uneasiness increased in spite of the fact that Kendrick was always sending people notes. It was a disease of the upper echelon to break out with paper work. The administrators had gotten so far away from the blackboard that they had forgotten their former problems. They liked to call you in and interrupt your work while they discussed their pet administrative ideas.

"Well, Alan," Kendrick would probably say, "I'm sorry to bother you but I need your opinion on the new house inspection form we've been considering." But he knew that Kendrick wouldn't say that or anything like it. On a Saturday morning when he had a thousand and one week-end plans to consider, Kendrick wasn't going to talk about the dirty clothes in the Carver closets. He was a martinet about some things, this man with his steel-trap mind and his powder-puff manners, but he wasn't a fool and he was never concerned with trivialities.

"Is that all, sir?" The boy was still standing there.

"Oh," Alan said, "yes. Thanks, Bill."

"It's Jack, sir."

Alan shook his head. "Of course. Sorry, Jack. I'm a little vague at the moment."

Alan hurriedly packed his brief case, stuffing in his textbooks along with a stack of uncorrected papers, a box of paper clips, a slide rule, and his grade book. He snapped off the light and started down the corridor, hearing from behind the closed doors the familiar droning of his colleagues' voices, each with its distinctive rhythm and pitch. At the end of the corridor he put his shoulder against the heavy door and lunged outward into the sunshine.

Walking up the hill, he passed the site where the new dormitory would be going up soon and suddenly he was thinking of his own future and of that letter from Hall & Crandon in his desk drawer. He would have to reply within the next few days. They were a top firm and this was their second letter. Were he to accept their offer, he could expect to be sitting in a New York office a year from now and in a little while he would lunch with his associates in a place where there would be no hungry, surging cohorts of young men attacking the platters of food at the long tables. After work he would go home on the train with his neighbors. Once little Bill was in bed, he and Nancy would have the evening to themselves and nobody was going to barge in and ask him how to do a chem problem. He would have the money to buy Nancy some clothes and bring her a present once in a while. At the moment she was making most of her own clothes and the last present he had bought her had been a gold pin that was part of a set with earrings to match. He was still saving up for the earrings.

As Alan approached the office, a boy passed him and noticed that he looked unusually stern with his deep-set eyes, his strong jaw, and the seriousness in his face which always made his smile so welcome. The boy said "Hi," but Mr. Richards didn't even look around, and the boy stopped a few yards farther on, puzzled and vaguely hurt. Someday maybe Mr. Richards would come down out of the clouds.

Kendrick was alone in his office, and Alan was astonished to see him peer out the door like an anxious old maid before he closed it.

"Sit down," Kendrick said.

Alan perched uneasily on the edge of a chair and watched Kendrick fold his hands, remembering that when you shook hands with Kendrick, his grip felt oddly boneless.

"Tommy Conway was killed this morning," Kendrick said.

Alan gasped under the impact of the shock wave that was spreading over him. For a moment he could only stare at Kendrick.

"My God, Justin," he said softly, "how awful! That poor little guy. What happened?"

"I don't know much yet. Hugh just called me a few minutes ago. I gathered that Tommy had fallen from the top of the Rock."

Alan shook his head. "Tommy Conway—He had breakfast at my table this morning. I can't believe he's—Accident, you say?"

"Yes."

"He was the nicest kid in our house by a mile. Nancy and I were very fond of him."

"Yes," Kendrick said, "Tommy was a fine boy." He pulled his chair close to his desk. "Well, we'd better get organized. The Head is on his way back now. Tommy's father probably won't get here until tomorrow but that will give us a little time to prepare ourselves. I called you in, Alan, because I thought you ought to be advised on how to handle Mr. Conway."

Alan frowned. "How to handle him? I don't get it."

"Well, what to say, for example."

"What to *say?*"

"Yes."

"Well, there isn't very much to say, is there, at a time like this?"

"You'd be surprised." Kendrick smiled tolerantly. "We've got to think of the school, Alan, and be consistent in our handling of this thing. Mr. Conway will not be an easy man to deal with."

"I agree with you there," Alan said. "I could see that on the first day he came up to school. There was something about the way he treated Tommy that I didn't like. I remember now that I—"

Kendrick had been looking at his watch. "I'm sorry to interrupt you, Alan, but I've got a pile of things to do this morning." He leaned forward over the spotless green blotter in the center of the big desk. "Now if Mr. Conway asks you a lot of questions, you had better answer them as simply and briefly as possible. I would avoid expressing any personal opinions and I would certainly not indulge in any speculation. After all, we can't do anything to help Tommy now, and there is no point in further upsetting or antagonizing his father. Remember, of course, that our official position must be that this was an accident."

Alan sat up suddenly. "Is there any doubt about it?"

Kendrick looked down at the cat's-eye ring. "Virtually no doubt."

"What did Hugh say?"

"He wasn't very coherent over the phone."

Alan nodded. "I can understand that. But you know, when you first said it was an accident, I wondered about that because Tommy wasn't the type to have accidents. He was much too careful. He even held on to the banister when he came down stairs. Good Lord, I hate to think that he might have—"

"I don't think we'd better pursue that possibility any further, Alan."

"You mean until Follensbee gets back?"

"I mean—"

"Of course," Alan interrupted, his expression clearing, "Hugh will know what happened. He must have been right there."

"Not necessarily."

"Well, if he wasn't looking just at that moment, one of the boys must have seen it happen."

"You can't rely on the boys at a time like this. They'll probably have a dozen different versions."

"Surely there must be some way to get at the truth?"

"The truth," Kendrick said, "is that the boy is dead."

Alan gave an uneasy laugh. "I know, Justin, but you must agree we've got to find out how he died. I mean, the actual circumstances."

"We'll know all we need to know," Kendrick said.

Kendrick's smile was meant to be reassuring but it wasn't.

"But, Justin," Alan persisted, "a thing like this *has* to be a matter of factual record. There will have to be an investigation, won't there? I think it's the law. And besides, Tommy's father will want to know how it happened."

"We'll tell him it was an accident."

"But supposing it *wasn't?*"

"We have no proof that it wasn't an accident."

"What if we did have proof?"

Kendrick gazed at the ceiling and for a moment he did not answer. Then he said, "Let me tell you something, Alan. The truth is not always the right answer for people. Most men can sleep more comfortably on a bed of lies. To tell Roger Conway, for instance, that his son committed suicide would be disastrous."

"For whom?"

"For all of us."

Alan could feel the tightening in his stomach. In place of his astonishment and disbelief there was anger now, a deep-down anger that would tolerate no compromise.

"Would you mind telling me, Justin," he said, "why Mr. Conway can't take the truth as well as the next man?"

"I could tell you why," Kendrick said blandly, "but I'm not going to."

Alan's jaw muscles stiffened. He leaned forward and clutched the arms of the chair. "I think I know the reason," he said, looking straight at Kendrick, "and I don't accept it. I don't care how many buildings Conway may give us. He and the rest of us ought to be deeply concerned about what really happened to Tommy."

"Sure, Alan, but don't forget we must deal with the realities of the situation."

"Isn't it a reality when a father ruins his own son?"

"Yes, but—"

"He was always giving the boy things," Alan rushed on, "even though Tommy didn't want them, forcing him to show off his old man's wealth and power, trying to make him act like a big shot. Tommy wasn't like that; he was quiet and shy and lonely. He didn't want to be a big shot; he just wanted to be himself, but that wasn't enough to satisfy his father. He made that poor kid drive up to the house the very first day in a new Jaguar with all the boys watching. Fourteen years old and driving *his own car!* Tommy was mortified; he looked sick when he shook hands with Nancy and me. I swear that he couldn't wait for his father to leave, but it was too late by then. The harm had already been done; the boys started riding him right away. There was nothing I could do about it. And every time a new present arrived, it just made matters worse. Tommy wouldn't even open the boxes after a while. There's a whole stack of them piled up in the back of his closet right now. That's a thoughtless, stupid, criminal way to bring up a child. The man's a complete jerk and somebody ought to tell him so!"

"Yes," Kendrick said quietly, "in some ways he is a jerk and he's been battling the knowledge ever since he was here at Carver. He is also doing a lot for this school."

"What does that matter?"

"It matters a great deal to some of us," Kendrick said and to Alan's amazement he saw that the cool eyes were blazing and the soft mouth had begun to tremble.

Alan was uncomfortably aware that he was setting himself against the most powerful man on the Carver faculty. Young masters did not prosper in that fashion, and Nancy would no doubt tell him that he was a fool. Still, he could not accept the idea that the truth should be compromised for any reason whatsoever. He believed that deeply himself, he taught it to his students, and he wasn't going to surrender his principles now. But a partial retreat was advisable at the moment.

"I didn't mean it that way, Justin," he said. "I know the school needs gifts. My whole point on this thing is that we owe it to Tommy to find out everything we can. We need to get all the facts and try to evaluate and understand them. Mr. Conway may be able to help our search in some way and therefore he cannot rightly be shielded from the truth. At this point we seem to be taking the position that Tommy's death was accidental before we even know what happened. That's what I object to."

Kendrick took a gold pencil from his pocket and tapped it thoughtfully against the green blotter. In the distance a bell rang. Once again the heedless feet echoed along the corridors, but this time the final class of the week was coming up. Already, in the voices drifting across the campus and sifting through the tired old walls of Kendrick's office, there was a note of Saturday-afternoon gaiety.

"Good luck today, Moose."

"Thanks, boy."

"Harland tough?"

"Yeah."

"We can beat 'em. Hear from Mary?"

"Got two this morning."

"She still love you?"

"Madly."

"You lucky stiff."

Kendrick gave no indication of having heard the voices.

He looked up from the blotter and his voice was deceptively smooth and mild, the way it was sometimes when he had a boy standing anxiously in front of the big desk.

"I think, Alan," he said, "that you had better leave the handling of this to my judgment. It happens to be a very complex situation."

Alan felt the sting in those words and they infuriated him. For a moment he thought wildly of telling Kendrick that he would never consent to any such glossing over of the facts, but he wasn't ready to do that yet. First he would have to try to arm himself with the truth about Tommy. He stood up, and his own voice was cold and formal.

"Do you want me for anything more?"

"Not at the moment. Tell Boucher, Beckett, Lindstrom and the rest of that crowd in your house that I don't want them running around talking about this thing. And tell Boucher he's not to touch anything in that room. He's to leave everything exactly as it is."

"I hope he'll co-operate," Alan said dryly.

"He will." Kendrick pointed to the disciplinary list. "Young Mr. Boucher has rather a large account to settle with me."

"You think of everything," Alan said, and Kendrick could take that any way he liked.

Kendrick's face was expressionless. "I have to," he said.

Alan walked quickly and purposefully back to his house. He and Nancy had a duplex apartment in one wing, and there were fourteen boys living in the other. Most of them were Tommy Conway's age, but there was a sprinkling of seniors to keep the place intact. Alan could see Nancy in the kitchen, giving the baby his bottle, but he went directly to the side entrance of the boys' wing and climbed the stairs. Fortunately, at this moment the younger boys were all in class or study hall, the seniors happened to be out, and he had the place to himself. He hesitated an instant in front of Room 204 and then opened the door.

One could tell at a glance that the two boys who occupied the room were quite different personalities. A scuffed brown shoe peeped out from under Boucher's bed, and his mud-stained windbreaker was lying across his pillow. On his desk the books and papers were strewn about, and on one corner of the wrinkled blotter there was a half-eaten cracker dabbed with peanut butter. A bosomy blonde swelled seductively from her pin-up portrait on the adjacent wall. By contrast, the other side of the room had a prim, austere formality. Tommy's desk top was clear except for the gold pen and pencil which his father had given him recently and which looked now as though they had been purposely placed at the exact center of the immaculate green blotter. On his part of the wall Tommy had hung a calendar whose upper portion was a colored picture of a huge, red-faced hunter watching in dismay as a young buck swam out of range across a northern wilderness lake. The picture was captioned: "The Quarry Escapes."

Alan disliked poking into a boy's personal effects and never did so under normal circumstances unless the boy was present during the inspection, but he worked swiftly now, searching Tommy's bureau, desk, and closet without finding what he wanted. The bureau yielded a picture book of nearly nude models and a small radio, both contraband but otherwise not significant. It was in keeping, Alan thought, that Boucher should display his sex interest openly while Tommy kept it hidden as he had most everything else. In the desk were several packets of letters neatly secured by rubber bands. One stack bore the letterhead of Roger Conway's New York office; another contained a variety of scrawled communications from friends in neighboring schools, and the remaining batch had all been written by a girl. They might well contain a clue but there was not time to read them now. Piled heedlessly in the very back of the closet were three unopened packages from Abercrombie & Fitch and one from Spalding's.

There was no proof of the thing that Alan was sure of, and for a moment he stood indecisively in the center of the room. He had not been successful, but he wasn't giving up yet. Tommy Conway had not died accidentally this morning; everything Alan knew about the boy refuted this explanation. He himself had scaled the Rock on several occasions, and he remembered that there was a kind of parapet at the top which one would have to deliberately mount before there was any possibility of falling from the summit. Tommy hadn't fallen, and Follensbee would know that, too. He must have been right there with them, probably talking about the geological wonders spread out below when the boy had edged toward the parapet and been too quick for him. At any rate, Follensbee would know what had happened, and if he chose to tell Conway the truth, there would be no way for Kendrick to gloss over the facts. As a matter of fact, Kendrick had a nerve to think there *was* any way to "line up" a thing like this.

On his way out Alan started to pull down the photo of the overstacked blonde but changed his mind. Such pin-ups were strictly illegal in the dormitory and Boucher knew it. He was a fat slob who needed to have his ears pinned back, but just at this time he could be a valuable ally and it was better not to antagonize him.

The last thing Alan noticed was the picture of Roger Conway in its silver frame on his son's bureau. The face was proud, boldly handsome, and completely self-assured.

5

ROGER CONWAY hadn't looked that way when he first came to Carver in 1926. Times were good in the U.S.A. that year and getting better. There was a man in the White House who didn't have much to say and didn't have to say much. The money kept rolling in anyway. *George White's Scandals* were on Broadway, Babe Ruth was in the ball park, and the bootleggers were all over the place. It was good to be alive and to know that wars were errors of the past.

Kendrick was master of Darrow House that year, and Carver's enrollment had climbed to a prosperous hundred. On the opening day of school he had waited on the steps of Darrow with a house list in one hand and a pencil in the other to check off the boys as they arrived. Most of them drove up in enormous touring cars, seven-passenger jobs with their tops down, piloted by smiling fathers who wore straw hats and smoked richly flavored cigars. The boys wore plus fours and soft sweaters and some of them smuggled in hip flasks just to prove that they knew what the world was all about. These boys were the cream of the crop in America and they knew it. They recognized each other by certain easy signs of wealth and position. There was much laughter and handshaking as they stepped down from the big cars. Upstairs in one of the rooms a gramophone was playing "I Want To Be Happy."

By suppertime Kendrick had checked in all of his boys except one and directed them to the dining hall. He saw by his list that the missing boy's name was Roger Conway and he remembered that Dr. Parsons had mentioned him briefly at the last faculty meeting. Conway, it seemed, was coming to Carver for just one year. He had graduated from high school in the Pennsylvania mining town of his birth, but his father had reasoned quite correctly that the boy would stand a better chance of getting into Yale if he applied from Carver. Mr. Conway could not afford the full tuition, and Roger had been granted a partial scholarship, a fact that was not for publication.

"He'll be something to leaven the bread with, Gentlemen," Dr. Parsons had said in his booming voice.

"The old man wants to build up the football team," someone had whispered at the back of the room.

The touring cars had all gone and the chill, autumn darkness was closing in on the campus when Kendrick gave up waiting and started over to dinner, hurrying because it was important to be on time at his table this first night of school. He was crossing the street in front of the headmaster's house when he saw a boy trudging up the hill from town. He was a big, raw-boned kid and the suitcase in his meaty grip resembled the disreputable valises carried by the villains in the old vaudeville skits. His suit was not becoming and even in the dusk the dirt streaks on his face from the long train ride were ridiculously apparent. Conway, for this was certainly the boy, was going to "leaven the bread" all right, Kendrick thought, walking toward him with a practiced smile.

"Sorry to be late, sir," Conway said after Kendrick had introduced himself. "I didn't figure it was so far from town."

"Why didn't you take a—?" Kendrick started to say and then caught himself.

"I didn't have the money, sir."

Kendrick winced. There were certain things about which gentlemen were never specific, and this bluntness shocked him. He was embarrassed at first and then angry with the boy for making him embarrassed.

"We're late for dinner," he said brusquely. "You can wash up in the cloakroom under the dining hall and leave your suitcase there for now."

He waited at the foot of the stairs while Conway washed off the worst of the dust. Another boy had been dispatched to tell the headmaster that the last of his sheep was in the fold. It was a tradition at Carver for Dr. Parsons to shake hands with every new boy on the first night of school, and Kendrick was sure that he would be especially anxious to include Conway.

Still clutching his napkin and having not quite swallowed his last mouthful, Dr. Parsons was waiting for them in the tiny alcove at the head of the stairs. He was a big man with a bald head, a long nose, and the eyes of a wise old hawk.

"Well, well, my boy," he boomed, "it's wonderful to have you here!" He pumped Conway's hand, smiling at him with his special start-of-the-year smile. "I trust you had a good trip."

"Not very, sir."

"Oh well, you'll be feeling better tomorrow. If you're a little homesick these first few days, Mr. Kendrick will be glad to talk to you any time, day or night."

"Homesick?" Conway looked astonished.

"Haven't you ever been homesick, my boy?"

"No, sir."

"Well, you will be. Heh! Guess I shouldn't say that, but I want you to know that we're all on your team, my boy. Come now. Your dinner's getting cold. We can't have a little fellow like you going hungry. Heh!"

Dr. Parsons headed back to his table. Conway glanced around at Kendrick and for a moment they exchanged the smiles of saboteurs. Kendrick recognized his mistake a second later. The faculty all knew that the Head was a fatuous old windbag at times; they also knew the penalties of allowing the boys to perceive their true feelings on this score. Kendrick admired Conway for refusing to be charmed by the old man's palaver, but he was also afraid that the boy might take further advantage of the situation. It was to make his own position unmistakably clear that he asked Conway to report to his study after lights that evening.

"Sit down, Roger," he said. Then he lied easily. "I just wanted to make sure that you're all set for tomorrow. Got your schedule and books?"

"Yes, sir."

"Good." Kendrick smiled. "Any problems?"

"No, sir."

"Like your roommate?"

"He's all right."

Kendrick laughed. "You don't sound enthusiastic, but I guess you haven't had time to get acquainted yet."

There was a silence and from the boy's rather amused expression Kendrick decided that he had better be careful or he would defeat his own purpose. It was difficult, however, to come to the point with Conway sitting right there, his big hands resting on the arms of the chair with a kind of clumsy ease. His pajama top was open, revealing the firm ridges of his chest muscles. He was handsome in an uncouth sort of way. He needed a good barber and a good tailor, but once he got that big, awkward body under control, he was going to be very impressive. Kendrick looked away. To cover his confusion, he picked up a paper knife and grasped the blade tightly, grateful for the sudden pain in his fingers. His voice was a little too loud.

"This is a great school, Roger. I hope you are going to take full advantage of your academic opportunities here." He paused, and chancing a look, saw that the boy was staring off across the room with the expression of one who is not privileged to interrupt but need not pay attention. Kendrick was suddenly aware of his own awkwardness and he could feel his anger rising again. "The headmaster," he said desperately, "is an outstanding educator."

"Yeah," Conway said.

Years later Kendrick was to remember the way Conway said that "yeah" and be unable to suppress his laughter. By then, with a skill gleaned from the years, he would know how to talk to a boy with humor and with that dramatic flair for the unexpected that was to become his trademark. But at the moment he was floundering with only the sense to know that he must terminate the thing at once while some dignity still clung to him. He pushed back his chair and stood up.

"You've had a long day, Roger. Better turn in. Don't hesitate to let me know if I can help you in any way."

Conway's voice clearly conveyed his relief. "Thanks, sir. I will."

He hadn't needed any help for quite some time and meanwhile he had established a formidable reputation for himself on the Carver campus. If the headmaster had really wanted to put a ringer on the football team, he couldn't have done any better. Conway's furious plunges through the line bowled over most of Carver's opponents who had the temerity to tackle him, and he led the team to an undefeated season. The boys cheered him wildly and called him "Old Ironsides" and he went on to further triumphs during the wrestling season, hurling other giants to the canvas while his classmates roared their approval. By the end of the first term it was apparent that Roger Conway was going to make an athletic success of his year at Carver, and he was capable of getting at least passing grades in all of his courses. But there was something else about the boy that Kendrick only suspected at first and then knew for sure: Roger Conway was a hero on the athletic field but away from it he was an outcast.

This curious dichotomy puzzled Kendrick until he faced up to a fact about the majority of the students at Carver in the golden year of 1926: a great lot of them were dreadful snobs. It was important to them to be successful athletes, but it was even more important to wear the right clothes and to know the right girls and to entertain them at the right places. A thing became "right" when it was accepted by a certain group, and everyone in that group knew almost instinctively what was "right." The way a man danced with a girl, the way he talked to her between dances, the way he escorted her home—these were important and showed up a man's knowledge of "right" and "wrong." They marked a man once and for all as belonging or not belonging. His family background, where he came from and how much money his father made—these were important, too, but they were the kind of thing you could fill in about a man with confidence once you observed that he belonged.

Conversely, any failure in etiquette, any fumbling or lack of know-how when it came to the demanding conventions of this exclusive group, and you were a marked man, undeserving of membership in the club no matter what your athletic prowess. After all, you could applaud a fighter in the ring without having to invite him to your table. And you could cheer a boy for winning your football games but you didn't have to accept him as a suitable date for your sister.

There was nothing strange or unworthy about this distinction as far as the boys were concerned. They were wholeheartedly loyal to Roger Conway on the athletic field, but only the least sophisticated of his admirers could overlook his deficiencies away from the locker room. It was too bad, of course, but at the same time it was perfectly obvious that the big, good-looking kid from the Pennsylvania mining town just didn't belong in your parlor.

Kendrick became acutely aware of the situation on a cold December night during the winter dance week end. He was off duty that night and catching up on some long deferred reading when he heard a gramophone playing softly in one of the rooms at the far end of the corridor. Under the impression that all of the boys in Darrow had gone to the dance, he put aside his book and went to investigate. He found Roger Conway sprawled on his bed, staring at the ceiling.

"Aren't you going to the dance?"

"No, sir."

Conway had made no effort to get to his feet, but Kendrick was learning to overlook the obvious. He moved quietly to the gramophone and turned it off. "Why aren't you going?" he asked.

"I don't have a tuxedo."

"But that's silly. You could have rented one."

"They would have known."

Kendrick sat on the edge of the bed. "What difference does that make? A lot of boys rent them. As a matter of fact, your own roommate rented one."

"They know Harvey has one at home."

"And so might you."

"But I don't, sir, and they know it." Conway sat up suddenly and the corners of his mouth sagged. "They don't want me down at the dance anyway."

"I'm sure that's not true," Kendrick said. "Where did you get a crazy idea like that?"

Conway gave him a pitying look. "You just wouldn't know, sir." He slid off the bed and began to pace up and down the room, kicking at the rug with his bare toes. "It's true and there's nothing you can do about it, you or anybody else. Only me." The big hands were clenched into fists. "And some day I will!"

"Roger—"

"Snob bastards," Conway said softly, "dirty snob bastards!"

"Roger, listen to me!"

The boy looked up, glaring at Kendrick through tears of hate.

"Get your clothes on," Kendrick said.

Conway stared, his jaw dropping. All at once he seemed to realize that a master was in the room. "I didn't mean to talk that way, sir, if you're gonna take me to the Head—"

"Don't be silly," Kendrick said. "I'll wait for you in my study. Put on an overcoat."

Kendrick went back to his room and sadly returned the book to its place on the shelf. But this was more important. He had the feeling that this was something that nobody else in school could handle and it was something that he could very easily muff himself. He was dressed warmly and sitting at his desk with the car keys in his hand when Conway came in.

"Where are we going, sir?"

"Out," Kendrick said.

He led the way down the drive and around to the back of Darrow where there was a flimsy shed which served as a garage. The isinglass curtains crackled with the cold when the car doors were opened, and the old Packard started reluctantly after considerable grumbling. They drove into the country without saying anything, huddled down against the cold, looking out at the winter stars and listening to the chill clanging of occasional stones striking the undersides of the mudguards. Presently, Kendrick turned off the main highway onto a dirt road that curved into the woods. Bumping and lurching, they came to a stone fence whose opening was blocked by a sturdy chain. Kendrick got out and lowered the chain, replacing it carefully as soon as they were inside.

"The police sometimes check this place," he explained to Conway. "I wouldn't want them to think we were trespassing."

Conway grinned. "Say, what is this place?" He sat up and peered through the windshield. There wasn't a trace of anger left in his voice.

"I'm surprised you haven't heard of it," Kendrick said. "This is known to Carver boys as 'Parsons' Palace.' Actually, as you'll see, it's a kind of hunting lodge."

"I didn't know that old—that the headmaster liked to hunt."

Kendrick laughed. "He doesn't as far as I know. He likes to write his sermons without being disturbed and to have a place where he can get away from the school once in a while."

"I don't blame him," Conway said.

Kendrick drove the last hundred yards in low gear and all at once the lodge loomed up in the glare of the headlights. It was a rambling, rough-hewn cabin, and when Kendrick turned off the headlights, he and the boy had to feel their way cautiously through the moonless night. Conway watched with admiration as Kendrick quickly located the key in its hiding place over the door. Once inside, Kendrick knelt quickly before the huge fireplace and struck a match. The fire came to life with amazing speed, pushing back the darkness and filling the room with warmth and cheer.

"Thank goodness he always leaves the fire freshly laid," Kendrick said. "We'll have to return the favor. There's plenty of kindling and logs in the woodbox."

Conway was surveying the room. He whistled softly. "This place is the bee's knees."

"It certainly is," Kendrick agreed. "Two bedrooms, bath and kitchen." He did not add that Dr. Parsons had built the whole thing with school labor and without a cent of cost to himself.

They pulled a couple of chairs within comfortable range of the fire and shed their overcoats. Kendrick waited patiently, knowing that eventually the boy would talk of his own accord and that it would be better that way.

"I wish I had a drink," Conway said abruptly.

Kendrick chuckled. "I'm afraid I couldn't go quite that far."

"I know, sir. It's just more like home here and I'd probably be havin' a beer or somethin' if I was back home."

"Tell me about home," Kendrick said.

Conway put his head back. "Well, I'd be out with my girl. Maybe we'd go over to somebody's house. Or if it was warmer, we'd just drive around the town in an old jalopy I got. We'd wave to people and they'd laugh and wave back. Everybody's friendly in my home town. It doesn't matter how much money you got or what your old man does for a livin'. Everybody gets along good with everybody else. Everybody's happy, at least until the siren goes up at the pits. Then everything stops and the whole town goes out there and waits. That doesn't happen very often, thank God."

There was another silence and then Conway said, "I figure I know why you brought me out here, sir. I guess I was just about ready to tear the place apart."

"Tell me some more about home," Kendrick said.

"Well," Conway continued, "like I said, it's a swell place. Big, shady streets and lots of good vegetable gardens out back of the houses. I guess I like the summer evenings best, the long twilight time when the men get home from work and families sit around on the front porches and talk. And the June nights when Karen, my girl, and I go driving down by the river. It's maybe a kind of muddy, dirty-looking river in the daytime but at night you don't notice it, not in the moonlight, anyway. Sometimes in the distance you hear a train whistling up the valley, the good old Pennsy chugging the silver rails—"

In the fireplace the logs broke one by one amid showers of sparks and after a while the glowing embers winked out. Conway's voice droned on. The boy was talking freely now, completely immersed in his own world, his hatred and despair forgotten. Kendrick was becoming dreadfully sleepy when suddenly Conway broke out of his reverie.

"Can I tell you something, Mr. Kendrick?"

Kendrick woke up a little, aware that Conway's tone had altered. "Go ahead, Roger," he said.

"I got a motorcycle here."

Kendrick was suddenly wide awake. "You mean here at school?"

"That's right, sir. It's not exactly at school. I got it in a garage downtown."

"Where?"

"Sawyer's."

"How long have you had it?"

"Since the first day."

"You mean, you rode it up here?"

"That's right, sir. My father didn't know whether we could have them or not, and I told him I wouldn't use it if we couldn't. That's why I was late when I saw you on the street that night. It took me a long time to find a garage."

"And you haven't used it since?"

"No, sir."

"Why are you telling me this? You could get yourself into a lot of trouble if the headmaster knew about it."

"You've done a lot for me, sir. More than anybody else around here. I just wanted you to know."

Kendrick could recognize a compliment of this sort from a boy. "Thank you, Roger," he said, "but what makes you think I won't tell the headmaster?"

"You won't, sir," Conway said with perfect confidence. "You're not that kind of a guy."

When they drove back to the campus a little while later, Kendrick was aware that his hands had been very neatly tied. He could not reveal the secret without forever losing the boy's confidence and teaching him the folly of trusting an adult. He was to find himself in this position many times as the years went by. It was the penalty for being a popular master. Gradually he would acquire a whole storehouse of secrets and they would become the basis of his negotiations, so that he and generations of Carver men would be bound together in a kind of mutual blackmail wherein he did things for them and they did things for him. Occasionally a boy would attempt to double-cross him, but it would be his last mistake. Kendrick always saw to that.

"I'll keep it to myself," he said, "providing you'll do something for the school."

Conway gave a little sigh of resignation as though he had known there would be a string attached. "What do you want me to do, sir?"

"Not now," Kendrick said. "Later on." There was no time to choose his words with care. He went on bluntly, "You're tough, Roger, and you're aggressive. You weren't born with the proverbial silver spoon in your mouth. In your case it was a coal shovel. You want certain things very much and I have a feeling you are going to get some of them. Money, for example."

"Sure," Conway said. "I'm gonna make a million dollars and give it all to Carver. Pardon me, sir, but you can tell that to the marines."

They were nearing the campus. Kendrick slowed down. The lights in the gym were still blazing and across the brittle silence of the winter night came faintly the lilting strains of "Valencia." Conway stiffened and his big hands became fists again. Kendrick turned to the boy. Perhaps the truth would be best right now.

"Maybe they don't want you down there now, Roger," he said gently, "but they will someday under different circumstances."

Conway didn't say anything for a long moment and then his voice was little more than a whisper, as though he were promising something to himself.

"Someday I'm gonna fix it so that a hundred guys like me can come here and be just as good as anybody else."

When Roger Conway stood up to receive his Carver diploma on a beautiful June day, Kendrick in cap and gown watched intently from his seat among the faculty. It seemed to him that alone among the boys Conway was tense and unsmiling. He towered over the headmaster and when he walked out in the procession, he clutched his diploma like a weapon. Only when he passed Kendrick and caught his eye for an instant did some of the coldness leave his face. By that time he and Kendrick had more than one secret between them.

6

I'M ALL RIGHT, Sam," Follensbee said.

He smiled, aware of the concern in the doctor's face, and then he looked toward the ambulance again. The back door was open and the blanket on the stretcher did not conceal the outlines of the body underneath. The blanket did not really conceal anything as far as he was concerned. He could still see the boy sprawled on his back in the rocky brook, his left leg twisted under him, the dark blood trickling from his open mouth.

The medical examiner had come and gone. The boys were clustered around the station wagon now. For once they were relatively quiet, and when they talked, it was in short, explosive bursts punctuated by nervous laughter. With the natural resilience of youth they were recovering quickly from the shock which had gripped them in a dumb, staring horror when Follensbee had at last reached the parapet, his own face like a piece of stone. And by the time they started down, stumbling in their haste, their fear had turned to curiosity and they boldly approached the thing in the brook as though it were a challenge to their manhood.

With Follensbee it had been rather the other way. He had gone from disbelief to dreadful awareness and now to a kind of numb and leaden despair. He had failed to meet a challenge and he felt somehow that he had lost a battle. At the same time and even as he reproached himself most bitterly, he was aware of his fundamental innocence and the futility of proclaiming it. There was simply no way to avoid the blame for what had happened. He felt the doctor's hand on his shoulder.

"Don't take this all on yourself, Hugh. I should have seen it coming myself. When I look back—"

"But I fell asleep," Follensbee said. "There's no getting around that."

"Yes, I know," the doctor said gently. "That's the tough part about it because I'm pretty sure this would have happened anyway sometime, somewhere." He jerked his head toward the ambulance. "When they get that way and make up their minds, it's almost impossible to stop them. I just wish to hell I had seen it coming and gone on record with the family. Then we could have shifted the responsibility."

"I wasn't up there at the time," Follensbee said. "Who is going to say what happened?"

The doctor did not reply. Follensbee glanced up at him and thought he saw a flash of pity in his eyes.

"It will work out," Whelden said. "We'd better get back now." He motioned to the ambulance driver. "All right, Jack, let's go."

Follensbee plodded toward the station wagon, dreading the ride back with the restless little mob grimacing in the seats behind him.

"You better take it easy the rest of the day," Sam Whelden called out to him just before the ambulance drove off.

"Are we going back now, sir?"

"That's right," Follensbee said. "Get in, everybody."

"Where are they gonna take *him*, sir?"

"I don't know."

"To the morgue, you dope," Boucher said to the boy.

"What morgue?"

"Any morgue, stupid. Haven't you ever seen where they got the bodies all in—?"

"All right," Follensbee said sharply, "that's enough of that. We'll talk about something else."

"Why do you think he did it, sir?"

"I don't know."

"Hey, the ambulance is out of sight already. The Doc sure is in a hurry."

"He wants to get home to lunch," Boucher said.

There was laughter, and Follensbee had a furious desire to slap the fat boy in the mouth. He bent closer over the wheel, trying not to hear the chattering voices, forcing himself to drive on through the autumn noonday without any of the delight that the New England countryside normally stirred in him.

"He was kind of a queer guy."

"You can say that again."

"I never did know him real well."

"Nobody did."

"Boucher did. What about him, Fatso?"

"Don't call me that, you fairy."

"I don't want to hear any more language like that," Follensbee said.

There was an unintelligible murmur in the back seat and then sudden, raucous laughter which Follensbee understood all too well.

"He must have been nuts to do a thing like that."

"I didn't think he had the guts."

"It doesn't take any guts."

"Sure it does."

"Not when you're crazy. You probably wanna do it."

"I still think it takes guts."

"That guy was *really* queer, wasn't he, Jim?"

Boucher nodded. "That's for sure."

"I hope I never get any ideas like that. Did he ever talk to you about it?"

"About what?"

"You know."

"No, sir. Any more questions, sir?"

Laughter again. Boucher could always get a laugh. He liked being top dog this way.

"No kidding, Jim. Didn't Tommy ever say anything?"

"Sure. He said, 'I'm gonna jump off the cliff tomorrow morning at ten o'clock.'"

"Okay, wise guy."

Boucher sensed that it was time to toss out a few crumbs. "Tommy never talked much," he said, turning to face the others. "The little creep studied all the time and wrote letters. After lights every night he did some other things."

"What other things?"

Boucher was ready with the punch line. "You're too young to know, Crampton," he said, and that one really hit the top of the laugh meter.

Follensbee could see the New Hampshire farmhouse and behind it the barn where the trailer was waiting for them. The pale blue exterior would be covered now with a thin film of dust, but inside, everything would be shining and clean, the way Emmy had left it. He wished that he didn't have to tell her about what had happened this morning, but she would have to know. The whole school would know in a little while.

He arrived with his noisy cargo a few minutes before the end of the last period. Kendrick had apparently been waiting for them. As he came toward the car, the boys stopped talking and eyed him apprehensively.

"I want to see all of you right now," Kendrick said. "There's a classroom we can use."

The boys scurried after him like frightened mice. Follensbee was so stiff that he could hardly get out of the car. The pell-mell descent down the Rock had overtaxed his muscles. He wanted a hot bath more than anything at the moment, but he trudged along after his class, feeling uncomfortably like a guilty boy himself.

Kendrick leaned against the master's desk and for almost a full minute he scanned the upturned faces. Watching him, Follensbee wished that he could command such rapt attention.

"I have just one or two things to say to you," Kendrick began, "about the tragic accident that happened this morning."

"Pardon me, Mr. Kendrick," Boucher said in his best apple-polishing voice, "but that was no accident, sir."

Instantly, Kendrick's arm shot out toward the fat boy. "I'll see you after this meeting, Boucher."

A radiator clanked, but there was no other sound in the room. Follensbee could see that Boucher's aplomb had been shattered and that this considerable feat was being silently applauded by the rest of the class. He himself felt a little flooding of satisfaction as he observed Boucher's flushed face and his grin which was a little wobbly now. On the other hand, Follensbee couldn't help feeling that Kendrick had been a bit harsh with the boy for simply trying to tell the truth.

"You boys are going to be asked a lot of questions," Kendrick said, "and you will hear a lot of rumors. Some people will not have the manners and the good sense to mind their own business. It is up to you to protect yourselves and your school from false impressions gained through certain statements of yours that may not be as accurate as you think. For example, what you *think* you saw this morning and what actually happened may well be two different things. It is quite possible that Tommy was *pretending to jump* in order to attract attention and then lost his balance. I'm almost sure that's exactly what did happen, as a matter of fact."

Kendrick paused and smiled reassuringly. "All of this doesn't really matter, you see. It won't help Tommy or his father for us to talk about it amongst ourselves. Of course, if you are asked by the headmaster or myself to give an opinion, you are free to do so, but I would again caution you against being too positive as to your recollections. The best thing we can do is to go on about our business and I know I can rely on each of you to act accordingly." He paused. "You'd better!"

Those last two words and the way Kendrick had said them delighted the boys and there was a murmur of appreciative laughter. This ability to come up with just the right touch at the crucial moment was one of Kendrick's chief talents, and Follensbee had seen its effectiveness hundreds of times. Watching the boys filing out now in good humor and completely under Kendrick's spell, Follensbee couldn't help admiring the performance himself. Sometimes it seemed to him that Kendrick was nothing so much as a superior ringmaster who cracked his whip and then looked on complacently while all of them, masters and boys alike, rushed to do his bidding. He was not physically powerful, nor was he gifted with any obvious reasons to command. And yet he did command and sometimes he made a boy squirm, the way Boucher was squirming now, like an overstuffed bug in the heat of a probing torch.

"You went to the movies yesterday afternoon, didn't you?"

Boucher's face turned the color of putty and his mouth gaped in a wordless circle of pure astonishment.

"Well—did you?"

"Yes—sir."

"You know that Third Formers don't have movie permission?"

Boucher could only nod weakly.

"And you are aware, Mr. Boucher, that you have already acquired ten latenesses this term and been put on report twice by your housemaster for roughhousing?"

"But I wasn't the only one who—"

"Answer yes or no."

"Well—yes, sir."

A thin, beady line of perspiration had appeared on Boucher's forehead and his little eyes were no longer crafty.

"And do you know what all this adds up to for you?"

"No, sir."

"You are restricted to the campus as of this moment. Tomorrow night your name will come up before the Discipline Committee and I wouldn't be at all surprised if they put you on probation for the remainder of the term."

"Does that mean I can't go home next week end?"

"It certainly does."

"But I asked a girl—"

"You should have thought about that before you went to the movies."

Boucher looked down at his hands. He was licked and he knew it. He was also very close to tears. Kendrick observed this and his voice softened.

"You didn't play it very smart, did you, Jim?"

"No, sir." Boucher smiled faintly. "I guess I didn't."

"I may be able to say a word in your behalf," Kendrick said, "provided you behave yourself from now on. With respect to this morning, I don't want you going around telling people that Tommy jumped. We have to be careful about statements like that."

Boucher looked up with new hope in his eyes and some of his natural guile returned. "I see what you mean, sir. But if I *could* prove that Tommy jumped, would you be interested?"

Kendrick blinked and moistened his lips. "Yes, of course. But I wouldn't bother with that." He glanced at his watch. "Lunch is in fifteen minutes. I suggest you be on time."

Kendrick made a gesture of dismissal and Boucher headed for the door with obvious relief. He stopped and looked around at Kendrick.

"How did you know I was in the movies, sir?"

"Never mind," Kendrick said.

A typical Kendrick performance, Follensbee was thinking. Kendrick had the fat boy right where he wanted him. And now it was to be his turn. Through the window he saw the Harland School bus lumbering up the hill on its way to the gym, bringing Harland's football team to the fray. The bell rang harshly and in the classroom next door there was an extra surge of joy because the week's work was done and the weather was perfect and the football game this afternoon would be a honey and the movie tonight was rumored to be a new one for a change.

Kendrick turned and smiled at the senior master. "Well, Hugh, you've had quite a time this morning."

Follensbee felt the black dismay flooding over him again. He dreaded what was coming now. "Yes," he said.

"It's a terrible thing," Kendrick said, his smile fading, "for you and for the school, but I know you couldn't have done anything about it."

"I might have," Follensbee said. He was looking down at his boots.

"What do you mean?"

"I fell asleep on the way up. I wasn't even there when it happened."

Follensbee decided later that it must have been his imagination but when he looked up a moment later, he thought that Kendrick seemed almost pleased. But only for an instant. Then his expression darkened and he said, "That's not so good, Hugh. It puts us in a pretty awkward position."

"I know," Follensbee said. "This is the first time in forty years that I haven't gone directly to the top with them."

"Please understand," Kendrick said quickly, "that I'm not blaming you for this. You shouldn't feel personally responsible."

"I'm afraid I can't help it."

"It's just that we have to be careful," Kendrick said, "about our liability when something like this happens. You never know when some slick lawyer may try to get you over the barrel."

Follensbee shook his head. "I hadn't thought of that."

He was too tired to think of it. His weariness was paramount now and it was impossible to worry about a lawsuit or to care what other perils might lie ahead. Follensbee wanted to go home, but first he had to set Kendrick straight about something.

"In spite of your remarks to the boys, Justin," he said, "I don't agree with you about it being an accident. Tommy just wasn't the sort of boy to show off that way in order to get attention. When he climbed up on that parapet this morning, I'm sure he had some other reason."

"Can you prove it?"

"Well, no. But the boys—"

"The boys," Kendrick said, patting his arm, "aren't reliable. You know that, Hugh. But don't worry about it. We'll work something out."

Kendrick's manner seemed rather odd, but Follensbee

wasn't going to worry about it now. Kendrick had already started for the dining hall which would no doubt be seething with the story by this time. Follensbee turned homeward, thinking to himself that after he had cleaned up and rested awhile, the whole situation would present itself to him in proper perspective. He saw Alan Richards wave to him from the doorway of Foster and then start toward him. Follensbee would have liked to avoid a meeting just then, but there had been an urgency in the young man's signal that he could scarcely ignore. He waited patiently while the boys streamed past him, engrossed in their own affairs.

"Good Lord, Hugh! Are you okay?"

"Yes."

"It wasn't any accident, was it?"

"I don't think so."

Alan was staring at him. "Don't you *know?*"

"I'm just going home now," Follensbee said.

Alan caught his arm. "Listen, Hugh," he said, and Follensbee could not mistake the fervor in his voice, "stick to your guns on this thing, will you?"

Follensbee gave him a bewildered look. "I don't think I know what you mean," he said.

How beautiful the morning had been with the trail swinging up toward the blue sky and the crimson wine of October spilling across the hills. How beautiful until . . .

Alan was starting to speak again, but Follensbee turned away abruptly. "Excuse me," he said, "but I must go home now."

7

THE BLACK limousine sped westward from Boston along the Worcester Turnpike, guided by the capable hands of Carver's chauffeur. In the back seat Carver's headmaster sat brooding over the terrible news he had received a little while ago. He was a tall man, very thin, slightly stooped and gray-haired at forty-four. At the moment his lean, ascetic face looked ten years older and wore a troubled frown as he fished his pipe and tobacco pouch from his overcoat pocket.

Nothing like this had ever happened before in Carver's history. It was still hard for him to believe that it actually had happened. Kendrick had not been able to say much over the phone, but it was perfectly clear that he considered Tommy Conway's death to be an accident. Even so, it was an accident that should never have had a chance to happen. As a faculty they had failed somewhere in the worst way possible. Schools did not slip up that way very often and survive. Even one bad mistake could leave a scar that would take years to heal. And Tommy Conway's father was the least likely man in the world to let them off easily. He wouldn't accept excuses and he was the sort of man who liked a fight. Pettengill remembered him as an arrogant, uncouth, loud-talking man whom he had disliked from their first meeting. Under the circumstances, he would almost certainly withdraw his recent gift to the school, but that was the least of Pettengill's worries. Carver could afford to lose a building, but not her good name and her reputation for being completely dedicated to the needs of each of her boys.

Right now they were on the spot. Conway would come storming up to school and when a man like that had to face tragedy and defeat, he rarely if ever took it well or even reasonably well. Kendrick, of course, was going to fall all over himself to placate Conway, because Kendrick, in spite of the circumstances, would still be after the money. Kendrick wanted to build Carver the way you built a town and he seemed to think that the school was simply a big business corporation whose primary purpose was the acquisition of new buildings. Kendrick was a materialist to the core of his competitive soul and he always had been. Dr. Parsons had known that, too, but Kendrick had made himself very useful to the old man in a number of ways and now he had that damnable security in schooling known as "tenure." In the private schools like Carver tenure was unofficial in its rights and privileges, but it was just as ironclad and unassailable as it was in the public school system. After a certain number of years at a school if a man had been reasonably competent and faithful in his work, he could not be dislodged from the faculty tree. He could be dead from the neck up but still cling to his departmental limb until he fell off in the ripeness of his retirement age.

Kendrick, of course, was far from being moribund in any sense of the word and he was still several years from retirement. Right now he was perhaps at the height of his prestige with the Carver alumni and trustees; the student body had always had an extraordinary respect for him. Ever since his appointment as headmaster, Pettengill had felt that he was fighting Kendrick in one way or another. They didn't want the same things. Kendrick would have him spend half his time traversing the country, pulling the money out of the pockets of the alumni, holding out his hand to every pluto-crat in the land who might like to have his name on a Carver building. If the money and the buildings came along in due course, he would accept them but damned if he was going out to get them. Kendrick himself buttered up the trustees in an outrageous fashion, flattering the dying manhood of old Henderson and Parkwell and that idiot, Sykes, all of them up to their necks in corporate armor. It was wrong, Petten-gill knew, all wrong when the mind had to defer to the pocketbook. Someday he was going to pick a few masters and start a school in the mountains somewhere. They would outlaw trustees and have no need of endowments. But mean-while he cared a great deal about Carver and its reputation and the job it had to do in the modern world, cared enough to be furious at the thought of a boor like Roger Conway rampaging around the campus. He wasn't going to be a wel-come sight from any angle.

He glanced at his watch. The gold-tipped hands pointed to one-thirty. He wasn't hungry but he knew that he should eat something. They were still an hour and a half from school, and when they arrived, he would have to make an appearance at the football game before he could talk with Kendrick and the others concerned. There would be no time for food then. He leaned toward the chauffeur.

"Is there a place to eat around here, Frank?"

"Yes, sir. There's a Howard Johnson up the road about two miles. We stopped there last time I was through here with the football team."

"Fine."

The place was crowded, but shortly after they walked in, the hostess waved them to a small table at the rear of the room. She appeared to see nothing strange in a gentleman's dining with his uniformed chauffeur. People didn't make those distinctions any more, Pettengill thought. He felt very democratic and he was ashamed of himself for feeling that way. Ever since his childhood he had been trying to shatter the notion of his own natural superiority. In the big house on Fifth Avenue the servants had moved quietly and discreetly. The nearest he had ever come to eating alone with one of them had been an occasional snack at the kitchen table on the maid's night out. When the family went on motor trips, his mother had avoided any possible embarrassment on this score by ordering a picnic lunch. A few extra sandwiches and a hard-boiled egg were always packed in a shoe box for their chauffeur, Jason. He had developed an ability to eat so quickly and unobtrusively on the other side of the car that the family almost believed he never ate anything at all.

Pettengill had gone eventually to St. Paul's and Harvard, and these places had done nothing much to uproot his innate acceptance of class distinctions, but by that time he had at least begun to doubt their validity. An army foxhole had been the real convincer, and having pierced the artificiality of the old aristocratic barriers, he had gone into teaching prepared to destroy snobbery in other little snobs with all the added zeal of the convert. But even now as he sat across from Frank, keenly aware of the intellectual absurdity of his embarrassment, he was nevertheless embarrassed as he would have been years ago had Jason suddenly opened his shoe box on *their* side of the car. It was an emotional reflex that he had come to detest and it made him all the more anxious to take Frank into his confidence and treat him like an equal. Frank was going to hear the news pretty soon anyway. He might as well have it straight.

The chauffeur's hand moved swiftly across and then down his chest. "That's a terrible thing, Mr. Pettengill."

"It certainly is," Pettengill said.

Frank shook his head. "Only last week I drove him to the dentist."

Pettengill looked up from his plate. "What did he talk about? Do you remember anything?"

"He didn't talk. I remember tryin' to kid him along a bit. You know, sometimes the boys get pretty worried about them tests and I try to get 'em to smile. I couldn't get nothin' outa him."

"I see. Did you notice whether he looked especially unhappy?"

"I couldn't really say about that, Mr. Pettengill. I just remember lookin' at him a couple of times in the mirror. He wasn't cryin' or nothin' like that. He was just lookin' out the window. Some of the older ones acts that way when they got a girl on their minds or somethin', but the little guys like him are usually full of pep."

"Tommy was always pretty quiet."

"You don't think he coulda done it on purpose, do you?" Frank said. He made the sign of the cross again.

"Yes," Pettengill said, "I'm very much afraid he might have."

He was thinking all of a sudden about Hugh Follensbee and what a loyal and painstaking teacher he was. And yet, if he had heard Kendrick correctly over the phone, Follensbee had not been right with the boys at the time of the tragedy. Kendrick hadn't known why, but the mere fact in itself was unfortunate, to say the least.

"He certainly wasn't like his father," Frank said.

"You've met Mr. Conway?"

"Not exactly, sir. I seen him down at the garage the first day of school."

"What was he doing down there?"

"Teachin' his son to drive, it looked like. He had the boy get behind the wheel of that new Jaguar of his, and then he had the kid backin' and turnin' all over the yard down there."

"Did Tommy like it?"

"No, sir. He sure didn't. After he'd tried it awhile, I heard his father tellin' him to go ahead and drive it up to the school. Tommy didn't want to do it. He said he'd look silly and the boys would think he was tryin' to show off. His father got kinda mad at him. Said he oughta be proud he had a father who would let him drive an expensive car like that. If you ask me, them two didn't get along so good."

Frank was certainly right about that, Pettengill reflected. There were letters from Mr. Conway in Tommy's file in the office which hinted at the tension that must have existed between father and son. Pettengill could remember sentences here and there from those letters: *I want Tommy to go out for football. . . . He's not aggressive enough. . . . I don't want him rooming alone. . . . He's got to learn to be a leader.* There were other detailed instructions in Roger Conway's blueprint for his son's success. Again his dislike for the man swept over Pettengill. How could any boy have survived such a parent? If it turned out that Carver in some way had failed Tommy Conway, then it would be equally true that his father had failed him, too.

"Maybe he got along better with his mother?" Frank said.

"As I recall," Pettengill said, "he hardly even knew her. She died when Tommy was very young."

"Poor kid. Looks like he didn't have nobody he could trust."

Pettengill's lips came together and all at once he looked very tired. "Yes," he said, "I'm afraid that was so."

After lunch they paused for a moment in the parking space to light their cigarettes. The sunshine was warm in the lea of the building and from somewhere the breeze carried a pungent whiff of wood smoke. Pettengill glanced at his watch again and saw that they wouldn't be in time for the kickoff against Harland, but it couldn't be helped. He wondered how the boys were taking the news and whether Kendrick had been able to reach Conway yet on the phone.

"We'd better roll, Mr. Pettengill, if you wanna see any of that game today."

"Right." Pettengill nodded.

He got into the front seat this time, but he kept silent and he was grateful to Frank for not attempting to start a conversation. In his mind he struggled to line up the situation in an orderly fashion under two headings: accident or suicide. If the boy had died as the result of an accident, then the school in general and Follensbee in particular could be accused of negligence. But if Tommy had deliberately taken his own life, the underlying reason would almost certainly be found outside of his experience at Carver, and his father would have to answer for that. He would try to blame it all on the school, of course, but if they should be lucky enough to come up with some incontrovertible proof of suicide, Roger Conway could hardly disclaim his responsibility. Nor could they disclaim theirs. That was the part that he must ferret out in spite of embarrassment and at the risk of hurting individual feelings. It was a terrible thing to have to search for a flaw in the skill and devotion of men like Hugh Follensbee who had given their lives to teaching, but he would have to do it. If they had indeed failed somehow, they would not hide the fact even from Roger Conway. On the other hand, no deference to material expediency would make them kowtow to Tommy Conway's father or anyone else.

Kendrick would probably not be of much help to him in this. Kendrick was not really a scholar. Although he had once taught in the classroom, academic matters were not his primary concern. Kendrick's executive abilities were obvious and in many ways he qualified as a headmaster, but Dr. Parsons had considered him to be too much of an opportunist.

Pettengill would never forget the afternoon he had talked with Dr. Parsons in a Boston hotel room. He had already had several interviews with Carver's headmaster and had recently learned of his appointment. Dr. Parsons had met him in the lobby this time and they had gone up to a stuffy little room on the fifth floor where incongruously they had talked more or less in the midst of a linen merchants' convention.

Actually, it was Dr. Parsons who had done the talking. For an hour or so he had rambled on about Carver's problems and finally he had come to a detailed description of the strong and weak points of the various faculty members.

"We've got one man who can be of great help to you. Name's Kendrick, Justin Kendrick. Been at school a long time, about thirty years. Hard to say exactly what he does. Handles all of our discipline for one thing and takes charge when I'm away. The boys go to him a great deal for one reason or another. Afraid he's going to be a bit disappointed."

Dr. Parsons paused and rubbed his chin while Pettengill recrossed his legs again and stared out the window into Beacon Street, wondering how this fellow Kendrick or any man could have stood thirty years of Dr. Parsons.

"Good man, Kendrick. Very competent. Only trouble with him, Pettengill, between you and me, he's too much for the main chance, if you know what I mean. Always has his eye out for money or a new building. Necessary concerns, of course, but we wanted someone who would be more concerned with scholarship and with moral and spiritual values. Boys need a lot of guidance, you know. Can't let them grow up too fast. That's Kendrick's trouble. Treats them like grownups half the time. Makes private commitments. Not good, Pettengill, not good at all. Must say I've never quite known where I was with the man."

Dr. Parsons paused again and gazed out the window for a moment while from somewhere a tiny breeze stirred the fuzzy white hairs in the lobes of his ears. "Tell me, Pettengill," he said, "what do you consider our most important aim as a school?"

"Scholarship," Pettengill said. "The development of sound mental habits."

"Yes. Anything else?"

"Good citizenship."

Dr. Parsons nodded vigorously. "I like that. Go on."

A frown of concentration darkened Pettengill's face. He sat tensely in his chair, trying to ignore the laughter that was coming from down the hall along with the unmistakable chuckle of ice cubes in tall glasses.

"I believe," he said, "that the world needs gentlemen. Not snobs, but educated gentlemen who will instantly recognize right from wrong, truth from falsehood, men who will act from the finest of motives. This war has taught us, I believe, the value of toughness and the importance of moral fiber. I hope we never lose it as individuals or as a nation."

"Splendid, sir!" Dr. Parsons said, his voice shaking with emotion. "Splendid."

"Intellectually we must—"

Dr. Parsons was no longer listening. He pulled out an enormous timepiece and after a quick glance returned it to his pocket.

"Sorry to interrupt you, Pettengill, but my train leaves in thirty minutes. One thing I want to be sure of: for appear-

ances' sake, you understand, I don't want Kendrick to think
I, eh—stood in his way. The trustees left the decision entirely
up to me, but as far as Kendrick is concerned, it's best he
think it was a majority decision. Majority rules, eh? Can't
go against the democratic process, can we?"

"I understand, Dr. Parsons."

"Good. Then it's all settled. You come down as soon as you
can and I'll show you around. Introduce you to Kendrick.
Extraordinary man in some ways, but watch out for him."

Since that time Pettengill had had much the same feeling
about Kendrick. He was intensely loyal to Carver after his
fashion, but it was impossible to tell how he was going to
operate in any given situation. He never played the game by
the book. He had known Roger Conway, for example, ever
since the latter had been a schoolboy at Carver. The exact
nature of that relationship was not clear to Pettengill, and he
could not deny his uneasy suspicion. It seemed to him that
Kendrick's private commitment here, whatever it might be,
had greatly increased the danger of the present situation as
far as the school was concerned. There were going to be no
private understandings and no special favors for Roger Conway from now on. Pettengill had already made up his mind
to that. Kendrick was going to have to play this one out in
the open.

The road twisted gently toward the foothills of the Berk-
shires, and through the golden haze of the October afternoon Carver's headmaster rode tensely now, anticipating the
clash that was to come. The more he thought about it, the
more it seemed to him that Tommy Conway had made his
own terrible decision to jump this morning and they had all
failed to read the signs of his aloneness and his despair.
Those signs were not always easy to read and sometimes
they could be very misleading. Pettengill himself had wit-
nessed an incident some time ago in which Tommy Conway's

estrangement from the group had seemed rather amusing.

About a week after the opening of school he had been driving leisurely around the campus one afternoon, looking in on the usual athletic contests that were in progress. He had stopped for a few minutes to watch a hotly contended football scrimmage between two teams of the younger boys. A single uniformed player had been sitting on the bench throughout the game, and when one of the boys had come trotting out to replace a broken chin strap, Pettengill had asked him the name of the solitary figure on the sideline.

"That's Tommy Conway, sir."

"Why isn't he playing?"

"He's a substitute, sir."

"But isn't he going to get into the game?"

"He doesn't want to play, sir; he just wants to be a substitute."

"Do you mean," Pettengill had said with increasing astonishment, "that he comes out here every afternoon and just sits on the bench?"

"Yes, sir."

"And *never* plays?"

"No, sir, but he does the exercises before the game. He could play if he wanted to, but he doesn't, and Mr. Richards says it's okay for him to be the official substitute."

The boy's teammates were anxiously waiting for him to return, and Pettengill let him go. Alan Richards was in charge out there and he was very effective with this age group. He was a champion of the individualist, and one could see why he had not forced Tommy to play football, no matter what his father had said about making him more aggressive. "Official substitute." Pettengill had smiled.

The delightful absurdity of the situation had appealed to him and as he had driven off he had not thought to look more closely at the small, hunched-over figure on the bench.

He blamed himself for that now because he had always believed that no boy at Carver could have the thoughts that Tommy Conway must have had without sharing at least some of his troubles with a master. It was a Carver boast that every boy felt close to at least one master, and that man, in Tommy's case, should have had some suspicions long ago and reported them. They had all been taken unawares and even though it was hard to believe that the boy wouldn't have done it anyway, their position as a school was a vulnerable one. Roger Conway would be quick to see that.

The limousine was climbing the last rise and soon the chapel spire would come into view. Frank reached into the breast pocket of his uniform and pulled out a pack of cigarettes.

"Have one, Mr. Pettengill?"

"Oh—thanks."

The chauffeur's black-grained mechanic's thumb spun the little wheel on his lighter. He moved the flame close to the headmaster's cigarette and then to his own. A moment later both men exhaled and their smokes drifted together. It was an intimacy, Pettengill thought, which old Jason would never have permitted.

8

KENDRICK'S announcement had caused less stir than he had feared, and now that lunch was over and the first stunning impact of the tragedy had been taken in stride, the school was rushing on toward the events of an exciting afternoon. Kendrick himself strolled back to his apartment where he hoped to catch a short nap before the headmaster arrived.

Kendrick's abode was a rambling set of rooms on the ground floor of one of the older houses. Although his apartment was neither as modern nor as conveniently located as some of the other bachelor quarters, it had the great advantage of being relatively hidden and remote compared with the average school accommodations for the faculty which had all the privacy of a goldfish bowl. In Kendrick's house there were two other masters, and he left all the supervision of the routine to them, taking on no official duties himself. Very occasionally he would invite the boys in small groups to come in after evening study hall. He would serve them some rather exotic sandwiches along with a punch of his own concoction for which the boys had an extremely derogatory name but which they invariably drank to the dregs. No boy on first seeing Mr. Kendrick's apartment could be persuaded that he was on school property, and afterwards he would be inclined to believe that he had simply dreamed about tropical fish cruising in their warm water prisons.

Kendrick's interest in his bright-finned captives dated back to his college days at Oberlin, not far from the small Ohio town of his birth. At college he had become acquainted with a biology professor who liked to spend his vacations poking around in southern swamps and bayous, occasionally venturing into the open sea. During the Christmas holidays of his senior year Kendrick had gone with him to Key West, where, cruising the tepid shoals of the Dry Tortugas, they had peered into fascinating underwater kingdoms. That was when Kendrick had begun the lifelong task of learning to recognize the various species and to study their habits. But it was not a laborious task for him. He had fallen in love not only with the amazing creatures but also with their surroundings. He loved the warm winds and the languorous, melting blue of the sky. The white sands and the graceful, whispering palms delighted him, and when he felt the hot sun on his back, he knew the contentment of the lizard sleeping on the warm rock and why the cat arched herself with such pleasure before the fire. His pale skin never tanned, but new colonies of freckles appeared; the tip of his nose got red and peeled and then got red again. With no desire to go north to steam heat and heavy clothing, he imagined that he wished to stay forever on the shell-strewn beaches.

But the vacation had ended and when he had come back again a year or so later for a much longer visit, he had fallen into the habit of staring at the wall of his beach house for hours at a time, a malady that was treated according to local custom with large quantities of rum. Kendrick decided that after all he preferred the more invigorating northern air for himself and he would duplicate artificially a tropical environment for his fish. The project had developed into a long-range hobby. Each of the glass-walled tanks in his apartment at Carver had its own thermostat and purifier. Now and then he bought new fish from various dealers and had them shipped to him at great expense. But the fish were worth it. With multicolored radiance they swam in and out of their man-made grottos and around their pebbled yards. Kendrick never tired of watching them. He could come home unnerved at the end of the day and look into their silent world and feel a kind of primordial serenity drift over him.

Approaching his apartment now, he was thinking about the new tank he had on order. Down on the football field there were thunderous cheers, but when he closed the door of his apartment, the silence was broken only by the faint and measured ticking of the ornate clock on the mantelpiece. The place was too hot. He opened a window and then checked the temperature of each of the tanks before he went to his bedroom and changed his brown tweed jacket for a pale blue silk dressing gown. Returning to the living room, he stretched out on the couch.

He lit one of the Turkish brand of cigarettes that he had smoked ever since the days when Roger Conway had been at Carver. The boy had done pretty well for himself since then, if you didn't trouble to look behind the facts of his astonishing career. Kendrick had kept careful track of that career from newspaper clippings, from the reports of other alumni who had crossed his path, and from Conway himself when, for example, Conway had first returned to Carver and they had sat together here in the apartment, drinking Scotch through most of the night. Conway, his handsome face coarse-fleshed now, thick-veined and a little too ruddy, had revealed all too plainly just how far the blind and terrible force within him had driven him since that June day of his graduation long ago.

There had been another graduation after that when four years later he had marched through the streets of New Haven in a much larger procession in which scarcely anyone even knew his name. His sojourn at Yale had been passed in almost complete obscurity where in the midst of a social feast and a bustling scholarship he had felt again the loneliness and the sullen anger of the misfit. His sole incentive for enduring the whole blundering and painful experience of college had been the acquisition of a diploma which he had regarded as the indispensable key to his future. He had used the key during the darkest days of the depression to unlock a series of doors in a small mining company in western Pennsylvania until one day just before his thirtieth birthday, he gained the office of the president and saw his own name stenciled on the door.

He had paused only briefly to get the feel of the place and to convince his employees and his stockholders that a man of thirty could actually run a company and run it well. Then he began to look around. He had gained a plateau, he was halfway up the mountain, but it was a mountain that could not be scaled by hard work alone. He needed more working capital, for by this time he had learned that it took a nickel to make a dime. Once again the Yale diploma served as a key and this time it opened a handsome door in a gracious, white-columned house in Charleston, West Virginia. This was the home of Abner Graham Fairfax. Out in the state's vast coal fields armies of men descended into the earth, locomotives puffed in the sooty dawn, and factory whistles blew because Abner Graham Fairfax said so.

Roger went to see the tycoon, hoping to obtain the backing he needed for a daring venture that would pay off handsomely if he could afford to take the risk. He came away not only with the money and the old pirate's blessing, but with his daughter, too. Louise Ann Fairfax was reputed to be the prettiest girl in Charleston, and her friends said that she fell in love with Roger Conway because he was so definitely not her type. Long accustomed to meeting men from the big eastern universities who had seemed to her like so many bits of polished paste, she saw in Roger Conway a rough diamond that was much more to her liking. She made up her mind very quickly. They were married three months later, and the guest list for their wedding was only slightly behind the record attendance at the annual horse show.

The school office staff scanned a great many newspapers in order to keep an up-to-date file on the alumni, and Kendrick had come across the clippings one afternoon in the course of other work. Conway had not invited him to the wedding and he had not expected an invitation. The boy's fortunes were on the rise now; he was climbing furiously and with clear intent. At the moment he had cast aside his former guides and confidants. He didn't think that he needed Kendrick now or would ever need him again. Kendrick knew better. Roger Conway was climbing dangerously fast for a sustained flight. Someday what was left of him would come back to his beginnings.

The girl in the newspaper photo was very lovely. Kendrick could tell just from reading the formal announcement that Conway was marrying over his head. Abner Graham Fairfax had probably had very little to say about the wedding, iron-fisted business executives being notoriously like so much putty in the hands of their beautiful daughters. As he entrusted more and more of his money to his son-in-law, the old man had probably expected that his daughter would teach her husband a little more about the social amenities that were expected in their environment. Kendrick had had his doubts as to her success on that score. Could even a bride teach a coal miner's son something that he would be too proud to admit he didn't know? Kendrick had put the clippings back in the file, wondering irrelevantly if Louise Ann Conway had ever ridden a motorcycle.

There had been a few more items from the society pages after that, but from Pearl Harbor until the end of the war, Kendrick had received only the sketchiest reports on the activities of Roger Conway. Piecing them together and guessing at the blank spots, Kendrick had written the story in his mind, complete with characters and dialogue as though he had actually been its author.

The story began on the morning after Pearl Harbor when Abner Graham Fairfax had called his son-in-law to assure him that coal mining was an essential industry and therefore Roger was clearly draft exempt. When this had not appealed to Roger, as he must have known it wouldn't, the old man had quietly arranged through powerful friends to get him an army commission and a desk job in Washington for the duration. Conway, meanwhile, in his usual hotheaded and impulsive way, had figured that the marines would be the first into combat and had joined up. His wife had suspected and feared what he was up to, but in the end she had been quietly proud of it. She moved into miserable quarters near his training camp, and six months later when he embarked with his division for the South Pacific, she was pregnant.

He came back two years later with a bullet crease in his shoulder and a recurrent case of malaria that was to go on ravaging him periodically. He was battle tough and weary but more aggressive than ever and explosive with rage over civilian lags in production and bureaucratic red tape. He might have gone right back again after his leave, had not Abner Graham Fairfax died quietly in his sleep one night, leaving all his vast holdings to his son-in-law. Fairfax Industries, Inc. or "the company," as Roger called it, was badly in need of consolidation and staff reorganization. As a result of the old man's weakening grip on the helm in the past few years, competitors had made serious inroads all along the line. It had been relatively easy for his wife to persuade Conway to obtain a medical discharge and go to live in the big house in Charleston.

He was thirty-five now and already at the top of one mountain, but Louise must have known by this time that it would not be enough for him. She had observed that he took far more delight in climbing than in reaching the top, and this worried her because she was growing weary of her husband's need to be something other than he was. She wanted to settle down again in her father's house and live the easygoing, quietly gay and comfortable existence of her childhood. She wanted her husband to stay home at least two days a week and putter around the place the way the other husbands did, and she wanted him to go out with her to the homes of their friends and to the parties which no one in their group would think of missing, business or no business. They had enough money as it was, more than enough; they had been through a war, and now with the loss of her father, she felt more and more the need to grow close again to her husband and for them to have the leisure to share their lives with their son. It was the part about Tommy that worried and hurt her most of all.

He was a beautiful child with large, dark eyes, a lovely clear skin and a most affectionate nature. Louise had rejoiced at the prospect of showing him to his father and she would never forget the first time that Roger had bent over the crib. He had looked almost as surprised and delighted as she had hoped he would, but then he had straightened up and turned to her.

"Isn't he a little peaked, dear? He should get out more."

His big hand had gripped the fragile crib. "After all, he has to exercise those muscles for the future, you know."

She had stared at him for a moment. "He's only a baby," she had said, a coldness in her voice. "He doesn't *have* to do anything."

Perhaps even then the first tiny fissures in their marriage had begun to open. They ran together and suddenly one day the chasm was there between them and they could not bridge it. She had pretended at first that the gulf was nonexistent and had gone to parties gaily and alone, if need be. When her husband wasn't working (there always seemed to be another merger in the offing nowadays), she would take his arm in public without the slightest hint of the stiffness in her fingers, and meanwhile she had lavished her love upon the little boy as though some dreadful intuition had warned her that what she gave him then and in the next few years would have to last him for the rest of his life.

There had been no need for Kendrick to guess at the next part of it or to make up a story. Harvey Blanton, Conway's former roommate at Carver, had returned for Alumni Day in 1949 and had told Kendrick exactly what had happened. The tragedy had occurred after a party, one that Louise Conway had not wished to attend because it was to be almost purely a business affair where, in a rented hotel suite, men would use their wives and their liquor to help set up "the big deal." Conway had prevailed upon his wife at the last minute, and it had been Harvey's opinion that Louise had sacrificed her evening to her husband's interests in the hope that he might in the future devote a little more time to hers. It wasn't to turn out that way.

Everything had gone wrong from the beginning The party was too large, too much liquor was consumed, and for some unaccountable reason dinner was served nearly an hour later than planned. Before the evening was over, Louise had developed one of the "sick headaches" that had been troubling her recently. She told Conway that he would have to take her home but that he was free to return if he wished. Conway, reluctant to leave while there was still a chance of some agreement being made in his absence, created an unpleasant scene and then stormed out of the room after his wife. Ten minutes later on one of the back roads over which he had been furiously speeding, Conway's big car went out of control and turned over in a ditch. The police highway patrol found Louise dead, pinned under the wreck, and Conway stumbling around with the blood pouring from a deep gash in his cheek. It was just two days before Tommy's sixth birthday.

It had soon become obvious to Kendrick that Conway had not been able to adjust to the consequences of that terrible night. In a way it had driven him back to Carver. He had had few friends in Charleston, and after Louise's death he had even fewer. On the day after the accident Louise's favorite aunt had swooped down upon the house and whisked Tommy away to her own home. Conway had not objected. He had felt, he explained later, completely alone. He lived in another world now from his own parents. His boyhood friends back home had regarded his meteoric rise first with envy and suspicion and, finally, with hostility. Shortly after the funeral he had sold the lovely, big house of Abner Graham Fairfax and moved to an apartment in New York where "the company" was setting up an office. He had appeared quite unexpectedly on the Carver campus one winter afternoon. A few of the boys had noticed him wandering around in the gym, a big, heavy-set man with a terrible scar on his cheek. That night he and Kendrick had sat drinking together, and Kendrick's long-range gamble had begun to pay off.

Kendrick stood up. He took a china figurine from its place

on top of the bookcase, looked at it thoughtfully for a moment, and then put it back. In the distance he could hear the strident efforts of the Carver band. The game would soon begin and he would have to look in on it and also check on the afternoon showing of the movie before the headmaster arrived. He sat down again and, full of memories, lit another cigarette, smoking this one in the sleek, amber holder which he had acquired around the time that Roger Conway had decided to enter his son.

That was in 1952 and Conway had looked much more relaxed when he returned this time. He had brought along some snapshots of Tommy and showed them to Kendrick with obvious pride. The boy was in the Fourth Grade at school and doing well in his studies. He was a bit timid on the athletic field, according to his father, but he would get over it. Conway was going to make sure of that. The boy would have to toughen up. You had to be tough in this world, able to give and to take physical punishment. Otherwise, the boys in school would gang up on you, Conway explained, the way they always ganged up on the weakling.

Kendrick had been listening in disapproving silence. "I think, Roger," he had said, "that you should marry again."

Conway had laughed hoarsely but that had not concealed his surprise. "Marry again? Why?"

"For the boy's sake, for one thing."

Conway had made a disparaging gesture. "Tommy doesn't need to be mothered any more. He got all he needed of that from his aunt, more than he needed. I can give him everything he needs now and I've already started." His voice rang out proudly. "I'll bet that boy of mine has more guns, knives, and fishing rods than any other kid in his school."

"Does he want them?"

More dark blood had surged into Conway's face, but he

had kept his voice smooth and easy. "Of course he wants them. What else would a normal boy of his age want?"

Kendrick had considered telling him and then decided to try another tack. "Well, you need a wife yourself, Roger. Don't you miss—?"

"A woman in the bed?"

Years ago Conway's bluntness had embarrassed Kendrick and it did so again.

Conway laughed. "There are always plenty of women if it's a piece you're after."

Kendrick had tried not to show his distaste for such unspeakable vulgarity. He saw that Conway was regarding him with amusement.

"I suppose that comes as rather a surprise to you cloistered schoolteachers," Conway said.

"I was referring," Kendrick said stiffly, "to something else that marriage might do for you and Tommy."

Conway was still laughing softly, "You fellows ought to come down to the city once in a while. Matter of fact, some of you guys really need a woman."

It was all Kendrick could do to keep from speaking sharply as he had years ago when a country bumpkin had come up the hill with a dirty face, but he reminded himself that the bumpkin was giving Carver one of the finest prep school dormitories in New England.

Conway recrossed his legs, and the beginnings of a paunch swelled out over his belt. "Don't worry about Tommy," he said. "He's going to have everything he could want. As a matter of fact, I get a lot of fun out of giving him things before he even asks for them. I figure he'll be ready to come here in '57. That's just thirty years after my time, isn't it? I certainly hope things are better for him."

"Things weren't so bad for you," Kendrick said.

"Yes, they were," Conway contradicted sharply. Then he looked down at the carpet. "It's very bad to be a poor boy in a rich man's school."

"Wait a minute!" Kendrick said. "This isn't a rich man's school, Roger."

"Aren't boarding schools for the rich?"

"Of course not."

Conway blinked.

"Boarding schools are for all who are lucky enough to get to them in one way or another."

"Then I suppose you'll say that money isn't important around here?" Conway flung out.

Kendrick leaned forward in his chair. "Money," he said, "is *very* important around here. We need money to maintain our plant and to add to it; we need money for our teachers and perhaps most of all we need money to increase our scholarship funds so that we can take a boy with brains and character from anywhere in the world, not because he can afford to come here but because we can afford to have him."

Kendrick could remember that Conway had had the effrontery to applaud at that point in mock approval. "Those are very worthy aims, Justin," he said, "very worthy indeed, but I'll be honest with you. I don't operate that way. Whatever I may give this school from now on will be primarily for my own benefit and for my son's."

Another tremendous cheer from the football field broke into Kendrick's reverie. He got up from the couch, thinking to himself that Roger Conway could do nothing more now for the benefit of his son. His opinion of the school at this point could be easily predicted and so could his personal reaction to the tragedy. There was only one possible chance of Conway's having a constructive reaction to what had happened and that possibility lay within the man himself. Meanwhile, the faculty members involved would almost inevitably further complicate matters. Pettengill, especially, with his front and center idealism and his boy scout notions of conduct would bring out the very worst in Conway. Kendrick frowned and glanced at his watch. He had work to do, but he stood there a little while longer in his soft silk dressing gown, considering ways and means of dealing with the situation.

9

THE BABY had been bottled, burped, and put to bed, his raucous, red-faced yelling muffled by angelic sleep. This miracle of repose occurred each midday and with luck it would last a couple of hours. Nancy had had a sandwich for lunch and having made enough of Bill's formula to last over the week end, she was enjoying her cigarette and coffee in the living room when Alan came in. She saw at once that he did not have his usual look of Saturday satisfaction.

"What's the matter, dear?"

Alan stopped in the doorway. He glanced at his wife and then looked away. "Nancy—Tommy Conway was killed this morning."

Nancy stood up, her coffee cup rattling in its saucer. "Oh no!"

Alan crossed the room and dropped heavily into a chair. He stared into the fireplace. "I couldn't believe it either."

"That poor little boy."

"That's what I'm thinking. Of all the kids in this house—"

"But what happened?"

"According to Kendrick it was an accident on Hugh's field

trip. Kendrick told me about it just before the last period. You were feeding Bill and I thought I'd better wait to tell you."

"It's just as well you did." Nancy frowned. "This must be awful for Hugh."

"Yes."

"Do you know exactly what happened?"

"Not yet."

"How could he have simply fallen, Alan?"

Alan looked up. "Exactly. He was the most careful boy in the house, wasn't he?"

"I certainly would have said so."

"Of course he was. He wasn't the type to take any chances on falling from up there."

"Alan, you don't think—?"

"Yes, I do."

"You really think he could have been *that* unhappy?"

"Yes, but I can't prove it. Nobody knows yet what really happened. I couldn't get anything out of Hugh just before lunch. He was exhausted. We've got to find out."

"But of course. Won't Hugh know?"

"Kendrick has already implied to me that we can't entirely trust Hugh's recollections or the boys', either. I think he suspects suicide just as I do but he insists on pretending the whole thing was an accident."

"Why?"

"Because he doesn't want to tell old man Conway the truth. He might get mad and not give Carver any more money."

"That sounds pretty farfetched to me," Nancy said. "I should think Mr. Conway would be even madder if he thought it was an accident, possibly caused by our carelessness."

"He doesn't react that way. You remember him, don't you?

Big, beefy guy. Very wealthy and very stuck on himself."

"I remember him all right," Nancy said dryly. "The day he brought Tommy up to school he asked me if I was prepared to give out tea and sympathy this year."

"Very funny."

"Yes, I know, but I felt rather sorry for him in a way. I think he means well."

"Maybe he does," Alan said, "but he's still a jerk for my money. I have an idea Kendrick feels the same way about him down deep. There's something between those two that goes back to Conway's student days here."

"Well, you don't have to worry about that, darling."

"Maybe I do."

"But why?"

"Because I have an idea it's tied in with something Kendrick's trying to promote."

Nancy looked incredulous. "I don't understand this sudden suspicion of Justin Kendrick."

"It's not sudden. I've always thought he was a pretty smooth operator and now he's up to something. It can't be any good if he's trying to hide the truth."

Nancy stubbed out her cigarette and then tucked her slim legs underneath her on the couch in a position which Alan would have thought horribly uncomfortable but which she always insisted was not. Alan leaned back and tried to relax a little himself. Normally on a Saturday afternoon he would have headed for the athletic fields or gone up to the lab for a little work on his own. The tension wouldn't flow away this afternoon, and soon he was sitting up straight again, remembering the tired and bewildered look on Hugh Follensbee's face when they had met just before lunch. Nancy seemed almost to echo his thoughts.

"I'm so sorry for Emmy and Hugh," she said. "Emmy and I had a wonderful visit together this morning. We went for a long walk and she told me lots of things about her first days here and about this life in general. She hopes you won't get too easily discouraged with teaching."

"You didn't tell her I was thinking of leaving?"

"Now just relax, Alan. Emmy doesn't blab like some of the others."

"Well, I certainly don't want any rumors like that flying around," Alan said. "At least not until we've made up our minds. By the way, that letter—"

"Yes, I know."

"What do you want to do?"

"It's up to you, dear."

"The wife is entitled to an opinion."

"The wife goes where the husband goes if she's the right kind of wife."

Alan came over, rumpled her hair, and then kissed her. "You're the right kind, Mrs. Richards," he said, "in case you're wondering."

Nancy squeezed his hand and suddenly he pulled her into his arms. For a moment she pressed against him and then, looking toward the living-room windows, she pulled away.

"The boys, darling. They can see everything in here."

"To hell with the boys."

"Oh sure," Nancy said ruefully. "I only wish we could say that once in a while."

"We could if we were anywhere else but here," Alan said. He took both her hands and looked intently into her eyes. "I'll answer that letter from Hall & Crandon tonight. I'll tell them I'll be ready the first of July. No, let's make it August. We'll take a month off and go someplace. How about it?"

"Fine," Nancy said, "but isn't a month rather long to go without eating?"

Alan grinned. "All right, wise guy. Now tell me seriously, what do you think?"

"How come you've made up your mind so suddenly?"

Alan thought a moment. "I guess it's a little of everything. For one thing, I'm fed up trying to teach spoiled brats like Larry Connors who just don't give a damn to begin with. I guess I want to feel that I'm working with people who care as much about the subject as I do. That would be true in business."

"Oh, I don't know. There are dedicated people wherever you go. And undedicated ones, too, if that's a word."

"I don't think it is."

"Well, you know what I mean. What else don't you like?"

"Oh, I guess you could call it politics. Special favors, deals, things like that."

"Wait a minute. Do you think in business—?"

"You expect that sort of thing in business. You're after material gains and there are bound to be deals."

"I don't know what you're referring to specifically," Nancy said, "but I think there are going to be deals and understandings in any activity."

"There shouldn't be here."

"Oh, come now! In a boarding school? Why even among the women we have certain agreements that you might as well call 'deals.' We give a little here, take a little there, press our advantages and try to strengthen our position. We have to do that to keep in with things."

"I'm talking about teaching," Alan said. "We deal with facts. It is our job to impart known facts and to teach the boys how to devise techniques that will help them to perceive new facts. I'm not giving a course in social behavior."

"How about when you elect a faculty committee of some sort? Don't tell me there aren't any politics involved there?"

"Well, that's not primarily an academic matter. Teaching is concerned with the ideals of truth and justice, not with hypocritical judgments and privileged people."

Nancy stared at him for a moment. "Really, darling, I admire your idealism and lofty concepts, but aren't you being just a little naïve? I mean, doesn't a teacher have to tell his students about reality, too? Don't you have to tell them out of your experience what the world is really like, as well as what it could be like or maybe should be like?"

Alan got up, stuffed his hands into his pockets, and began to pace slowly up and down the room, something his classes often saw him do when he was teaching most intently.

"I agree with you," he said, "that we must somewhere tell the boys the sordid details, but I don't think that means I should be using *The Daily News* as a textbook. Now, what I meant about politics—"

Nancy spoke very quietly and without looking at her husband. "I think it's even more important for the boys to be able to tell the teacher the sordid details once in a while and to know that he will listen. Anyway," she went on quickly, "let's don't try to decide today about leaving. Let's think it over and say you'll write that company one way or the other next week. That will be final."

"All right," Alan said. "That's fine with me."

He sat down again and lay back against the worn upholstery, thinking to himself that his wife was a darn sensible woman and a pretty one, too. Her brunette, patrician good looks were bone deep, and she had the kind of figure that made the boys turn around to look at her when she walked through the dining room to their table. Nancy fitted well into the school life. The boys liked her, and she knew how to talk to them on equal terms and still keep their respect. In this business a man's wife could make all the difference. The right woman sometimes accounted for his success; the wrong one invariably ruined him.

"I wouldn't get into a fight with Kendrick if I were you," Nancy said.

Alan's complacency vanished and he stiffened abruptly. "Why not?"

"I just wouldn't. He's been here a lot longer than we have."

"What difference does that make?"

"And he has a great deal of power."

"So what? He can't fire me."

"No, but he can make things unpleasant for you. He does that to people who cause trouble."

"But I'm not *causing* trouble, for Pete's sake!"

"You don't have to shout," Nancy said. "I'm only telling you what I know happens. Sally Tingue told me that Bill got extra study-hall duty all last spring just because he argued too much with Kendrick. It isn't worth it."

Alan's jaw muscles stiffened and his face was suddenly dark and tense. "Well, I think it is," he said.

"But what good will it do?"

"It isn't a question of good; it's a matter of getting at the truth."

"But what if the truth doesn't help in this case?" Nancy persisted.

"You don't understand," Alan said, "any more than Kendrick does. The truth is the truth whether it helps or not. It can't be compromised. I respect the truth; Kendrick doesn't. He simply acts on whatever premise best suits his purpose."

"He must have a reason."

"Of course he has a reason!" Alan shouted. "I've already pointed out why he won't tell Conway the hard fact that it was suicide."

"But you don't know it was suicide."

"Even if we did, I doubt if Kendrick would tell him."

"I don't understand," Nancy said, "why you should be so angry with Justin before you know what he's actually doing. You always tell me to act on the facts." She smiled. "How about you?"

"But—"

"You're taking an awful chance on getting in wrong with the important people around here before you're even sure there's anything to make a fuss about. That's not exactly smart, darling."

"Listen," Alan said, "Kendrick has no desire to look for the truth here. I already know that. You should have seen the way he acted when he called me in this morning, as though I were some sort of backward child who couldn't understand the situation."

"Honestly?"

"You're darn right. He told me how I should react to Tommy's death and just what to say to old man Conway. You can imagine how I felt, listening to him go on that way as though Tommy were some kind of a stick that had slipped off a cliff and we didn't have to concern ourselves about it any more. He means to handle the whole thing his way and to hell with the horrible mess that must be behind it."

"It's hard to believe that, Alan."

"Maybe it is, but he's been running the show around here for years and I think it's time somebody challenged his methods."

"Did it ever occur to you that he might have his own reasons for what he's doing?"

"I'm sure he has."

"And they might be good reasons?"

"I don't believe it. Not after the line he took with me."

"He also might be a little wiser than you, Alan, under the circumstances."

"Wiser! Because Conway has a lot of money—is that what you mean?"

"Stop shouting! You'll wake the baby."

"I don't care!"

"Well, I do!"

Nancy looked down at the cigarette which was trembling between her fingers. Alan turned and stared out the window. A referee's whistle shrilled in the distance, and from the packed and frenzied stands came a rhythmic, husky-throated cheer.

"Why don't you go to the game?" Nancy said.

Alan was still looking out the window. "I am going. How about you?"

"And just leave the baby?"

"I'm sorry, I forgot. I'll wait."

"Don't be silly. I don't know when he'll wake up. He was pretty tired. I'll bring him down later."

Alan swung around. "I'm sorry, honey. I just wanted you to see my point."

"I do see it."

"Are you sure?"

"I still think Justin may be doing what is best."

"Best for whom?"

"Best for the school. Best for all of us."

"All right," Alan said, "supposing he is. Now I just want you to answer me one question without getting mad. Is it right for a man to deliberately ignore the truth?"

"That depends."

"On what?"

"Well—the situation. His reasons."

"Then there are certain situations when we can dispense with truth for our own reasons?"

"I—"

"In other words," Alan rushed on triumphantly, "it's all right someday if our son isn't truthful at times?"

Nancy put her hands to her face. "Go to the game," she said.

"But I was only trying to show you—"

"Go to the game!"

Alan did not move for a moment. Then he shrugged and walked out the door, knowing that Nancy was crying softly behind her hands. He wanted to comfort her, but he knew from experience that it would be best to leave her alone now. He fumbled in the hall closet for his overshoes and the heavy, fleece-lined overcoat. It would be cold in the stands when the sun went down behind the gym.

On his way out he stopped by the living-room doorway. Nancy was still sitting on the couch. She did not look at him.

"I didn't mean to shout at you, honey," he said. He paused hopefully and then added, "I'll save you a seat."

Nancy didn't say a word. Alan shrugged. A man would have accepted his apology on the spot; a woman had to wait for the right time and place.

Carver was trailing by one touchdown in the declining minutes of the first half when he arrived at the game. In a dark mood he walked along behind the overburdened bleachers, wondering what Nancy was doing now. He should have kept this business to himself and not drawn her into it at all. There was no reason why she should share his deep distrust of Kendrick, but she might at least have shared his respect for the truth. It worried him that she hadn't.

In one corner of the stands where the faculty usually congregated, he managed to squeeze into a top row seat between Harry Rogers and Bill Tingue. Tingue's thin, long-nosed face was pinched with cold and he was huddled down in his sheepskin coat. It passed through Alan's mind that Tingue always looked cold and thin and tired, probably because he spent too much time at his typewriter, grinding out stories that didn't sell. Harry Rogers, on the other hand, was always barging around the countryside, and today he was simply wearing a wool sweater under his sport coat. His fleshy, good-humored face seemed to exude a glow of its own which pushed back the cold. He gave Alan a quizzical look.

"Where have you been, boy?" He nudged Alan in the ribs. "This one's a humdinger." Leaning forward, he cupped his hands and bellowed encouragement so fiercely that several of the boys sitting nearby turned to stare at him.

Alan smiled to himself. Harry Rogers had been teaching history for twelve years at Carver, but he was a kind of perennial sophomore who invariably behaved like a wild man at a football game, yelling at the officials and pounding spectators on the back whether he knew them or not, much to his wife's disgust.

The big Harland team was only a few feet from another touchdown when after a furious scramble the whistle blew and the half ended. Alan felt Harry Rogers' fists thudding against his arm.

"We stopped 'em, boy! We'll get 'em in the second half when we open up with the passes." He looked disapprovingly at Tingue. "What's the matter, Bill? Haven't heard a peep out of you."

"I've got a cold," Tingue said.

"Oh." There was a faint note of contempt in Harry's voice. "I thought maybe you had your mind on one of those stories you're always writing."

"As a matter of fact, I *was* thinking about a story," Tingue said. He reached for his handkerchief and blew his nose vigorously. "But not one of mine."

"What?" Harry said. He was watching two small boys who had run out on the field of glory and were playing catch with a varsity football.

"I said the story wasn't mine," Tingue repeated. With a surreptitious movement he opened a small box of pills and slipped one into his mouth.

"You damned hypochondriac," Harry said good-humoredly. "Whose story was it, then?"

"Tommy Conway's."

"What was it about?"

Tingue swallowed the pill. "Death," he said.

Harry looked at him reproachfully. "Don't be morbid, Bill."

Harry's attention was distracted a moment later by the Carver band which was performing an intricate maneuver in the center of the field. Alan touched Tingue's sleeve.

"Tell me a little about that story, will you, Bill?"

"Why, sure." Tingue looked surprised. "It was a pretty good yarn, as a matter of fact. Very realistic for a kid of his age. It was about a married couple who don't get along. They have an automobile accident and the wife is killed. The point of the story was that it should have been the other way around."

"Would you let me see it?"

Tingue blew his nose again. "I'd be glad to, Alan, but I handed it back to him several days ago. I have no idea what he did with it."

"Oh."

"May I ask why this sudden interest?"

Alan wasn't sure just how Tingue would play it if the chips were ever down. "No special reason," he said, as casually as he could. "Tommy was in my house. I knew him pretty well and I can't help wondering what happened this morning. How do you figure it?"

Tingue shrugged. "To tell you the truth, I didn't know a thing about it until Kendrick made that announcement at lunch. Naturally I was shocked. I liked Tommy. I haven't thought much about how it happened. I suppose it was an accident . . ." His voice trailed off.

"Supposing," Alan said, "just supposing you were asked your opinion on the chances of its *not* being an accident. What would you say?"

Tingue offered his pillbox. "Have one? I've got kind of a rough throat. Had it all week."

"No, thanks."

Tingue helped himself and then closed the box with a decisive little click. "Who's to say about a thing like that? You've got to have some positive evidence. Tommy was a nice little guy—rather sad, overly sensitive, very intense, but those are often the stripes of a writer. I really think he might have done something pretty fine someday. On the other hand, he was maybe a little too introspective. Frankly, I can't answer your question."

"I only asked you," Alan said, "because I knew he'd been having a rough time of it this year. He wasn't happy and I thought you might have noticed it, too."

"Not especially, but then he liked English."

"Who's this?" Harry said. The band was leaving the field and there was a moment of vacuum now before the teams returned from the locker room.

"Tommy Conway," Alan said.

"Oh, *him*." There was a sneer in Harry's voice. "Little odd ball. I had that guy in my fifth period ancient history class. He sat in the back row and I can still see those big eyes of his staring at me. Looked like he was in a trance. I may put 'em to sleep, but I sure as hell don't hypnotize 'em!" He laughed his big, extrovert laugh. "If you asked me, I'd say that no normal kid of fourteen would look like that."

"Wait a minute!" Tingue said. "Just because he was shy—"

"I don't mean that," Harry said. "I honestly think that kid was a case and we didn't know it. I wouldn't even be surprised if it wasn't any accident this morning." He shrugged. "Not that it would make any difference now."

Alan started to speak but at that moment the Carver team trotted out of the gym and a roar went up from the stands.

"Let's go get 'em, Carver!" Harry shouted.

It was hopeless, Alan knew, to try to get Harry's attention now. He looked away and just then saw Kendrick standing at the edge of the crowd. Kendrick's pudgy face turned, and his eyes, omniscient and calculating, seemed to observe in a single glance the number of boys in the stands, their dress and general behavior, the presence of parents and guests, the campus police at their posts and no one knew what else before he moved on, heavy and thick-waisted, his soft hands dangling below the cuffs of his camel's-hair coat. Alan watched him go and then looked around for Nancy. He wished she would come but knew somehow that she wasn't coming. He was going to leave in a little while and have another look in Tommy's room. That composition might still be in his desk. There had to be a clue somewhere, a place where the boy had given himself away.

He was aware all at once of the stunned silence around him as one of the big Harland ends caught a pass and ran through the Carver secondary for a touchdown. Alan's glance strayed toward the cheering section and there like a fat tub was Jim Boucher. It was somehow typical, Alan thought, that in the midst of defeat and collective despair Boucher should be unconcernedly picking his nose.

10

BOUCHER was bored. The feeling had been coming over him since the start of the second quarter and it had settled upon him now in a kind of heavy pall from which he could see no escape. Pro football was worthy of attention, but these school games were mostly a succession of fumbles and other stupid errors. Boucher had come to the Harland game only because he had been unable to find anything else to do that was sufficiently diverting. He regarded his companions who yelled and cheered at these games with contemptuous amusement. "School spirit" was a synthetic frenzy whipped up by the headmaster to impress people with what a great place Carver was. That stuff was for weenies. Sophisticated men never yelled themselves hoarse at one of these games unless they had never grown up. Mr. Rogers, for example, was certainly good at making a fool of himself. Boucher dug a finger into his nose and stared moodily at the thick lips of the tuba player.

In spite of the all-pervading dullness of the moment, his mind was not a total blank. Unpleasant images and bits of memory kept intruding themselves so that he was obliged to

see again his roommate's face before and after the awful
thing that had happened this morning. The first memory
went back to when they had all gotten out of the car and old
"Stinger" was giving them the usual spiel about being careful. Tommy had been standing on the outer edge of the
circle and he had looked different somehow. The nearest
Boucher could come to describing him in his own mind had
been to say that his roommate actually looked happy, and no
one at Carver had ever seen him look that way before. His
eyes had been unusually bright and he had darted glances
around him, looking at the woods and the sky and everything
as though he had never seen them until this morning. And
when they had all raced for the trail up the Rock, Tommy
had not hung back as usual, afraid that they might lay for
him or give him a pink belly as they had done last night. He
had just walked along as calm as could be, slinging the strap
of that nifty camera of his over his shoulder. When Boucher
had said something to him, Tommy's eyes had seemed to
look right through him as though he was in kind of a
trance. It had given Boucher a spooky feeling just to look at
him.

There was another part which had happened at the top.
All the way up when they had been horsing around in the
underbrush, Boucher had been wondering about the strange
and invulnerable armor which his roommate had acquired
all of a sudden. For a boy who cried at night in his bed and
sat for hours alone, staring out the window, he was unbelievably calm this morning and sort of "high," the way
they said dope could make you. There had been no time to
see if the others had observed this phenomenon, for as soon
as they reached the top each of them had participated in a
defiant and dangerous little ritual. Each in turn had climbed
the parapet and forced himself to look straight down at the
brook below. Then, feeling exhilarated and having thor-

oughly disobeyed instructions, they had gathered in a smirking circle to look at some trick cards which Georgie Lindstrom had brought along. The cards had a picture of a naked woman on them and if you shuffled them in the right way, she would wiggle her bot at you.

At one point when Boucher had chanced to glance up from the cards, he had seen his roommate standing on the parapet, not looking down as the rest of them had, but out at the distant hills, at the horizon, or perhaps at nothing at all. Boucher, in wordless astonishment and gripped all of a sudden by a horrible awareness of what was going to happen, had been unable to move or even to bring forth the scream that was lodged in his throat. Seconds later, there was nothing on the parapet or beyond it but the emptiness of space.

Afterwards, approaching the brook with his knees shaking and the nausea flooding into his throat, he had glanced at the blood-choked mouth and the staring eyes and then turned quickly away. For a while he had been afraid that he would never see anything else, but by the time the doctor had arrived and lifted the body out of the brook and put the blanket over the face, he had begun to feel a little better. It was still hard to believe that Tommy had done it, but Boucher was absolutely certain that it had not been an accident. There had been no one near Tommy to push him or scare him. He had just climbed up there and jumped; he must have been planning to do it all along. But why should a guy look so happy when he was planning to kill himself? It didn't make sense.

Boucher came out of his reverie and looked toward the faculty end of the bleachers. Mr. Kendrick had appeared and was making a quick check of the stands. Their eyes met and Boucher smiled inwardly. He could leave any time now because Mr. Kendrick's mind would have registered his presence at the game. He purposely delayed a few minutes and then stood up.

"I gotta go now," he announced loudly to no one in particular. "Kendrick wants to see me." He began to push his way toward the end of the row where he could easily drop to the ground.

"Stop shovin', you fat slob!"

Boucher ignored the speaker who was one of the seniors in his house. "Bastard!" he said under his breath.

He walked along slowly, eying all the new cars in the parking space. He wished that he had the nerve to hop into one of them and drive off. More than anything else right now he wanted to escape from school, from his thoughts, from everything. He paused to stare at a new Jag. It was exactly like the one in which Tommy and his father had driven up to school. Mr. Conway was a man who looked as though he had made out all right for himself. Everything about him—the big ruby ring, the expensive cut of his clothes, the way he took the crisp new bills from his wallet— all added up to having plenty of the green stuff and being able to buy anything you wanted. That was Boucher's idea of living and he had already decided that Mr. Conway would be a swell guy to know if he liked you but not if he didn't. It was hard to believe that a big guy like that could have had such a little worm for a son.

Boucher was halfway to his room before he thought of something that would give him at least a momentary satisfaction. He slouched across the campus to the school canteen, known to generations of Carver men as the one place where you could get away from the masters. By tradition the faculty never entered this vanilla, chocolate, and strawberry retreat. After a quick check of his resources, Boucher ordered a double-rich hot fudge sundae with an extra portion of chopped nuts and whipped cream. He sat alone in a dark corner of the old room whose oak-paneled walls were defaced with countless crudely carved initials, letting the warm, sweet fudge scrape pleasantly against his tongue and sluice down his throat. There was a place near his home which made these sundaes even bigger and better. The thought of them made him nostalgic all of a sudden for slender pines against a sunset sky and hunting dogs baying wistfully to the autumn moon. He sat morosely before his empty dish until he had brought up a very satisfactory belch and then pushed back his chair. Outside, the long shadows were beginning to place their dark tentacles across the paths.

For no particular reason he sauntered into his house through the locker-room entrance in the basement. He stood for a moment looking at the rows of lockers, but these redolent metal boxes crammed with sweat-stained T-shirts and muddy socks were depressing. He had decided to go to his room and listen to a few records when he caught a glimpse of a magazine, half-concealed in the trash barrel at the foot of the stairs. This particular magazine, having been expressly forbidden by the school authorities, was read more carefully by the boys than any other. Along with its sister publications it was bought in countless furtive purchasings at a grimy little smoke shop near the railroad station. This copy, Boucher observed at once as he pulled it from the barrel, had recently been in contact with a pizza that had not been entirely consumed. Holding the sodden treasure by his finger tips and at some distance from his nose, Boucher studied the cover. The girl was sexy enough but nothing out of the ordinary. Then the pages seemed to fall open by themselves to reveal the blond girl kneeling in the sand. Her head was thrown back, her mouth was half-open, and her arms were raised in mysterious supplication. But it was what the pose did to her swelling breasts that made Boucher stare and the way it flattened her belly and tautened the flesh of her thighs and legs. Boucher gave a little exclamation and moistened his lips several times.

He wondered if a naked woman really looked that good. He had never seen one without any clothes on except his sister and she was awful skinny. There was a girl he had been seeing lately without his parents' approval. Her name was Phyllis and she had been letting him go a little further each time. She had hard little breasts and when he slipped his hand inside her dress, the nipples would come up stiff and pointed against his palm. Phyllis had been sent to a boarding school like himself and after considerable difficulty they had recently arranged a date in New York for the coming weekend. She would stay with an aunt and uncle who went out most every evening, and they would have the apartment to themselves. Phyllis was sixteen, about nine months older than himself. She had wonderful brown eyes, nice legs, and a big, soft mouth. All week long he had been thinking about her. . . .

Abruptly he flung the magazine into the trash barrel. Mr. Kendrick had ruined everything. It was impossible to see how he could have found out about the movie. They had all gone in the usual way and there had been no hitch. Beckett had bought the lone ticket this time and then opened the door so that the rest of them could enter from the fire escape. No one had seen them come in and they had sat quietly in the blessed darkness of the balcony until just before the final clinch on the screen when they had left by the same door. Kendrick couldn't have known; he must have taken a guess, and Boucher, unnerved by the morning's events, had not even tried to deny it. He had let Mr. Kendrick bluff him out of what probably would have been the best week end of his life. He wasn't going to tell Phyllis the bad news yet. There was still a chance that Mr. Kendrick might change his mind. But he wouldn't fall for any sob stuff. It would have to be for some other reason.

Boucher went on up the stairs, kicking methodically at the cracked and peeling paint on the banisters. When he reached the first-floor landing, he could hear the Richards' baby yelling in their apartment and the voice of Mrs. Richards, trying to calm it down. Mr. Richards was a pretty good housemaster, but he was too strict and all he cared about were rules and regulations. You couldn't really talk to him about anything because he expected everybody to be perfect all the time. He could be a very nice guy if only he would wise up a little. His wife was quite a dish. She looked like a model and when she came to the dining hall on Saturday nights in one of those real tight dresses of hers, every guy in the room was thinking the same thing. Mr. Richards might be able to help him get back that weekend by putting in a good word for him with Kendrick. It probably wouldn't do any good, but it was worth a try.

He sprawled full length on his bed, feeling too lazy and disgusted even to turn on his phonograph. He stared at the ceiling and thought about Phyllis. So many of the guys here at school were under the impression that they were really making out with a girl if she just let them kiss her. A guy like Tommy Conway had probably never even done that. On sudden impulse, Boucher shut the door and went over to Tommy's desk. Mr. Richards had told him at lunchtime not to touch anything of Tommy's, but nobody would know the difference. For a long time he had been curious as to the contents of Tommy's desk drawer and especially the faintly scented letters in their soft blue envelopes. He skimmed through five or six of them as quickly as he could, keeping his ear cocked toward the door.

To his astonishment and vague disappointment the letters were all from some girl named "Ann" who wrote very much as Phyllis did. All the letters began with "Darling" and ended with "All my love." Boucher felt a little more respect for his former roommate. There were also letters from his father and from guys in other schools. Boucher read a few, but they were all decidedly dull and he soon lost interest in them. He replaced the rubber bands carefully and helped himself to a box of paper clips before closing the drawer. He wondered if the school would give him a new roommate or if they might let him have the room as a "single" for the rest of the year. He hoped it would be the latter. He could make this into a pretty swell place once they moved out Tommy's stuff. They might even let him keep an extra chair. On the chance that it might be a good idea to swap beds he sat down on the edge of Tommy's. The springs squeaked the way they had sometimes late at night when Tommy must have thought that everybody else in the house was asleep.

Boucher decided that the bed was not as comfortable as his own. He happened just then to glance up through the top of the window. Outside, tucked under the sloping roof and cleverly fastened to the eaves, was a small wooden box that from a distance might easily have been mistakened for a birdhouse. But, peering closely at it now, Boucher saw that the box had a solid little door which was hinged at one end and which locked at the other with a hook and eye. No one in the room would have thought to look up there under the eaves, and only from one or two angles was the hiding place visible at all. Boucher opened the window and, reaching up, shoved his thumb against the metal hook. The instant that the little door swung open, he knew that the leather-bound volume tucked away inside was a diary. He grabbed it quickly, and with all of his senses alert now, relatched the door, shut the window, and smoothed the wrinkled bedspread. He left the door of the room ajar before dropping heavily upon his own bed. Then with greater excitement than he had felt all afternoon he opened the diary.

The entries in Tommy's neat handwriting were each preceded by the date in the upper right-hand corner. As the present volume had been started on the first day of school, it was easy for Boucher to orient himself. He did not know what he expected to find and he had only a guilty sense of intrusion as he began to read:

Sept. 27

Well, I'm here and I hate it. Dad said I would love it in a few days, but he just doesn't know me. He made me drive the car up to this house and I felt like such a dope. Nice housemaster and wife, but Dad had to ruin everything with remarks about how much the car cost and everything.

Sept. 28

I don't belong here. I KNOW it. I guess I don't belong anywhere and never will.

Sept. 29

I think I might have found a friend. His name is Mr. Tingue. He is my English teacher. I found out he likes music and books and he said to come and see him any time I liked.

Sept. 30

Worked all day. Dad sent new football. I don't WANT it.

Oct. 3

I am writing this after lights. Missed a few days but nothing good has happened. Just bad. My roommate tells dirty stories all the time and everybody likes him. They don't like me. They found out I had tea with Mr. Tingue and tonight they gave me a pink belley (belly—sp.?). A whole bunch of guys get you down and rub you with a hair brush. It still hurts. Next time they said they were going to rub alcohol on my   I tried not to cry but couldn't help it. Damn them!

Oct. 4

Letter from Dad. He says he'll be satisfied if I make a team this year and get on the Honor Roll. I don't want to make a team and I'm not good enough for the Honor Roll. I guess I just don't want to be a big shot in school like he was. I like writing and reading and listening to music. Sometimes I just like to sit and look out the window by my bed. There is a maple tree outside. I like to watch the red leaves drifting down. A bluebird comes and sits on my window sill. Beauty! That's what I really want—the beauty of the world and not just things.

Oct. 7

Letter from Ann. She says not to mind being lonely, but she's very popalar(popular—sp.?) and it's easy for popalar people to say that. Dad sent me a copy of his letter to the Head. All about how I'm not aggressive enough and must learn to be a leader. Won't he ever leave me alone? He also sent me new football shoes and a book about judo. Says he's coming up to see a game pretty soon—one of MY games. I just pray he doesn't. When he sees me sitting on the bench, I know he'll say something awful to Mr. Richards and then even he won't be friends with me.

Oct. 10

After lights again. Haven't had time to write every day, but I'm glad there's at least some place where I can say what I really think. Right HERE. My roommate certainly has a dirty mind. We had a bull session in here tonight (not me but the others) and he said he   a girl on the beach last summer. I told him not to talk so loud because Mrs. Richards might hear him. He laughed and said he would do it to her too if he could. Then everybody laughed and they asked me "didn't I approve?" and I said "no" and so they all jumped on me and ripped off my pajamas. I started to yell and finally Mr. Richards came up and gave us all hours, me extra for yelling so loud. It's no use.

Oct. 11

My marks are getting worse and worse. I'm flunking math and history. Only good thing is a B in English. Mr. Tingue writes stories for magazines. I would like to do that some day but oh, I just can't stand it much longer. I shouldn't cry like this but I just can't help it.

Oct. 13

Today in history class I wasn't paying attention. Mr. Rogers stopped and stared at me and made some sarcastic remark. He's always making sarcastic remarks. Everybody laughed and he wanted to know if he had hipnotized me or something. I said "no," but as a matter of fact his voice does make you sleepy. I was thinking about my mother. She was killed a long time ago in an automobile accident. Aunt Margaret told me about it. She said my mother was beautiful and liked all the things I do. Tonight I said a prayer to her.

Oct. 14

Too tired to write. Feel tired all the time now.

Oct. 16

Tonight Mr. Richards called me in and wanted to know how I was getting along. He ought to know and if he doesn't I don't know how I can explain it to him. Why do masters always act as if they didn't know anything about you? My roommate is as awful as usual. I don't believe he's done half the things he says. More packages from Dad. I don't even open them any more. The guys know I get them and tell me I'm just a spoiled little rich kid. I don't care what they say, but I wish Dad would stop giving me things. There's nothing I want but he keeps sending me things anyway. Maybe some day I'll find something I really want and I'm gonna fix it so he can't give it to me.

Oct. 19

Too tired to write the last few days. I'm tired but I can't sleep and that makes me more tired. Spent most of the day at the infirmary. I got a slip to have some kind of metalbosim or something test. Dr. Whelden tried to be funny all the time. He said I was underweight and did I have any problems? That's a good one. I just hate my father, that's all. Oh, I guess I don't really HATE him the way I do J B, but I wish there was some way to get away from him forever. After the test they told me to rest awhile. I lay on the bed and looked up at the sky and thought about Mother. I wonder if she knows about me?

Oct. 20

Letter from Ann. She says she and her whole family are going to Bermuda for Christmas. That's just great. Marks getting worse and worse. I'm flunking just about everything and I guess they'll kick me out. I wouldn't care except for Aunt Margaret. She keeps writing me how proud she is of me and I don't want to let her down even though she is gonna find out sooner or later that I'm a failure. I can't run away either on account of her. I don't know where to go or what to do. Oh, Mother, I wish I could talk to you. I wish I was dead. I WISH I WAS DEAD.

Oct. 21

Dad's coming! In about ten days. He's going on a business trip first. Then he wants to spend a whole day here, see me play football, and talk to my masters. He says why don't I ask some of the fellows on the team to have lunch with us. Wait till he find out I don't play football, am flunking almost all my subjects and don't have any friends. What am I gonna do? I'm not afraid of him, but I know he'll tell me all over again that I have to learn to fight people and be a good mixer. Be a BIG SHOT, he means, like himself and I'm sick of hearing that. SICK of it and I know I'm gonna hear it all my life. Where can I go? What can I do? I lost more weight and I feel awful. If only there was some way. . . .

Oct. 22

Only nine days! Maybe I will run away after all. Terrible wind blowing all day. All the beautiful leaves on the maple tree have fallen off and the bluebird has gone away.

Oct. 23

Something's just happened. It's so wonderful I can hardly believe it. It must be about two o'clock now. We're supposed to go on a field trip tomorrow up some mountain, but I couldn't sleep and I was lying here looking at the moon when something started me crying again. Then, all of a sudden I heard this voice. I swear I did. Just as clear as anything. It was my mother's voice and it said, "I love you, Tommy, and I understand." I KNOW it was her voice and now I think that sometime I will see her out there in the sky. Then I'll be all right.

The diary ended there in a watery, ink-stained blot. Boucher closed the book with a feeling of disbelief. His former roommate had been crazy as a bedbug. That was for sure. Nobody could write that way about his dead mother unless he was definitely bats. But the thing that really astonished Boucher was that his roommate had been able to achieve such distinction even in that way. Tommy was just too ordinary to hear voices, and the fact that he should have objected to a father who gave him everything was the final proof of his unworthiness.

Boucher fastened the metal clasp and wondered what he should do about the diary. He had half a mind to show it to the other fellows for laughs, but some native caution warned him that it would be better to wait awhile. He decided to return it to Tommy's hiding place which would now be his own. He was just closing the window and smoothing out the imprints of his knees in the bedspread when he heard Mr. Richards coming up the stairs.

11

BOUCHER made it to his own bed. He was turning the pages of *A Tale of Two Cities* when Mr. Richards
came in. The housemaster was so preoccupied that he didn't
even notice anything strange about a boy doing his outside
reading assignment on a Saturday afternoon. Boucher
smiled on the inside of his face and stood up with mechani-
cal politeness.

"Don't get up, Jim," Mr. Richards said in his man-to-
man voice. "I just want to look around a bit." He stared at
the book. "Reading?"

"Yes, sir."

"I thought you'd be at the game."

"I was, sir, but I got behind in this book and we're gonna
have a test next week."

"I see," said Mr. Richards, but he wasn't paying attention. "This is Tommy's desk, isn't it?"

"That's right, sir. Lookin' for somethin'?"

"Well, perhaps. You just go ahead with your reading."

Boucher made a pretense of it but he wondered what Mr.

Richards was looking for and his curiosity increased as the master pawed over the scented letters and then shifted his search to the shelves behind the desk.

"Did Tommy keep all of his papers here?"

"What papers, sir?"

"School work. Notebooks. Old themes—things like that."

"Yes, sir."

"Doesn't seem to be much here."

"Well, I know he threw a lot of old papers out."

Mr. Richards stiffened like a hound-dog on a point. "Threw them out? When?"

"Last week. When you had that inspection."

"But I told you to throw out the trash, not your work!"

"Well, me and Tommy had a big pile of papers messin' up the place, so we threw 'em out."

"Down in the trash barrel?"

"Yes, sir."

Mr. Richards looked grim. "Gone long ago," he said softly. He stared hard at Boucher. "It wasn't like Tommy to throw things out. He was always saving things."

Boucher's face was expressionless. "I know, sir, but we wanted to have the neatest room in the house, so we figgered we'd better get rid of a lot of that stuff."

The story wasn't true, but Boucher saw to his relief that Mr. Richards was apparently going to swallow it. Actually, Boucher, Beckett and Georgie Lindstrom had grown weary of Tommy's habit of preserving and classifying all manner of papers. His very neatness and thoroughness had goaded them into pitching a whole stack of his files into the trash barrel one night. Tommy had been out at the time and hadn't noticed his loss but he would have any day now, and they had all been looking forward to his reaction. Now the others would keep their mouths shut, of course, and there would be no way for Mr. Richards or anybody else to expose them. Boucher felt safe enough to pursue the matter further.

"Were you lookin' for anythin' in particular, sir?"

Mr. Richards sat down at Tommy's desk. He looked tired all of a sudden. "I want you," he said, "to tell me everything that happened from the time you left here this morning until the accident."

"Sure," Boucher said, "but that wasn't any accident, sir." A moment later, remembering Mr. Kendrick's warning, he could have bitten off his tongue.

Mr. Richards' face lit up. He leaned forward and suddenly drove his right fist into his left palm. "I thought not. Are you sure? Can you prove it?"

"No, sir."

"Did you see him jump?"

"No, sir."

"Then what made you think—?"

"I don't know, sir. I mean, I shouldn't have said it wasn't an accident because maybe it was."

"But you said—"

"I'm sorry, sir." It was getting very warm in the room. Boucher wiped his forehead.

"Now, look here," Mr. Richards said, "I don't want any smart-alecky stuff, Boucher. This is a very serious matter. You understand?"

"Yes, sir. I—"

"All right. Now we'll just go over this calmly and I want the exact truth. You say you didn't see Tommy jump?"

"No, sir."

"Where was he when you last saw him?"

"Standin' on the parapet."

"Just standing there?"

"Yes, sir."

"What were you doing?"

"Sittin' on a rock."

"Near him?"

"Pretty near."

"How near?"

"About from here to the window."

"All by yourself?"

"No, sir. A whole bunch of us were sittin' there."

"Watching Tommy?"

"No, sir. We were lookin' at, uh—some rock formations."

"Then how did you know that Tommy was standing on the parapet?"

Boucher wiped his forehead again. He hadn't expected anything like this. Mr. Richards wanted to pin him down to saying one thing and Mr. Kendrick wanted him to say the other. Boucher couldn't figure out the reason for this, but it was clear to him that for the time being, at least, he had better stay in the middle as much as he could.

"I want the truth, Boucher."

"I just looked up, sir, and he was standin' there."

"Then what happened?"

"I don't know."

"Well, did he jump or didn't he?"

"I told you I don't know. I wasn't lookin' at him and when I did, he wasn't there."

"You mean you looked away for an instant and when you looked back, Tommy had disappeared?"

"That's right."

"Were there any other boys near him at the time?"

"I don't think so."

"You don't *think* so! Surely you can remember *something* accurately?"

"I'm tryin' to, sir."

Outside, surrounding the lonely, leafless maple in the center of the Quad, the lights were winking on in the dormitories. The autumn night was bleak and cheerless, but in-

side the cozy, cluttered rooms there was warmth and laughter. Boucher fidgeted, tapping his foot to the intoxicating
beat of a hi-fi down the hall, wanting to join Beckett and
Georgie and the others for their customary bull session before supper. He was beginning to resent this questioning
which seemed to have no purpose. Why should Mr. Richards
care whether Tommy had jumped or not?

"All right now," Mr. Richards said briskly, "we'll try another tack. How did Tommy feel about high places?"

"He didn't like 'em."

"Exactly. And how do you know that?"

Boucher could scarcely conceal his mounting displeasure
with this inquisition. Everybody knew that Tommy was
"chicken" about climbing trees or anything like that. It was
a stupid question to ask.

"There were lots of ways to see it, sir. I don't know
what—"

"All right," said Mr. Richards. "We can leave it at that.
We know that Tommy wasn't the kind of boy who would
climb a parapet just for the fun of it."

Boucher very pointedly looked at his watch.

"One more thing," Mr. Richards said. "What was Mr.
Follensbee doing at the time this happened?"

Boucher considered lying, but they were going to find out
about the Stinger sooner or later. He looked at a point just
above his housemaster's head. "I don't know, sir. He wasn't
there."

"You mean he wasn't *anywhere in the vicinity?*"

"No, sir."

Mr. Richards looked as though he had been hit over the
head. "Good Lord!" he said softly. "Then no one saw it."
He seemed to be talking to himself.

Boucher looked at his watch again. Mr. Richards stood up.
His shoulders sagged and he looked the way the football

coach did when the team had lost. He opened the door and then turned back.

"You don't know of any records Tommy might have kept, do you? Any journal or diary or anything like that?"

Boucher hesitated only a fraction of a second. "No, sir."

"He might have kept it hidden. Let me know if you come across anything. We'll make a check when we pack up Tommy's things."

"Am I goin' to have another roommate, sir?"

"Who cares about that now?" Mr. Richards said and slammed the door.

Boucher sat quite still for a moment or two. What was going on here? Why had Mr. Richards asked him so many questions and why had Mr. Kendrick told him to keep his mouth shut? Why was everybody being so mysterious? Mr. Richards would certainly like to see that diary and so would Mr. Kendrick, probably. That diary was just about the best thing he could have found. It was worth plenty, maybe even a weekend. Boucher felt a sudden excitement. But which one of them should he give it to? Mr. Kendrick was a bigger wheel than Mr. Richards, but on the other hand Mr. Richards wasn't mad at him already and might really go to bat for him if he had a good enough reason.

Boucher got up, scratched his belly, and sauntered down the hall to Georgie Lindstrom's room. The diary could stay where it was until tomorrow. That would give him time to figure all the angles. He was feeling good when he barged into the room.

"Hey Georgie," he said, "lemme see those cards again."

12

WHEN Alan Richards reached the bottom of the stairs, he saw Larry Connors standing at the door of his apartment.

"Can I talk to you for a minute, sir?"

Alan stared at the boy. He didn't have his usual blasé appearance and there had been a strangely humble note in his voice.

"Why—yes," Alan said. "I suppose so."

"Would some other time be better, sir?"

"As a matter of fact, it would."

"All right, sir," Connors said. He sounded rather relieved. "Maybe some other time."

"Sure," Alan said. "Any time, Larry."

"I wish you could have seen him," Nancy said when he came into the living room. "He's been waiting out there at least half an hour. I asked him to come in, but he seemed embarrassed."

"Strange kid. Most of the time he's a wise guy, but every now and then he surprises you." Alan moved closer, but

Nancy stepped back and he saw that the storm signals were still flying.

"I wish you had seen him, Alan. I think you should have."

"I would have but I want to go over and see Hugh before supper."

"Isn't it more important to see the boys when they come over here especially to talk to you?"

Alan flushed. "Now, wait a minute, honey. Are you telling me how to handle my job?"

"Yes, I suppose I am."

"Well, don't."

"It's not your business, Alan."

"What isn't?"

"This fight with Kendrick."

Alan could feel the tension again like a big fist in his stomach. "Since you know my business so well," he said, "suppose you teach my classes."

"This has nothing to do with your teaching," Nancy said. "I'm not talking about that."

It was all Alan could do to keep from shaking her like an impudent child. "Listen," he said, "teaching isn't just chemistry and mathematics and history. It's concerned with living, too, reality in all its shapes as you said yourself. All this business about power and money came up in class today. I tried to deal with it there and I've got to deal with it here."

"But, Alan, do you actually *know* that Mr. Conway's money has anything to do with Justin's handling of the situation?"

"It's quite obvious to me," Alan said. His face darkened. "Money and power," he said grimly, "how I hate that combination."

"I must say you sound like a schoolteacher," Nancy said. "Or can't you take a joke any more?"

"What do you mean by that?"

Nancy bent over the coffee table and helped herself to a cigarette from the silver box which had been a wedding present from Alan's ushers. He made no attempt to strike a match for her.

"I mean," Nancy said, "that I have a peculiar feeling you're trying to ruin yourself."

"Don't be silly."

"But you *are* going to ruin yourself, you know. You've got some idealistic bug in your head that you're going to save the Carver School, but you won't. You'll just ruin yourself."

"All right," Alan said, "if that's the way you interpret what I'm trying to do, I guess there's nothing more to say."

Nancy gave him a searching look. "You really believe in this—this crusade of yours, don't you?" She reached out her hand to him, but this time it was Alan who wouldn't sign the peace.

"I'm going over to see Hugh," he said. "It might interest you to know that he wasn't even there when it happened this morning."

"Where was he?"

"I don't know yet."

"I'm afraid that's not so good."

"You can imagine," Alan said, "what Kendrick and Conway can do to him for that one mistake."

"You sound as though everyone was against Hugh."

"Well, Conway certainly isn't going to take the blame for this, and the way Kendrick operates I wouldn't put anything past him. Poor Hugh."

"I agree," Nancy said, "but there isn't anything you can do about it."

"You just wait and see," Alan said grimly.

Nancy crushed out her cigarette. "I wish," she said, "I just wish, Alan, that you understood your own job and where you fit in and who really needs your help around here."

"I'll see you in the dining hall," Alan said. Then he walked out.

A cold wind was blowing and the stars were flecks of gleaming gold. Alan turned up his collar and headed toward the north boundary of the campus where Hugh and Emmy Follensbee had a small cottage to themselves. There were a number of similar houses in that area and all were occupied by senior masters who were approaching retirement. The boys, with their particular genius for irreverent baptism, had named that part of the campus "The Last Resort."

The lights in the Follensbee cottage were determinedly gay and so was Emmy's smile when she opened the door.

"How nice to see you, Alan. Come in."

He saw the weariness behind her smile. "I'm afraid this isn't a very good time to call," he said. Through the doorway he could see Hugh Follensbee stretched out in an easy chair before the fire.

"Of course it is," Emmy said. "We aren't going to dinner. Are you?"

"I've got to. I'm on duty. I just wanted to talk to Hugh for a minute."

"You go right ahead. I have some things to do upstairs." She lowered her voice. "I wish you could cheer him up a bit. This thing has been a terrible blow."

Alan nodded. "I knew it would be. I'll do my best."

Follensbee started to get up but Alan waved him back. "You just sit still, Hugh."

"I had to answer the telephone a minute ago," Follensbee said. "Did you know that there's a faculty meeting at eight o'clock tonight?"

"No, I hadn't heard."

"Mrs. Henry is apparently calling all the houses now." He smiled. "I'm glad to see you, Alan. Sit down. How's that handsome wife of yours?"

"She's fine," Alan said. He stared into the fire. "Hugh, I'm damned sorry this thing had to happen to you. I wish there was some way I could help."

"Thank you, Alan, but there isn't."

"Are you sure?"

"Quite sure. You see, I fell asleep out there today."

"Oh."

"Exactly, my boy. There's no getting around that, is there?"

"How did you happen to fall asleep?"

"I was tired climbing. The sun was hot and I found a comfortable place to sit for a moment. I was thinking back over my life and I guess I just went off."

"But that doesn't make you responsible for what happened."

"Not entirely and not really, in my opinion, but I won't be able to explain that. In a way I was responsible. You know that."

"But I think Tommy deliberately jumped."

"So do I, Alan."

"Doesn't that make a difference?"

"No."

"Not even if we could prove it?"

"Well, if we knew that the boy had been mentally ill and had planned to do this terrible thing, it would ease my conscience a bit but that's about all. The fact remains that I might have been able to stop him."

"He would have tried it again. Looking back, Hugh, I'm sure there was a conflict with his father. The poor kid was all mixed up."

"I know. Sam Whelden feels the same way. But even if Tommy had tried it again, it wouldn't have been on *my* field trip, you see."

"Kendrick seems intent on making it appear to be an accident."

"Naturally."

"Why?"

Follensbee reached for his pipe and tamped the bowl with his forefinger. His voice, to Alan, sounded strangely matter of fact.

"Suicide is an awful thing anywhere, Alan. In a school it is especially so. Certainly it's best to consider it an accident as far as outsiders are concerned and best for the boy's father, too."

"Even if all our evidence were to point to suicide?"

"Yes, I think so."

"I can't see that. To me the facts are of paramount importance and I can't see any reason for compromising the truth."

"You think we should tell the truth at all costs?"

"Yes."

"I don't know, Alan. That's a tough one. Anyway it doesn't look as though we are going to know the whole truth in this case."

"I think we *can* know it," Alan said, leaning forward tensely. "If we put together all we know about the boy, the facts will make clear what really happened this morning."

"That may be what the Head has in mind for the meeting tonight."

"If Sam Whelden will support us," Alan went on, "and if Tommy's class masters are willing to lay it on the line—"

"Us?" said Follensbee. "What do you mean by us?"

"I think of us," Alan said, "as the ones who want to see the truth come out in this thing, whether it will be pleasing to Mr. Conway or not. I'm also thinking of you."

Follensbee puffed on his pipe for a moment. "Thank you,

Alan, but I'm afraid it isn't what's best for me that has to be considered."

"Certainly you have the right to protect yourself."

"From what? Can I protect myself from the knowledge that I was the responsible person up there this morning?"

"No, but—"

"Forty times," Follensbee said, looking into the fire, "I took a bunch of kids up that trail, and thirty-nine times I brought them all down safely."

"What I mean," Alan said, "is that this could have happened to anybody, a veteran like yourself or a beginner like me. It has nothing to do with professional competence. You could have been right there at the top and turned your head for a minute to speak to another boy."

"You talk about the truth, Alan. Face it yourself. I *wasn't* right there at the top. I took a chance that I had no business to take. I agree with you that I was unlucky."

"Are you going to tell Conway the truth?"

"I'll have to."

"I mean about the suicide?"

"I have no proof of that."

"But supposing we found a note or some irrefutable evidence?"

"I don't know. A thing like that might even be worse for the school." He leaned forward to tap his pipe against one of the andirons. "As to whether the truth should be told under any and all circumstances, that's ethics, not science. Out of my field."

They were both silent for a moment. Alan could hear the chapel clock chiming five-thirty. In an hour the school would go to dinner in the big hall and shortly after that the masters would leave their houses and gather in the faculty room. Follensbee would be there in his usual seat in the midst of the science department and he must know even now that it was going to be an ordeal for him. And yet he seemed unnaturally calm and resigned, an old man awaiting his fate without making any attempt to shape the forces that might deliver him. He needed help.

"The point that bothers me about this whole thing," Alan said, "is that you are willing to let Kendrick get away with it."

"With what?"

"Telling Conway any story he likes in order to keep from offending him and risk losing the money."

"I don't think Justin operates that way."

"I'm afraid he does. In fact, he told me this morning that it would be 'disastrous' for all of us if Conway was told that his son had committed suicide. What else could that mean but that we might not get any more money?"

"He could have meant a lot of things. Don't you think we'd better just leave it up to him?"

"No, I don't!" Alan burst out, his face reddening. "I certainly don't. That's what people around here have been doing for years—just leaving it to Kendrick to make his own arrangements. Well, I say it's time somebody challenged his right to gloss over the truth to suit his purposes."

Follensbee made an impatient gesture. "Alan, I certainly don't know the truth here and I don't think Kendrick does, either. No one does. We've just got to grapple with this thing as best we can."

"That's just what I mean," Alan said. "Nobody's even trying to grapple with it."

Follensbee looked into the fire for a moment. Then he said, "I know you feel strongly about this, Alan, but if you will pardon a word of caution from an old man, don't rush in here too quickly."

Alan smiled to himself. How like an older man, he thought, to exercise caution and to steer clear of conflict.

Follensbee was old and tired and habituated to letting Kendrick run the show without question. He probably knew it was wrong and that Kendrick should be challenged, but he no longer had the vitality to stand up and fight. Kendrick was going to maneuver him at will unless somebody arose in his defense.

"Do you know Conway, Hugh?"

"No, only by reputation."

"Well, that's nothing," Alan said, "compared with the man himself. He will insist on having his own way at any cost and he won't care how many people he crushes to get it. That's what he did to his own son and that's what he'll try to do to you. I just want you to know, Hugh, that I'm more than ready to take your side and that I'd like nothing better than to show this man that there are stronger forces than his money and his power."

In the firelight Follensbee's pink scalp glowed right through his cottony white hair. "I certainly appreciate your support, Alan, but—"

"As a matter of fact," Alan interrupted eagerly, "maybe we ought to plan our strategy right now. Get the jump on him and Kendrick. Take the offensive. Blow this thing wide open."

Follensbee stood up and began to poke at the fire although it was burning well.

"Cherry wood," he said. "Makes a good, hot fire. I still have some on my place in New Hampshire." He fussed with the fire a little while longer and then turned to Alan, his face reflecting his embarrassment.

"At the risk of your misunderstanding me, Alan, I'm going to ask you not to do anything in my behalf."

"Alan sat up, gaping in astonishment. "You mean *nothing* at all?"

"Yes."

"But—"

"Some things are final, Alan. They are over and done with. There is nothing we can do about them."

"But I'm not talking about Tommy. I'm talking about—"

"I know, Alan." Follensbee shook his head. "I was afraid you wouldn't understand," he added gently.

Alan stood up. "I certainly don't. I thought that you of all people, Hugh. Well—I was sure that you would—"

Follensbee stepped forward suddenly and put out his hand. "Alan, I wish that I could explain something to you."

"There's nothing to explain," Alan broke in stiffly. "Do as you like. I'm going ahead on my own. You can't expect me not to do that."

Follensbee gave a helpless little shrug. "No. I'm sorry, Alan, because I don't think this is going to help you."

"I don't care about myself," Alan said. He walked to the door and then turned back, feeling the righteous anger surging over him again. "Everybody around here is afraid," he said, his voice shaking. "They hide in their houses and make brave speeches, but when the time comes to take a stand on an issue like this, they won't commit themselves. Well, somebody has to be willing to stick his neck out."

Outside, with the night air cooling his burning cheeks, it occurred to him that he had left very abruptly and rudely. It did not seem possible that he had spoken angrily to Hugh Follensbee. There was no finer man on the campus as far as Alan was concerned, and no finer friend. But somehow all at once their ordered little world here at Carver had been knocked off balance and was now wobbling uncertainly so that former relationships were no longer the same. He and Hugh Follensbee could have a misunderstanding now that neither of them would have dreamed of yesterday. No doubt the older man had found it upsetting, but for Alan their disagreement was a far more painful reality. Hugh Follens-

bee was actually content to accept the most expedient explanation of Tommy Conway's death. Alan was almost to
the dining hall before he could see any reason for this in-
credible fact.

Follensbee, he told himself, was going to retire in about
eight months. This was his last year and the smart thing for
him to do was to keep his mouth shut and hope to go right on
through. He had admittedly slipped up this morning. There
was no point in making Conway even uglier by trying to pick
a fight with him. That was probably what Hugh had been
trying to explain to him a few minutes ago. Hugh was privately certain that Tommy had taken his own life this morning and he was aware that Kendrick was going to ignore that
probability in order to soothe an important man's pride. He
must know that this was wrong, but he had sold out to expediency and he wanted Alan to do the same.

The lights of the dining hall were blazing up ahead and
as Alan approached there was wafted to him unmistakably
from the chipped, unlovely serving dishes the steamy, sour
greeting of overcooked cabbage. He scowled and then, plod-
ding grimly up the steps, bawled out one of the boys for
making a crack about the food.

13

T HE BOYS at the afternoon showing of the movie had been unusually quiet as they always were when Carver lost the Harland game, but the fact that it was a war picture had been even more sobering. They would smirk at sex, cheer for violence, and laugh uproariously at anything pious or sentimental in an ordinary picture, but let some hammy hero in a war picture embrace every cliché in the book, and they would sit there like rapt choir boys, scarcely daring to breathe. Kendrick smiled to himself and plodded along the path, his feet plumping squarely on the ancient flagstones. He was on his way back to his apartment to change before dinner and at the moment he was methodically summarizing the events of the day, pulling everything together like a general equating the opposing forces in the field.

First of all, there was Roger Conway. They had not yet been able to reach him but they would almost certainly succeed within the next few hours. His reaction to the news would be part genuine grief, but there would also be a sense of personal outrage as his old, dormant bitterness was stirred up again. His conduct would be violent and very likely insulting, especially to the headmaster. Pettengill, for his part, was shocked and deeply concerned for the good name of the school. His dislike of Conway was evident and he was ready to fight him. Disaster loomed that way for both sides and he, Kendrick, must forestall the encounter. And then there was Richards, young, hotheaded, zealous and naïve. He had the makings of a good man, but at the moment he was confused and he needed to learn which side his bread was buttered on. Meanwhile, he could very easily ruin everything because he thought of Truth and Justice only in capital letters. Follensbee, on the other hand, was much too mild and quiet to irritate Roger Conway unless by some unfortunate chance Follensbee's negligence became an issue. That, too, was a dangerous shoal to be avoided. Finally, there was Boucher who had apparently seen more than any of the others and was for that reason a source of interest. That big mouth of his could cause a lot of trouble and he was cagey enough to use it to his advantage if he could. There remained Tommy's class masters. No reason to worry about them, but he would have to discourage Dr. Whelden from elaborating on the psychological factors.

He decided to stop by his office and see what his secretary might have left for his attention. From the distance came the usual frantic cacophony of cutlery and glassware in the dining hall as the tables were set for the next onslaught. Kendrick glanced at his watch and then hurried in to examine the neatly penciled notes which had been placed in the center of his desk:

1. Faculty meeting at 8:00 P.M. Masters have been advised.

2. Bobbie Randall's mother called. She wants to know if he can go home week end of the 29th. His sister is getting married.

3. Mrs. Henry called to say that Mr. Conway has reservation for tonight at the Hotel Tarleton in Chicago. She has left word for him to call the school.

It was five o'clock in Chicago now. Conway could be almost anywhere—on a train, in an office, at a club—but the chances were that he would not check into his hotel until later. Once he learned what had happened, he would catch a late plane to New York and arrive at the school shortly after breakfast, possibly even sooner.

Kendrick stood by his desk for a moment, thinking back to that night years ago when the dance music had floated up from the gym and Roger Conway had kept to his room with a bitter and vengeful heart. Kendrick had succeeded in relieving the boy's tension temporarily, but in the long run he had failed to make him understand himself and the world. Roger Conway had never outgrown his bitterness; he had never come to terms with the overwhelming sense of inferiority that still drove him in a restless, aggressive, never-ending need to prove his worth. But what had once been childish and rather pathetic in the boy was dangerous and unforgivable in the man. It had cost him his wife and now his son. Kendrick wanted Roger Conway's money for Carver because he knew that it could be pumped like a life-giving blood into certain arteries of the school, but there was something else he wanted even more to accomplish with the man. It wouldn't have done any good to try to explain it to anyone.

He stuffed the notes into his pocket, snapped off the light and left the building, wincing slightly at the dissonances of competing phonographs in the flimsy old rooms of Darrow House. He hunched his shoulders against the wind and walked head down along the path to his own house. Near it but on the other side of the highway was a special cluster of lights partially hidden in a little copse of spruce. The lights came from a trim, white cottage which had a New England simplicity in its clean painted clapboards, its black shutters, and its steeply canted roof. This had always been the home of Carver's headmaster, and sometimes when Kendrick approached it at night this way he would remember vividly another night almost ten years ago, just before Dr. Parsons had retired.

That night Kendrick had waited tensely in the drafty front parlor. Dr. Parsons liked to keep his house at an inhumanly low temperature except for his study where an enormous fireplace was always well stocked with seasoned hickory logs that glowed with the devil's own heat. So great, in fact, was the temperature variation between the study and the world outside that a summons from the Head on a wintry night was virtually certain to be followed by a nasty cold in the morning.

Kendrick had already guessed at the import of the meeting. He had in fact waited a long time for this night, and having endured the patient years of service, he was at last to reap his reward. Dr. Parson's regime had been successful in many ways, but there had been times when the old man would have huffed and puffed and blown the school down had not Kendrick been on hand to mend frayed tempers and restore a measure of equanimity. Dr. Parsons was among the last of the old-timers whose very absurdities had enhanced their reputations and who, like the unforgettable dinosaurs before them, had blundered their way to success by the simple expedient of being magnificently themselves. To counterbalance his extraordinary unreasonableness in certain areas, the Head had possessed an almost infallible understanding of when to give way to others and this had kept his faculty remarkably loyal. All of them were aware, however, of the part that Kendrick had played behind the scenes and as he sat now, shivering slightly in the dismal parlor, he was pleasantly visualizing what was surely going to happen in the next few minutes. One of his first acts as the new headmaster would be to maintain a decent temperature in this room.

All of a sudden, Dr. Parsons flung open the door of his study and a blast of hot air swept out from the blazing fireplace. The headmaster's massive pate gleamed dully in the flickering light, and for a moment he remained in the doorway, studying his subordinate with his fierce old eyes. Age had slowed his thinking a bit, but he had become more windbaggy than ever.

"Come right in, Justin. It was good of you to come down here tonight. Middle of a busy week for you, I know." He waved at a chair. Sit down. Smoke if you like."

Kendrick would have liked very much to have a cigarette but everyone knew how the old man abhorred tobacco, and no one on the faculty ever accepted his invitation to indulge. Kendrick examined his fingernails and hoped that the fire wouldn't get any hotter. On his forehead a fine mist of perspiration was already gathering.

Dr. Parsons sat down at his cluttered desk and for an inordinately long time fussed with a mound of papers. Then he said, "You have been my right hand all these years, Justin. We've been quite a team, haven't we?"

"Yes, sir," Kendrick said. His anticipation was dreadfully keen now, but Dr. Parsons always insisted on preliminaries, no matter what the occasion. Kendrick could feel his shoes getting unpleasantly warm. He tried to mop his forehead unobtrusively.

"Too warm in here?"

"Oh no, sir," Kendrick said. He managed to move his feet a little further out of range.

"Old bones have to bake a little more, you know," Dr.

Parsons said. "Well, I won't keep you long. Fact is, I wanted you to know before publication that this will be my last year as headmaster of Carver."

"I'm sorry to hear that, sir," Kendrick said. His tone, he thought, had been perfect.

"I could go on, of course, if I wanted to, but I think it's time I stepped aside for a younger man."

Kendrick knew, as they all did, that the trustees had been trying for several years to ease the old man out of the saddle, but he had refused to take the hint. It was quite possible that they had finally been obliged to demand his resignation.

"Naturally," Dr. Parsons continued, "I don't want this to be known until an official announcement is made by the trustees, probably in a week or so."

He rose, picked up an enormous poker, and stirred a little more vigor into the ashes.

"As to my successor, you can be sure that the trustees and myself have conducted an exhaustive search for the right man. I can also assure you that from the very beginning I have hoped that we could select someone from our own faculty."

Well, Kendrick thought, it was coming now at last and it wouldn't be necessary to sit here much longer and stew in more ways than one. It was the man's damnable circumlocutions that had always been so irritating.

"Unfortunately, I was outvoted."

"*What?*"

"I was outvoted, Justin."

Kendrick sat very still. He no longer felt the heat. There was no possible way to express the feeling of outrage and the disappointment that was flooding up inside him. This was an absolutely unbelievable piece of injustice but it was somehow true.

"Do you mean to say—?"

"There was nothing I could do about it, Justin."

Kendrick's lower lip was trembling and as he sat looking down at his hands, his face sagged with defeat. Dr. Parsons observed this and as so often with the boys when he was embarrassed or temporarily baffled, he assumed a jovial approach.

"This thing has its good side, Justin. Good side to everything, you know. We're getting a fine man, but we need you more than ever behind the scenes. Always a good man standing under for the man on top, you know. Heh, heh. Disappointment for you, I know, but maybe best in the long run."

Dr. Parsons kept on talking and pouring the oil for quite a while. Kendrick heard him as one might hear a distant surf booming monotonously while he recovered some of his poise. He was still shattered inside but that was damage which Dr. Parsons could not repair.

"I wasn't counting on anything, sir," Kendrick said. "As a matter of fact, I prefer my present work."

The old man's relief was absurdly transparent. "Well, I'm certainly happy to hear that, Justin. The new man will need help from both of us. Think you'll like him as much as I do. Name's Pettengill, Kenneth Pettengill. Harvard man with considerable teaching and administrative experience. Comes to us very highly recommended."

Dr. Parsons stood up. The fire was crackling merrily. "Glad we understand each other, Justin. I won't detain you any longer. Be sure to keep this under your hat. When Pettengill arrives, I'll want him to meet you first."

The numbing cold of the front parlor was almost pleasant by contrast. Dr. Parsons had already closed his study door and presently Kendrick heard the thud of another log tumbling into the inferno. He put on his hat and coat and walked quickly out to the sidewalk.

There had been hours of turmoil for him that night. He told no one where he was going but trudged on across the athletic fields and up the hill into the woods. There he began to walk almost blindly along a series of trails that blundered across the countryside under the uncaring stars. Over and over he reviewed his qualifications and asked himself why he had failed. Was it because he was not married and a headmaster should have a wife? Was it some ugly bit of gossip that had prejudiced the trustees against him? They had nothing really to go on there. He had been careful to see to that. The women on the campus talked, of course, talked and speculated and drew conclusions about him because he did not respond in ways to which they were accustomed. It could have been one of them; men had less desire to kill what they did not understand. Waves of bitterness and anger beat against him and surged over him but he stormed ahead against the wind, kicking at rocks and bits of trees in his path, now and then plunging heedlessly through briars that scratched his face and tore at his clothes. It was a long time before calmness and acceptance came.

There was a predawn grayness in the sky when he returned to his room. His future was clear to him now. He would never be headmaster at Carver, nor would he accept the job anywhere else. He had been with the school from her early days and he would go on with her, building and shaping and controlling behind the scenes in ways which would not be possible for a headmaster and in these he would find his compensation. He washed and got into bed. In the morning he had made certain that no one saw his torn and muddy clothes.

"Justin!"

Kendrick snapped out of his reverie. Pettengill had come out the door of the headmaster's house and was now hurrying down the steps. He hadn't bothered to put on an over-coat.

"I just had a call from the newspapers." Pettengill's face had a haggard look.

Kendrick shook his head. "I guess they were bound to find out about it sooner or later."

"I had to tell them it was apparently an accident but I didn't like to commit myself that way. I just talked with Hugh and he certainly doesn't think it was. Neither does Sam Whelden."

"It's just as well this way," Kendrick said quietly.

"I'm worried about the publicity. Any word from Conway yet?"

"Not yet."

"I don't look forward to his arrival."

"I'll take care of him," Kendrick said.

Pettengill glanced up quickly. "He'd better act like a gentleman, Justin. I won't tolerate that cheap streak of his. We're too fine an outfit for that and we aren't dependent on his money. I feel very strongly about this."

"So do I," Kendrick said.

14

THE MASTERS' clubroom was inconveniently located on the second floor of one of the older buildings. In spite of several comfortable couches, numerous chairs, tables, magazine racks and the bright red curtains selected by the Ladies' Faculty Committee, the room was not attractive. The masters used it primarily as a retreat from the boys and as a place where they could inhale a steadying cigarette between classes. Once a week and when especially summoned as was the case tonight, the faculty met here in conclave.

Most of the men were already in their seats when Kendrick arrived. He was aware at once of the abnormally subdued atmosphere and of the way the masters glanced every now and then toward the headmaster's chair at the front of the room. From his own seat nearby Kendrick was able to survey a large portion of the room without turning his head. The faculty sat together by departments, each in a designated spot so that it was easy now for Kendrick, glancing around, to locate Follensbee and Rogers and Bill Tingue and Alan Richards. Kendrick looked a little longer at Richards who was obviously keyed up tonight, his face flushed and his eyes very bright. He met Kendrick's eye for an instant and then quickly looked away. Kendrick wondered just how much of a mess Richards was going to make of things. Probably a considerable one unless the others grew tired of him or had opinions of their own which might even things up a bit. Rogers, if he said anything, would be loud and good-humored, Follensbee taciturn and quiet, and Bill Tingue would probably take up his favorite cudgels for the rights of the individual. Sam Whelden at the back of the room with his chair nonchalantly tilted against the wall would be the least emotional and the most objective of them all. Kendrick sat back in his chair and twisted the cat's-eye ring until all at once the buzz of conversation died away and he saw Ken Pettengill close the door carefully and then walk purposefully toward his chair. On the way he stopped beside Kendrick.

"Anything new from Chicago, Justin?"

"Not yet."

"If the call comes during the meeting, I'd better take it."

"All right," Kendrick said, "unless you prefer my talking to him."

"No, thanks, I'll do it."

Kendrick glanced toward the clock on the wall. That first breaking of the news was going to be very important. The wrong approach would trigger Roger Conway like a bomb. Kendrick could only gamble now that Conway would not call until later, and as all incoming calls to the school were automatically transferred to his extension after Mrs. Henry went home, he would with luck be able to talk with Roger Conway first from the privacy of his own apartment.

Dr. Parsons had always sat heavily in the massive, black walnut chair, but the present headmaster liked to stand behind it and only occasionally did he rest his weight momentarily on one of the sturdy arms while he looked for something in the sheaf of papers he normally brought with him. Old hands on the faculty could generally estimate the duration of a meeting simply by noting the size of the headmaster's burden. Tonight as he took his accustomed stance, there wasn't even a scrap of paper in his hand, and this extraordinary occurrence together with the grimness of his expression made the room all at once almost oppressively quiet.

"Gentlemen," Pettengill's voice was measured and solemn, "I regret having to impose an additional meeting upon you this week but I know you understand the reason and appreciate how vital it is for us all to gather here tonight. All of you know, of course, what happened today and are as shocked and saddened by it as I am. I want to say a little about this tragedy, for of course it is a tragic and terrible thing which has never happened before in the history of our school. Then I think it would help us all to hear briefly from the men who were most closely associated with Tommy. Finally, we must prepare for Mr. Conway's arrival. We haven't been able to get in touch with him yet, but we've left word at a Chicago hotel and I expect he may call before this meeting is over." Pettengill smiled grimly. "I don't know how many of you have met Mr. Conway but of all our parents I can't think of any I'd be less happy to deal with."

Kendrick could see that Richards was poised on the edge of his chair now, ready at the first possible moment to rush into an argument. That remark about Conway being difficult to deal with was ill-timed and thoughtless. Pettengill should know that deep in the heart of every teacher was a basic envy and dislike of successful men like Roger Conway, and a remark of that sort was not going to help matters any.

"I want to say first," Pettengill continued, "that we are all of us aware of Mr. Follensbee's long and devoted service to this school. As our senior master, he has behind him a record of accomplishment which has won the admiration and respect of all who have served with him. I want him to know that nothing that happened today in any way alters our regard for him."

Follensbee did not look up to acknowledge the compliment and the only sign that he had heard was a slow deepening of the color in his face. He was too much of a pro, Kendrick knew, to be comforted by these assurances. Hugh Follensbee understood the hopelessness of his position and the awful finality of his mistake. Sitting there now and staring hard at the floor, he looked like a man who had seen a lifetime's labor lost in a moment.

"Unfortunately," Pettengill went on, "Mr. Follensbee was not at the scene this morning, and although he has blamed himself for the consequences much more severely than I think he should, the hard fact is that no adult was present. As the school was technically responsible for Tommy, we are in trouble here. There is no concrete evidence of an accident, and when you consider the fact that Tommy would have had to climb up on the parapet before he could have slipped or been pushed, it is hard to understand why he got up there in the first place. I certainly can't believe that he was *pushed* off and don't think we even have to consider anything like that. There remains the possibility of suicide but here again we have no positive evidence—"

"Mr. Pettengill?"

Pettengill turned and looked toward the science department. "Yes, Mr. Richards?"

"May I say something?"

"Well, I wasn't quite finished but go ahead."

Kendrick looked at the ceiling. Here comes goodness,

he thought, rushing in with a righteous sword. But goodness alone was not enough. Without intelligence and understanding, goodness was going to get clobbered every time.

"I am absolutely certain, sir, in view of Tommy's behavior recently in the house and what we know about his family background, that he killed himself. After all, he was not exactly a normal Third Former."

"Mr. Pettengill?"

The headmaster swung toward the other side of the room. "Yes, Mr. Tingue?"

"I disagree with that, sir. Tommy was a perfectly normal boy. He just wasn't like everybody else. Nowadays, if a boy is a little different and doesn't run around with the herd, we think he's not normal."

"Sir?"

"Mr. Rogers."

"I agree with Mr. Richards about Tommy's being a kind of odd ball. I never saw a kid his age look so dreamy and far off all the time."

"What's the matter with that?" Tingue challenged, jumping to his feet again. "Wordsworth daydreamed, didn't he, and probably Shakespeare and Keats and—?"

"Not in my class they wouldn't have."

The rest of the faculty welcomed an excuse to laugh even briefly and rather nervously tonight, but Tingue didn't join in. He took a small metal tube from his pocket, and pressing it against each nostril in turn, inhaled deeply several times. He and Rogers, Kendrick thought, had a kind of basic antipathy. One was animal and the other vegetable. Tingue was obviously ready to enter upon a serious discussion, but Harry Rogers never took anything seriously.

"I still say, Mr. Pettengill," Tingue insisted, "that just because Tommy was shy, sensitive, gifted and very much of an individual is no reason to assume that he was abnormal or anything like that."

"Was he gifted, Mr. Tingue?"

"Yes, I'd say he was as far as writing goes. He had a great deal of creative writing ability."

"You knew him quite well, didn't you?"

"Yes, sir. He came over to the house a good deal. He liked to listen to my records and we'd talk about writing. My wife was always stuffing him with cookies. She thought he looked bad."

"Was there anything in the writing he did for your class, Mr. Tingue, that would throw any light on his state of mind recently?"

"No, I can't think of anything especially except that his last theme was about an automobile accident."

"His mother died in an automobile accident, I believe. Am I not right about that, Mr. Kendrick?"

"Yes, that's right, sir."

"I just thought there might have been some connection in Tommy's mind. I know he didn't get along well with his father and it just occurred to me that in his unhappiness he probably missed his mother more than ever. Did you notice that at all?"

Tingue had been using his inhaler again and there was a strong odor of menthol surrounding his chair.

"I can't say I did, sir."

"Did he ever criticize his father?"

"Yes, but usually indirectly. He'd say, 'We don't have any books in our apartment' or 'We never listen to classical music.' Things like that."

"When did you last see him?"

"Yesterday in class."

"Notice anything unusual about him?"

'No, sir. Of course he liked English and he was doing very well—at least a B. I do remember now that he looked rather pale and I asked him if he was getting a cold because there's been a bug going around."

"Thank you," Pettengill said. He straightened, took his hands from the back of the chair, and looked around the room. "I can't help thinking that there are clues, gentlemen, but we have missed them. I wonder if Tommy kept a diary? His imaginative, articulate type often do."

"Sir?"

"Mr. Richards?"

"I've already checked his room but I couldn't find a diary or anything like that. There's a pile of letters but I haven't had time to go through them yet. I still think we'll find something, because Tommy was always keeping notes and records in various files. I talked with his roommate who admitted they threw out a lot of papers last week, but I'm sure Tommy wouldn't throw out a diary or anything like that."

"Who's his roommate?"

"Jim Boucher. And what a dumb combination that was!"

Kendrick exchanged a wink with the chairman of the Rooming Committee who over the years had been obliged to develop an immunity to such criticisms. The clock on the wall indicated that an hour had gone by already. It was eight o'clock in Chicago. Conway should certainly have registered at his hotel by now.

"While we are on the subject," Richards said, and he was still holding the floor, "Boucher was right there when it happened. I had a talk with him before supper. He said Tommy climbed up on the parapet with nobody near him and just suddenly disappeared. There's absolutely no doubt he jumped, and I think we should make this perfectly clear to his father whether he likes it or not."

The headmaster had already shifted his attention to Hugh Follensbee. "Anything to add?" he asked gently.

"No, sir."

"Any change in Tommy this morning?"

Follensbee hesitated, obviously trying to concentrate. "To tell the truth, he seemed if anything a little happier. On the way out he appeared to be more at ease with the boys and when they rushed on ahead of me, he didn't hang back the way he usually did. I got the impression somehow that he was easier in his mind and not so preoccupied with his own inner problems." Follensbee's lips tightened. "How wrong I was. I remember now that I did see him walking alone sometime after that. He had his head down and there was something about those bowed shoulders of his that should have warned me. How wrong I was."

"How wrong we all were, Mr. Follensbee."

"I know, but I often noticed that unnatural, starey sort of look in his eyes and it should have occurred to me that he wasn't failing my course for lack of ability."

"Mr. Pettengill?"

"Yes, Mr. Rogers."

"I don't want to inject a wrong note here and I don't like to say anything derogatory about the boy under the circumstances, but I honestly don't think it was all just unhappiness. I think Tommy was good at the things he liked to do such as English, but he didn't try very hard in my class. Names and dates just weren't his cup of tea and he didn't want to bother with them. I tried to kid him out of it but he never could take a joke very well. I still can't agree with Mr. Tingue that he was a perfectly normal boy. Lots of times he would just stare off into space and once or twice I thought he was going to pass out. I wonder if there was anything wrong with him physically?"

Pettengill looked toward the back of the room. "What do you think about that, Doctor?"

Sam Whelden's chair came down on four legs. His bulldog face was expressionless.

"No evidence of any organic disease. His white count was up a bit recently but that could go along with a cold or any other minor disturbance."

"Do you yourself feel that this is a case of suicide?"

"I don't know. It certainly could have been, but there was no evidence on the body. Without some proof of what the boy was actually thinking and how he was reacting psychologically, it's impossible to come to any definite conclusion. On the other hand, I saw quite a lot of Tommy lately at the infirmary. Symptoms of nervousness and depression were present along with loss of weight and vitality. We did a BMT on him which was negative, and it occurred to me at the time that he might have some psychosomatic difficulties. Looking back on it now, I wish I had ordered a psychiatric evaluation or at least advised the father that it was our recommendation."

Pettengill nodded. "Yes, we slipped up here in more ways than one. I mean all of us. We just didn't know the boy well enough. If a boy could feel as he must have and yet go on from day to day without our being sufficiently aware to take any action, then we weren't doing the job we should have. I'll have to admit that to his father, much as I hate the idea."

"Sir?"

"Yes, Mr. Richards?" Pettengill said, a trace of weariness in his voice.

"I don't see why we have to admit anything. The whole thing is Conway's fault. He ruined his son, absolutely ruined him. Everybody who has met the man can see that right away. I know for a fact that Tommy hated him and I'm willing to bet that when the poor kid couldn't find any other way to escape from his father, he killed himself. Why do we have to take the blame for a man like this? Why can't we just tell him the truth?"

Alan stopped and looked hopefully around the room for some equally outraged ally to join his cause, but in the silent upturned faces there was only a kind of shocked dismay as though something unspeakable had just occurred. And then all at once Hugh Follensbee was on his feet and speaking so quietly that the men at the back of the room had to bend forward to hear him.

"Alan, I think what the headmaster means, and quite correctly, is that we were responsible for Tommy Conway during all of his school activities. My field trip this morning is a case in point. I was representing the school and it is perfectly clear that I was derelict in my duty, something I shall regret for the rest of my life. Regardless of Mr. Conway's treatment of his son, we cannot deny our negligence, *my* negligence, and to do so would only make our position all the more vulnerable and open to criticism."

Follensbee sat down amid a general murmur of approval. To his astonishment Kendrick saw Richards get to his feet again. He looked puzzled but he certainly wasn't chastened. He was actually going to press his point further.

"I agree with Mr. Follensbee as to our responsibility," Alan said earnestly, "but don't we have an equal responsibility to find out as much as we can about Tommy Conway's death? Maybe he was only one little boy out of many and maybe we can't help him now, but surely everyone agrees that even the death of a child has meaning. We should at least care enough to look into the causes of this tragedy. I think most of us feel in our hearts that Tommy took his own life this morning, but officially we're just skimming over it. I object to that. I also object to being told that it would be quite 'disastrous' for Mr. Conway to hear that his son may well have committed suicide. As near as I can figure, that's because Conway might be offended and might withdraw his financial support."

He paused and looked around at the silent faces. "I know I'm sticking my neck out here," he finished, "but I will fight for a set of principles ahead of a set of new buildings any day."

Richards sat down, his face flushed, his jaw set. There was a strange silence in the room. Kendrick understood. The men were embarrassed. They were also, he suspected, rather impressed. Richards had a point there in his zeal to probe after the truth for the boy's sake. Pettengill would be sympathetic to any approach which stressed the school's responsibility. Neither he nor Richards would understand why this matter had to be handled in a different way.

"Mr. Richards," Pettengill said, "I think you must have misunderstood. I can assure you that we will not permit Mr. Conway to pressure us into anything and that we will deal with him as we would with any parent under similar circumstances. I share your concern for principles ahead of new buildings. By the way, who told you that it would be 'disastrous' to tell Mr. Conway the truth?"

"Mr. Kendrick."

Even before he saw the headmaster's expression, Kendrick knew that Pettengill would ponder that accusation but he was too smart to make an issue of it here. They had been circling each other warily for years and now this blundering young crusader was threatening to push them into open conflict. That was not Kendrick's way. He rose to his feet and after a nod from Pettengill walked toward the center of the room where he stood for a moment with his hands clasped behind his back, looking down at his shoes. The silence seemed about to explode.

"When we are young," Kendrick began, his green eyes blinking slowly, "we like to meet our problems head on like a tackler on the football field. As we grow up and mature in our understanding of people, we learn that there are less painful but equally effective ways of going about it. I did not expect Mr. Richards to refer to our private conversation of this morning; he leaves me no choice but to clarify a word that he has taken out of context. I was referring to the fact that we would gain nothing by treating Mr. Conway as an opponent whom we must crush at all costs and said, in effect, that it would be 'disastrous' to fling our personal convictions in his face when we are attempting here to deal with a situation that is extremely unfortunate for all of us."

"Excuse my interrupting," Pettengill said, "but of course you did not mean that we should give Mr. Conway a false picture of the situation, did you?"

"That's exactly what he meant, sir!" Richards said and his voice stung the silence like a whiplash.

Kendrick's face paled and the mottled patches of freckles were suddenly more prominent, but his voice was even milder than before, smooth and unruffled as an older man's might be when dealing with an impetuous child. He gave no indication of having heard Richards at all.

"There is a vast difference between established facts and circumstantial evidence. At the moment we have nothing to give Mr. Conway but the medical examiner's report which makes no reference to suicide. I think it would falsify the picture for us to impose our own theories upon Mr. Conway and I am certainly not in favor of that, sir."

Pettengill nodded in agreement, and Kendrick's glance flicked over Richards for the barest instant before he continued.

"Finally, although I am naturally concerned that Mr. Richards should be suspicious of my motives, I do not feel that this is the time or place for personal conflicts. We should all pull together at a time like this and I propose that we leave the matter of what is said to Mr. Conway entirely to the headmaster and stand by to help in any way we can."

The silence was different now. It was as though a door had been closed somewhere, an ugly vista blocked from view. Kendrick had restored dignity and confidence to a meeting which had almost lost both because of a young and inexperienced member who talked too much. Kendrick had wielded a sledge hammer in the gentlest of hands. No one looked at Mr. Richards.

"Thank you, Mr. Kendrick," Pettengill said. "I'm certainly going to need the support of all of you in what I anticipate will be a very difficult task. Mr. Conway will undoubtedly arrive tomorrow, and I must ask Tommy's class masters and housemaster to remain on the campus in case Mr. Conway wants to talk to them. I frankly don't know what he'll want. I don't want to discuss any of this with the boys if we can help it. I have a feeling they are going to recover from the shock long before we do, anyway. One more thing: please don't talk to any newspaperman who may show up in the next few days. We don't plan to issue any further statements to the press. Does anyone have anything else to bring up at this time?" Pettengill scanned the room and then stepped back from the walnut chair. "Thank you, gentlemen. We are adjourned."

Out of the corner of his eye Kendrick saw Alan Richards rush stiffly from the room. Four of the masters sat down to a bridge game, and a couple of others wandered over to the magazine racks. Harry Rogers was talking to Pettengill. Kendrick waited patiently, knowing that the headmaster would want to talk with him. He nodded to Follensbee who was about to depart.

"Good night, Justin."

"Good night, Hugh," Kendrick said. He smiled. "Have a drink before you turn in. It's a cold night."

"I believe I will, Justin. Yes, it is a cold night."

Follensbee's voice was flat and he looked terribly tired. There wasn't anyone more loyal to Carver. After all these years he and Emmy deserved a happier ending. He's in a daze, Kendrick thought, watching Follensbee leave the room, and then he saw that Pettengill had finished his conversation and was approaching.

"I'm sorry you had that run-in with Alan Richards, Justin. What's the matter with him?"

"Case of a misguided missile," Kendrick said. He smiled. "Alan's going to be one of the best men we've got if he survives this week end."

"I thought you handled it very well," Pettengill said. He looked at his watch. "Why doesn't that fellow call?"

"I don't know."

"Well, if I don't hear in the next hour or so, I'm going to phone his hotel again. They might have mislaid the message."

"I doubt it," Kendrick said.

"I'll have him come directly to my house tomorrow. He can make all his arrangements from there. You'll be around, won't you?"

"Oh, yes."

"Well, good night, Justin." Pettengill started to go and then turned back. "You know, I hope the faculty won't get the idea that I'm going to let Conway push us around just because he's giving us a new building."

"Don't worry about that," Kendrick said.

As he was about to leave, Harry Rogers came up with a knowing grin. "Boy, talk about trying to hang yourself!" He laughed.

Kendrick's face betrayed no reaction to this comment. He had long since learned the dangers of talking about one faculty member to another and he was a little annoyed now with Harry Rogers for attempting to draw him out this way.

"I sent you a note about a boy in your house," Kendrick said. "You should get it in the morning."

"Anything wrong?" Rogers' grin was fading rapidly.

"To some extent," Kendrick said. "Excuse me, but I do have to get back to my house."

He walked off, thinking to himself that it was a rather dirty trick to let Harry Rogers worry all night about a trifle, but perhaps from now on he wouldn't enjoy the discomfort of others so much. As for Alan Richards, there was nothing more dangerous than a truly inspired young man who was determined to do all the wrong things for the right reasons. Approaching his apartment, Kendrick knew that when Roger Conway arrived tomorrow he was going to need all the skill he had acquired over the years.

15

THE WINTER winds sweeping down from northern tundras could chill through to the bone, but Alan was not wearing his overcoat. He was still clutching it in the fingers of his right hand, exactly as he had snatched it from the cloakroom after the faculty meeting. In his haste to get out of there he had not noticed the cold and as he churned toward his house now, his anger kept him warm. Up above in the great, black, October night the moon was a polished pebble infinitely far from the Berkshire hills and the affairs of men.

When Alan came into the apartment, Nancy in pajamas and negligee was curled up at one corner of the sofa with a fashion magazine. The school oil burner went off at ten o'clock, but they always put the thermostat up during the last hour and trapped enough extra heat to keep the living room pleasantly warm. Alan flung his overcoat into the hall closet and slammed the door.

"What's the matter?" Nancy said.

"Plenty. I'll tell you."

"Come and sit down."

"I want to check the rooms first. I thought I saw a light from outside. Boucher's room, I think." He started out the door and then added, "If they think I'm squelched, they're crazy."

Nancy frowned, tossed aside the magazine and went into the kitchen to make a fresh pot of coffee. She had bathed and fixed her hair and put on lipstick and her prettiest negligee for his pleasure, hoping they would make up their quarrel tonight in bed together. But Alan was still in a black mood over something. He hadn't even noticed her.

Alan climbed the stairs swiftly, his anger transferred for the moment to the offending member of the house who must be reading after 'lights.' He moved stealthily past Beckett and Lindstrom's room and then saw a momentary glow under Boucher's door. A few seconds later he was in the room, and the hall light was shining in Boucher's startled eyes.

"What have you got under the covers?"

"Nothing, sir."

"Don't lie to me!"

"Just a flashlight, sir."

"What else?"

"Well—a magazine."

"Let me have it."

"Oh, sir—"

"You heard me."

With extreme reluctance Boucher reached under the covers and came up with another well-worn magazine that featured naked girls and advertisements for bust developers. Alan glanced at the cover and then stuffed the magazine into his coat pocket.

"Where did you get this thing?"

"I—found it, sir."

"What do you want to read this junk for?"

Boucher hung his head, but even in the dim light Alan could see the grin on his face and it was especially infuriating tonight.

"I'm giving you two hours," Alan said, "for reading after lights. If I catch you with anything like this again, you go straight to the headmaster. Understand?"

"Yes, sir."

Alan turned and looked into the shadows across the room at the empty, silent bed and the clean-topped desk beside it.

"Sir," Boucher said, "why did you come up here this afternoon?"

"That's none of your business."

Boucher stared at him for a moment. Then he spun around and flopped down on his stomach with a sigh of resignation. "Okay," he said, "have it your way."

"Don't be rude, Boucher."

"I'm not, sir. You don't understand. I just thought I might be able to help."

"You can help by going to sleep," Alan said, "when you're supposed to."

He shut the door firmly. What help could Boucher possibly be now? He had already told all he knew about Tommy. This was probably just another of his innumerable stratagems to confuse the faculty.

Nancy poured the coffee as soon as he came in and when he sat down beside her, she saw the magazine. "What's that?"

"Boucher's bedtime stories. That guy's a dirty-minded little cuss."

Nancy plucked the magazine from his pocket and turned the pages. "Wow!" she said. "Look at that bo-zoom!"

"What about it?"

"What do you mean, what about it? It's phenomenal!"

"So what?"

"Oh, Alan. Just look at these pictures!"

"I know. Trust Boucher."

"Well, he's not my favorite character but I can't blame him for being curious. All the boys probably look at these magazines."

"Not necessarily."

"Didn't you when you were his age?"

"I suppose so, but only once in a while."

"So there."

"What do you want me to do—hand them out to the boys each night?"

"No, but I wouldn't act so shocked, either. I think I'd just ignore them, outwardly anyway, and then maybe the boys wouldn't think they were so scandalous and exciting after all."

"They shouldn't even be allowed to buy them."

"You know, Mr. Richards," Nancy said, "sometimes I think you're just a wee bit stuffy. Oh, look at that one, darling! Do you think she's *really* sexy?"

"What do you care?"

"I don't," Nancy said. She moved closer and placed his arm around her waist. "And you don't, either. You have me."

"That's right."

"Such enthusiasm."

"I'm sorry," Alan said. "I guess I'm just not in the mood tonight."

Nancy got up to reach for a cigarette and when she sat down again, it was at the other end of the couch. "All right," she said, "tell me about it."

Alan crossed his long legs, and toyed with a shoelace. His face with its strong, aquiline features took on a tenseness as he began to recall the meeting.

"There isn't much to tell. It was just damned humiliating, that's all."

"What happened?"

"Well, we were talking about Tommy and I said that as most of us were convinced that he had committed suicide, we ought to tell Conway the truth."

"Yes, go on."

"I don't remember the exact sequence, but the thing that did it was my saying that I had been told it would be disastrous to tell Conway the truth. The Head asked me who said that and I told him it was Kendrick."

"Oh, Alan! You said that right at the meeting?"

"Well, why shouldn't I?"

"Right out in front of everybody?"

"Yes."

"Oh, Alan, how could you?"

"How could I what?"

"Make such a fool of yourself."

He swung toward her fiercely. "I knew you'd say that. 'Don't speak up. Don't take a chance on offending anybody.' Well, somebody's *got* to speak up. The rest of them sat there like a lot of mummies."

Nancy looked away. "Then what happened?"

"Kendrick got up to speak. He was very smooth about it. No rancor, no bitterness. You know—the usual cool as a cucumber Kendrick approach. According to him I'm very young and headstrong and we just shouldn't go about things this way. He said we have nothing to go on but the medical examiner's report which says nothing about suicide and so we should not 'impose,' get that word, our personal opinions on Mr. Conway. The Head broke in to say that of course Kendrick was not in favor of giving Conway a false picture of the situation, was he, and I—" Alan stopped and glanced over at his wife—"I said that was exactly what he meant to do."

"Alan, you're a fool."

"Thanks."

"But you are." Nancy stubbed out her cigarette. "Can't you understand why?" She looked up at him. "No, you can't," she said. Then she burst into tears.

Alan stared at her. "Listen—"

"Go ahead, ruin yourself," Nancy said, "ruin me and your son, too."

Alan made a helpless gesture. "It seems to me," he said, "that this is where I came in earlier today."

"We've got to live on this campus," Nancy rushed on. "We can't live here or anywhere until you stop being so— so blindly sure of yourself."

"Isn't Conway pretty sure of himself?"

"Yes, and he's wrong, too."

"And what about Kendrick?"

"Kendrick's different. He has something else that tempers his certainty. I don't know what to call it, but it's there."

Alan laughed harshly. "It's there, all right, and the Irish call it blarney. You'll be glad to know at the end of his little speech he cut me down to size or thought he did, anyway. He said that we should all stick together at a time like this and just leave everything up to the headmaster."

"I think you should."

Alan gave her a quizzical look. "Maybe I am naïve, but so are you. Kendrick *says* that, but he has no intention of leaving everything up to the headmaster. Tomorrow he will be in his old place behind the scenes, pulling all the strings as usual. Only—"

Alan's voice trailed off and he stood up. He seemed to be secretly pleased about something.

"Only what?"

"There's going to be one puppet who won't dance. To-morrow morning when I get the chance, and believe me I'll get it, I'm going to tell Conway the plain, cold truth about the death of his son."

Nancy opened her mouth to protest and then recognized the futility of it. Earlier tonight she had felt warm and loving and yielding and wanting, but the room seemed cold now and the feeling was gone.

"I'm going to bed," she said. "Good night."

"Now, don't get all upset about this, Nancy."

"I'm not in the least upset. I just happen to have an awful headache."

"I'm sorry," Alan said in a preoccupied way. All at once he noticed the negligee and it flashed upon him too late what Nancy had intended for tonight. He turned, but she had gone and a moment later the bedroom door closed with a decisive little click.

After a while he went to the kitchen and made himself a drink. He carried it back to the living room and sat there alone for a long time.

16

KENDRICK couldn't get to sleep. He lay on his back and stared into the darkness, trying not to hear a shutter that was banging somewhere. The night watchman, like some mechanized figure in a clock, swung into view each hour and he had just gone down the cellar stairs. Why, Kendrick was thinking, hadn't Conway called?

Several times he had been on the verge of going to the telephone, but he had resisted the temptation to anticipate the headmaster. Pettengill had insisted that he himself would initiate the call if need be and in all probability he was still trying to make contact. Conway could be at a party somewhere or he could be with a woman. It wouldn't be the first time.

In the spring of Conway's year at Carver a school maid had dropped dead in one of the houses. Her replacement, hustled in from a neighboring town, had been a full-bodied woman of about forty. Kendrick had noticed on several occasions that she seemed to go out of her way to speak to the boys. She had a husky, ringing laugh and when she walked, the stained white uniform would swing with a slow, deliberate provocation.

Kendrick's suspicions had not been confirmed until the night he had knocked on the door of her dingy room over the garage and then, hearing the frantic scramble inside the room, had walked in with his flashlight puncturing the darkness. Conway had tried to roll to the side of the bed away from the terrible beam of light, but the woman had sat up and groped for the sheet to cover her nakedness. Kendrick had looked with distaste at the bold, voluptuous symmetry of her body and had then coldly ordered her to pack up and leave that very night. Conway, as it turned out, had not been the only offender, but Kendrick had somehow managed to conceal the scandal from Dr. Parsons whose wrath, had he known, would probably have assumed ridiculous proportions.

Kendrick snapped on the light and reached for his dressing gown. Sleep was impossible at the moment. He wanted a drink. The hands of the clock in the kitchenette pointed to one o'clock. It was midnight in Chicago. Tommy Conway had been dead almost twelve hours. Kendrick was getting some ice out of the refrigerator when a knock on his front door startled him so much that he nearly dropped the tray. He hastened to open the door and then found himself staring at the headmaster.

"Justin, I'm sorry—"

"Not at all. Come in."

"I just happened to see your light on."

"Of course."

Pettengill crossed the threshold and stood in the center of the room, blinking in the light and looking at the fish.

"Won't you sit down?" Kendrick said.

"Well, for just a minute." Pettengill grinned rather sheepishly. "I've been wandering around a bit. Richards has his light on and Follensbee, too. I guess we're all stewing over this thing in one way or another."

"Would you like a drink?"

"I would if it's convenient."

"It is," Kendrick said. "I was just going to have one myself. Scotch, bourbon?"

"Scotch would be fine. A little water." Pettengill settled back in his chair and closed his eyes. "What a day, Justin. Can I help you there?"

"No, thanks," Kendrick said. He was thinking that in the ten years Ken Pettengill had been at Carver he had never dropped in like this before. Kendrick had often attended Mary Pettengill's charming dinner parties and there had been the usual faculty receptions and business conferences in which he and the headmaster had participated, but this was the first time they had sat down and had a drink together.

Pettengill accepted his glass with a grateful smile. "You'll be interested to know, Justin, that I talked to Conway a little while ago."

Kendrick's eyes widened, and the drink paused halfway to his lips. "How did he take it?"

"Very badly. He didn't believe me at first. Then he began to swear and make accusations. It was awful. I honestly think the man was drunk."

"It's quite possible," Kendrick said. "What did you tell him?"

"Simply the facts as we know them. I broke it to him as easily as I could. Told him it was apparently an accident although we couldn't be sure."

Kendrick had picked up a wooden match. It snapped suddenly between his fingers. "What did he say to that?"

Pettengill took a drink from his glass. "He wanted to know what else it could have been but an accident. I told him we would prefer to discuss the matter later. With considerable profanity he insisted that we discuss the whole thing right then and there. I flatly refused to do it over the telephone."

Kendrick was staring into his glass. "I was afraid of that."

"Of what?"

"That his anger would get in the way. Psychologically, he responds to every crisis in his life by getting mad. It's a protective reaction of his."

Pettengill frowned. "I know you're probably right, Justin, but I'm not a psychiatrist. As far as I'm concerned, the man is simply a mucker. That's a word my father always used when he wanted to describe anyone who was obviously crude and without manners. I think it describes Conway perfectly."

There was a pause. Kendrick studied the ice cubes in his glass. "I know what you mean," he said.

Pettengill sat up and banged the arm of his chair. "I've said this before, Justin, but I'm more determined than ever not to have our school and our faculty subjected to the arrogance and foul temper of this man a moment longer than is necessary. I almost wish that he wasn't giving us a new building. As a matter of fact, I wouldn't be surprised if he withdrew his gift after what's happened."

"Not if I can help it," Kendrick said.

Pettengill smiled but there was an extra alertness in his eyes, the way he looked when he expected an argument to be coming up. He pulled out his pipe and pouch and began to tamp the golden-leafed tobacco into the black, cake-encrusted bowl. The strain of the day was evident in the deepening lines of his face and in the dark hollows under his eyes. To Kendrick, who was fifteen years his senior, Pettengill brought to mind a very earnest young man who was muddling through on his own pretty well, but he was going to need an older, steadier hand to help him before it was over.

"I know how you feel about that building," Pettengill said, "and the ones you hope are to come in the future." He held a match to the pipe and then puffed vigorously. "Ever since I've been at Carver, Justin, I've been aware that you and I placed different values on such things. It's much too late tonight for us to get into a long discussion, but I hope we haven't been working at cross purposes."

"I'm sure we haven't," Kendrick said.

There was a silence and for several moments each man pursued his own thoughts. Kendrick was certain this was not the time for them to air their differences; it was probably best that they never did so. To define and explain and openly debate his purposes was not Kendrick's way of doing things. He had never seen a game worth playing in which all the cards were placed face up on the table. Besides, his differences with the headmaster were in the long run not so much a matter of objectives as of approach. Kendrick's approach depended for its very life upon his playing his cards close to his chest.

"You see, I won't kowtow to the man," Pettengill continued. "It's against every one of my instincts and all the traditions of my upbringing. I don't care if he wants to give us a solid gold dormitory. I won't sacrifice a single principle to get it. Richards was right about that."

"Richards is not yet dry behind the ears as far as this business is concerned," Kendrick said more sharply than he meant to. "He doesn't yet understand the problems of running a school and he can't solve them until he learns." He paused and then more gently and for Pettengill's benefit he said, "I don't see why we should have to sacrifice any principles."

"Good." Pettengill was obviously pleased. "Then we'll

hold the line together on that." He smiled and looked at his watch. "I've got to be going. I'm sorry about this fellow, Justin, but he gets my dander up."

"He may be better after this."

"What makes you think so?"

"Well, I don't see how a man can go through anything like this without it changing him. In Roger's case I think it will eventually be for the better."

"I understand you knew him pretty well when he was a boy here."

"Yes," Kendrick said.

Pettengill drained his glass and stood up. "Thanks, Justin. I didn't mean to stay so long, but I feel better now." He smiled. "I think I'll even sleep."

"You'll need it," Kendrick said.

Pettengill laughed. "By the way, Conway told me over the phone that he was taking the first plane out. I told him to come to my house. He said he wanted to talk to people about this, not wanted to but was 'damn well going to.' I think we'd better get Tommy's class masters together with Richards, you and me. Nine-thirty tomorrow morning at my house. Will you set it up?"

"Right," Kendrick said. He opened the door.

They had been talking in a little cell of warmth and light, but outside and all around them the rest of Carver was huddled down now against the cold and the darkness and the uncertainties of the night. Pettengill turned up the collar of his coat and looked into the blackness.

"Hugh has put his light out. Good. But I don't think he'll get much sleep tonight. I'll stand up for him all I can tomorrow. Good night, Justin."

"Good night, Ken."

Kendrick closed the door, glad for the warmth that still remained in the apartment. He carried the glasses out to the sink, then washed and dried them. Returning to the living room, he stood for a minute looking at the fish. They were always deep down in the tank at this time of night, somnolent and secure. It passed through his mind that it would be a good idea if he were to intercept Conway before the meeting in the morning. Conway would probably be in one of his blind rages but it might be possible to calm him down a bit.

When Kendrick turned off the lights and went into his bedroom, the night watchman's steps were echoing on the cellar stairs again.

17

MR. KENDRICK?"

Kendrick had been dreaming that he was in a big plane winging eastward into the dawn but when he opened his eyes he was back in the darkness again. Awareness came slowly.

"Mr. Kendrick?"

There was an urgency in the voice. Kendrick sat up and peered into the shadowy direction of his bedroom doorway.

"Who's that?"

"Boucher, sir?"

"What the devil do you want?"

"I gotta talk to you, sir."

"What time is it?"

"Well, I think it's about six-thirty, sir."

"What do you mean by walking in here at this time of the morning?"

"I knocked, sir, but you didn't hear me."

Six-thirty and the rising bell wasn't until eight-thirty on Sunday mornings! Kendrick swung his legs over the edge of the bed and turned on the light.

"All right," he said. "I'll be out in a minute."

Boucher's round face disappeared from the doorway as Kendrick reached for his dressing gown and slippers. This was one day he hadn't wished to start a minute ahead of schedule, but something very unusual must have occurred to get Boucher out of bed and over here at this hour. Kendrick padded into the living room and put on one of the table lamps. "Now what's the trouble?" he said.

"It's about Mr. Conway, sir."

Kendrick blinked. "What about him?" he said, suddenly alert.

"He's over at our house."

"Now?"

"Yes, sir."

"What's he doing over there?"

"Having a fight with Mr. Richards from the sound of it, sir."

"Damn!" Kendrick said softly. Mechanically he reached out and took Boucher by the arm. "You'd better sit down," he said. He indicated a chair. "Over there."

Boucher was looking at the fish tanks as he edged toward the chair. "Do those fish ever sleep?"

"Never mind about them now," Kendrick said.

He took a seat opposite Boucher. In his dressing gown, unshaven and with his hair uncombed, he knew that his appearance could hardly have been less imposing. But there was certainly no slyness in the fat boy's face just now. The little eyes were uneasy and as they glanced up at Kendrick they seemed to find him no less formidable than usual.

"All right," Kendrick said, "suppose you tell me just what this is all about."

"Well, I woke up about six o'clock, sir, and heard voices downstairs. They sort of mumbled for a while and then I heard Mr. Richards say, 'Well, it's only six o'clock. My wife and I aren't up yet.' Then Mr. Conway said—"

"How do you know it was Mr. Conway?"

"I got out of bed and went to the top of the stairs. From there you can see the door to Mr. Richards' apartment. The hall light was on and he was standing in his doorway in his pajamas and bare feet. Mr. Conway—I recognized him from when he brought Tommy up at the beginning of school—had his overcoat on and he was sort of crumpling his hat with his fingers. They didn't see me and—"

"What did Mr. Conway say?"

"Well, sir, you'll pardon me for saying this, but he said, 'God-damn it! I don't care what time it is.' Then Mr. Richards said something about he thought that Mr. Conway was supposed to go to the headmaster's house. Mr. Conway got real mad then. He said, 'Don't you tell me where I'm supposed to go. I'll go exactly where I please until I find out who's responsible for my son's death.' "

Boucher stopped and shook his head. "He didn't sound at all sorry about Tommy. Just mad. Georgie Lindstrom and Pete Beckett woke up, too, and some of the other guys. We were all watching and listening together." Boucher shook his head again and a faraway look of admiration came into his eyes. "I gotta hand it to Mr. Richards," he said. "And Mr. Conway is a lot bigger than him, too."

Boucher had been looking down at his hands when he told this part of it and so he did not see the look of horrified anticipation that crossed Kendrick's face. "What do you mean?" Kendrick said.

"I mean Mr. Richards really told him off, sir. We couldn't hear what they were saying for a minute but then Mr. Richards blew his top. 'All right,' he yelled, 'you just come in here and I'll tell you who's really responsible for Tommy's death.' "

Boucher sat back with a reflective smile. "We couldn't hear any more after that," he added with obvious disappointment. "Mr. Conway took him up on it and they shut the door."

"Is Mr. Conway still over there?"

"As far as I know, sir."

"Hmm." Kendrick stood up and with his hands clenched inside the pockets of his dressing gown, he strode over to the window and remained there for a minute or two with his back to Boucher, who was beginning to look at him now with growing apprehension.

It was clear to Kendrick from the relish with which Boucher had told the story that it was perfectly true. If there was anything the boys enjoyed, it was to see responsible adults collide without dignity or restraint. It was equally evident that the very worst had happened. Richards, infuriated by Conway's manner and spurred on by his own notions of right and wrong, had thrown all common sense to the winds and with it perhaps the only chance they had of preserving everything that Kendrick had been working toward all these years. Standing there at the window, he had a moment of overwhelming despair. It had not occurred to him that Conway would wander around the campus so early in the morning, and yet he should have known that it was just like the man to barge in wherever he pleased and to expect others to accommodate him at once. Surely everything was lost now. Kendrick grimaced like a man who sees a carefully constructed mosaic suddenly dashed to pieces, but it was in his nature to stoop and pick up the pieces and go thoughtfully to work again.

He turned from the window and looked at Boucher. The rest of it was clear, but Boucher's reason for coming over here at six-thirty in the morning to tell him about it was not. He put the question to the boy very directly.

Boucher did not answer at once. He ran his tongue back and forth over his lips while in his little eyes fear and cupidity wrestled. Then his right hand moved slowly down to the pocket of his wrinkled sports jacket.

"It was mostly on account of this, sir. I thought you might like to see it." Then, as Kendrick's arm shot out toward him, he added, "It's Tommy's, sir."

Kendrick turned the pages rapidly, reading only in snatches here and there, but perceiving the tone of the diary and the full implication of its contents immediately. Presently he refastened the metal clasp and concealing his excitement put the diary casually on the arm of his chair.

"Anyone else see this?"

"No, sir."

"No one?"

"No, sir."

"Not even Mr. Richards?"

"No, sir."

"When did you find it?"

"Last evening."

"Why didn't you show it to Mr. Richards?"

Boucher hesitated. "Well, I was going to but—"

Kendrick's tone softened a little. "Go ahead, Jim, you can tell me."

"Well—he caught me reading after lights last night and he got pretty mad about it. Even then I was willing to help him because I knew he was looking for something, but he told me it was none of my business."

"He was looking for something?"

"Yes, sir. I thought maybe it was the letters in Tommy's desk. From his father and his girl." Boucher stopped and his fat face flushed. "At least I think they were."

Kendrick smiled. "But you say you didn't tell Mr. Richards about this diary?"

"No, sir. He didn't give me a chance and this morning he and Mr. Conway were both so mad I—" Boucher stopped and then he looked at Kendrick out of the corner of his eye. "Also, sir, I thought that you might want to have it."

Kendrick had seen that sidelong glance. "Is that all?" he said.

Boucher was starting to squirm. "Practically all, sir."

"No, it isn't," Kendrick said. "And you know it isn't. I'll come back to that. First I have something else to say to you."

Kendrick sat back in his chair and for a long moment he simply stared at Boucher, scrutinizing in turn the little, beady eyes, the white dough flesh of the cheeks, the guppy mouth. And then as Boucher stared back at him, tense and uncomprehending, Kendrick leaned toward him and began to speak quietly.

"Now listen carefully, Jim. We haven't much time. You knew I wanted this diary; you also wanted something for yourself. That's all right. Perfectly natural. I trust you also knew that it would be a mistake to try to bribe me."

"Oh yes, sir."

"I know you very well, Jim Boucher," Kendrick went on. "You are vulgar, lazy, selfish and thoroughly impossible a good deal of the time, but there is hope for you. There is a chance you may not always be governed by your glands, that you may come to love something more than your stomach, that you may even grow up some day to be something more than a walking sack of gluttony. For in spite of your many faults, Mr. Boucher, you have one outstanding virtue: you know very well which side your bread is buttered on. Am I correct?"

Boucher's eyes had a glazed look but he managed to nod his head.

"All right," Kendrick went on, "I propose to make an agreement with you. For reasons best known to me which you must not question, I want you to forget that you ever saw this diary. It doesn't exist as far as you are concerned and it actually won't in a little while. You are not to mention this to your friends, to the masters, to your family, to anyone, understand?"

"Yes, sir."

Kendrick continued to look at Boucher as closely as a surgeon checking the progress of an operation.

"A great deal more depends on this than you can understand right now. Someday you should ask yourself whether it is ever right to tell a lie or wrong to tell the truth; at the moment you must take my word that what we are doing here is best for the school and for all concerned. I have one thing to add: if you are asked about any other part of this affair such as what happened at the Rock yesterday, I want you to tell the exact truth, bearing in mind as I said before that you can only guess as to whether Tommy slipped or jumped. Have you any questions?"

"No, sir."

"Good." Kendrick smiled. "Now for what you want. I am willing to reconsider your request for a week end, providing you first work off any hours which are standing against you, and providing your conduct next week proves that you deserve the privilege. After all, your girl wants a man, you know, not a silly little boy."

Boucher acknowledged this with an embarrassed grin.

"Did the others know you were coming over here?"

"No, sir. They went back to bed."

"Then I trust," Kendrick said dryly, "that you are sufficiently practiced to return to your room unobserved. Better get going."

Boucher was on his feet at once. "Thank you, Mr. Kendrick."

Kendrick held up the diary. "Are you man enough, Jim?"

"What, sir?"

"Are you man enough to stick to our agreement?"

"Yes, sir."

"You'd better be."

Boucher caught the characteristic intonation and already as he walked out the door he looked like more of a man. Kendrick had seen it happen before. Even a fat blob of protoplasm like Boucher had a backbone somewhere.

Kendrick sat thoughtfully still for a few minutes and then, clutching the diary, he walked over to the window. It was just getting light outside. A heavy frost glistened on the campus, and the sky was going to have again the deep blue, limitless horizon so typical of these beautiful autumn days.

He could be grateful that Boucher's selfish interests had led him to make the right decision as far as the diary was concerned. Richards had botched things almost beyond repair, but with the diary in his possession, the ruin would have been complete. Kendrick looked down at the metal clasp. Sad, pathetic little book, it was eloquent testimony to a boy's despair and to the school's failure to help him when and where he needed it most. But if they had failed to see what was happening to the boy and to meet the crisis when it came, the diary left no doubt that Roger Conway had been the blindest and the most blundering of them all.

Kendrick was about to dress and go look for Conway when he saw him coming across the campus. There was no mistaking the hulking figure with the big shoulders and the powerful arms. Conway had at least learned where to buy his clothes. Everything about the man—the hairy wrists, the bulging chest, the ruddy face, the big, strong teeth—had always had an overwhelming physical reality for Kendrick. It was in some confusion that he hurried into his bedroom and locked the diary in a strongbox that he kept in the back of his closet. Then he sat down on the edge of the bed to wait for the knock on his door that he knew was coming.

"You aren't up, either," were Conway's first words. He pushed past Kendrick into the room, his fingers tugging at the heavy buttons on his coat.

Kendrick closed the door. The boys had another hour to sleep, and nothing short of an earthquake was going to wake them sooner. He watched Conway fling his overcoat heedlessly onto a chair. He was unshaven and bleary-eyed and his face was like a ravaged battleground where fatigue and grief and anger had struggled. Kendrick pulled his dressing gown more closely around him.

"Roger, I can't tell you how sorry—"

"Never mind that," Conway cut in. "Condolences are in order, I know, but they won't bring my boy back. All I want to know is how a thing like this could have happened in a place that calls itself a school."

Conway's tone was challenging, just as it must have been for Alan Richards, but Kendrick knew better than to accept the challenge at this particular time. He tried instead to keep his voice pleasant and matter of fact.

"We're going to have a meeting at the headmaster's this morning of all the men who were closely associated with Tommy in any way. I'm sure they'll be glad to answer any questions you have."

Conway laughed harshly. "No, they won't," he said. "What time is that meeting?"

"Nine-thirty."

"Why so late?"

"We sleep longer on Sunday. You remember?"

"Sure, I remember. You fellows don't let anything interfere with your schedule, do you?"

Kendrick smiled. "How did you get here so soon?"

"What difference does that make?" Conway's tone was still truculent. "I chartered a plane at La Guardia and he got me to Taylorville. I had to wake up half the town before I could hire a car. Damned little hick burg."

It was on the tip of Kendrick's tongue to remind Roger Conway of an equally small town in Pennsylvania but instead he said, "You must be tired. If you'd like a shave and a shower before breakfast, I'd be glad—"

"Damn it!" Conway burst out. In typical fashion he leaned forward and banged his fist on the arm of the chair. His face with its livid scar was contorted and his voice had dropped to a rasping whisper. "Will you stop talking like a polite schoolmaster? Will you forget your God-damned diplomacy for a minute? This is not part of the old routine, Justin. You can't give me the usual Father's Day crap this time. None of you can, and that goes for Ken Pettengill, too. My son is dead. The school is to blame. You can forget your God-damned good-fellow approach. I want to know what happened and why it couldn't have been prevented."

Kendrick's lower lip was trembling exactly as it had thirty years ago, but he wouldn't have known how to handle this man back in those days. It was apparent to him now that Conway needed an immediate target for his anger but it would not do to confront him with the real enemy. There would be a time for that battle later.

"Did you come directly here?" Kendrick said.

Conway shook his head. "No, I went to see Tommy's housemaster. I figured he would know the score on this thing. Do you know what that Richards had the nerve to tell me? He said that Tommy killed himself. Now, isn't that pretty ridiculous, Justin? I mean, for a boy who had everything. I told that stupid son-of-a-bitch Richards that if he didn't know anything more than that about human nature, he'd never succeed in his job or any job. Do you have to hire people with as little brains as that?"

"This is only his second year. He's still learning the ropes."

"Well, sure, but it doesn't take experience to see that Tommy wasn't exactly a poor boy. I mean, he wasn't like me when I came here without a decent suit of clothes or a nickel to spend as I pleased. My God, I even told Tommy last year that I was going to give him a quarter of a million dollars when he was twenty-one. That's right—two hundred and fifty thousand dollars. Some kids start with nothing; he was going to start with a small fortune. It doesn't matter what you start with; it's what you make out of it, what you produce. I would have expected Tommy to double that easily in a year or two. So isn't that pretty ridiculous, Justin? I mean, is a boy who knows he'll have a quarter of a million in five or six years going to kill himself? Honestly, Justin, you agree with me, don't you? I mean, of course you do, but wasn't that a pretty half-ass statement for Richards to make?"

"There are a lot of angles, Roger, to most situations."

"Not to this one," Conway said. He stood up quickly. "I'll make that perfectly clear in the meeting you're talking about." He reached for his overcoat.

"Where are you going?"

Conway turned. "I want to see Tommy."

"But—" Kendrick stopped. There was no use trying to tell Roger Conway that it was only seven-thirty and that regardless of personal grief and tragedy the rest of the world did not care to be awakened at this hour of the morning. He said, "Will you come back to breakfast at my table?"

"I don't know."

In the silence the two men faced each other, further

words unsaid between them. Then Conway yanked open the door and stalked off down the hall. Kendrick closed the door gently. He was shaking when he went into the bathroom to shave, but there was comfort in the habitual actions of lathering his face and fitting a new blade into his razor.

Grief, he told himself, took many strange guises, but there was something else inside of Roger Conway, churning like a blind flood against a stubborn dam. Grief, when it was deep and true, when there was love at the heart of it, would almost always spill over eventually and there would be a cleansing of the body and sometimes an exaltation of the spirit. But in Roger Conway's case, love had never had a chance and perhaps the dam behind which it struggled was too strong.

Kendrick finished shaving, dressed, and sat down to make out a list of the masters who would be asked to attend the meeting this morning. In spite of what Conway had said, the routine of the school had to go on. There was Sunday chapel at noon today, for example, and a visiting preacher to be met at the railroad station. There were other scheduled events to prepare for and there would be unscheduled ones, too, as there always had been—the parents and guests forever cheerfully dropping in, the homesick boy, the electric power failure at the beginning of study hall—the list was endless. But even as Kendrick's mind automatically ranged over his duties, his thoughts kept coming back to the battle that loomed ahead. It would be all over, one way or the other, before this day was finished.

18

THEY came for Boucher shortly after nine-thirty. Two husky seniors had spotted him lounging on the fringe of a touch football game. They gave him the message. Boucher did not believe them and told them so in language that was not gracious. The seniors took him then, one at each arm, and hauled him twisting and cursing and purple with rage all the way back to his house where they set him down in front of Mrs. Richards.

"You had better change your clothes, Jim," she said quietly. "They want you at the headmaster's house."

Boucher's lower jaw sagged. "Me?"

The seniors were grinning. "I guess they finally caught up with you, Fatso," one of them said.

Boucher was too shocked to respond in his normal fashion. He stared at the seniors and then at Mrs. Richards. "What did I do?"

"I don't think you did anything, Jim," Mrs. Richards said. "Some of the masters are down there and they probably want to ask you a few questions. Now you'd better hurry."

Bewildered, Boucher turned toward the stairs. He was in a fog, the way he had been earlier this morning after he had left Mr. Kendrick's apartment and had nearly bumped right into Mr. Conway. At the last instant he had managed to avert his head, and Mr. Conway had stalked by him on the path, looking like a thundercloud. Safe in his own room a few minutes later, Boucher had experienced a queer sort of exaltation for a little while. In a momentary glow of inspired resolution he had decided to quit hacking around and become a paragon of virtue. Momentarily, Mr. Kendrick had made him feel very grown-up and responsible, but on more sober reflection Boucher had seen the folly of becoming a leader of men. Any such radical conversion would strip him of his present prestige and he would almost surely lose all his friends whose greatest scorn was reserved for apple polishers. Boucher had shuddered at the mere thought of being consigned to that category. He had played it smart so far with the diary and regained his chance to take a week end. That was all that really mattered. He would have to be careful next week but that was a different thing from actually helping the masters to run the school. To regain his composure he had gone into Beckett's room and tossed his knife a couple of times into the closet door they used for target practice. Then he and Beckett had sat together hashing over the scene between Mr. Conway and Mr. Richards until the rising bell.

Now as he pulled off his sweat shirt and mudstained khaki pants, Boucher was confused again. What did they want with him? The meeting must surely have something to do with Tommy Conway, but what was all the fuss about? Why didn't they just have the funeral and be done with it? He kicked resentfully at a bureau drawer that was sticking. He felt a little scared as he always did when the masters wanted to see him. Experience had taught him that no good ever came of these sessions. Mr. Kendrick had told him to tell the truth, but the whole thing was like a nightmare now and he wished they would let him forget it. He was tying his necktie when one of the seniors poked his head in the door.

"Come on, Boucher, get the lead out."

The senior went off whistling down the hall. Boucher glanced at himself in the mirror and then with a half-audible groan he leaned closer to the glass. There was a small pimple blossoming on the left side of his chin. He wondered if he could get rid of it before he saw Phyllis again. Taking one more look at the hateful blemish, he trudged out of the room and down the stairs.

For once in his life he tried not to be conspicuous. The fellows would think he was nuts, walking around in his best clothes almost three whole hours before chapel. Only the real queers did things like that. Boucher planned to tell the gang all about this later on and with suitable embellishments, but at the moment he did not want the word to get around about his being summoned to the Head's house. Those crummy seniors who lived down the hall would probably yack about it some, but he couldn't do anything about that now. Pursuing a circuitous route through basement passageways that he used when necessary, he came at last to his destination and rang the front-door bell. The butler answered and looked down at him with obvious dislike.

"The headmaster—"

"I know," the man said. He gestured. "In the study there."

"Okay, Ruggles," Boucher said but his derisive grin vanished as soon as he opened the study door.

The scene was too much for him to take in all at once. He saw Mr. Conway first, standing in front of the fireplace.

The Head and Mr. Kendrick were sitting on a couch nearby and grouped around them in a semicircle of chairs were Mr. Richards, Mr. Tingue, Mr. Rogers—That was as far as he got when he heard Mr. Kendrick's voice.

"Come in, Jim. And close the door, please."

Mr. Kendrick's voice was different somehow, and Boucher observed now that all of the faces looked very serious and Mr. Richards' jaw was sticking out the way it did when he was mad as hell about something.

"You!" Mr. Conway said, his right forefinger jutting at Boucher. "I've got some questions to ask you."

"Now, just a minute, Conway," the headmaster said, and Boucher had once heard his father use that tone to a man just before he hit him.

"I want you to know, Jim," the Head was saying to him, "that this meeting does not concern you primarily. You're in no trouble at the moment so far as I know." He smiled. "Mr. Conway has a few questions to ask you and it will help us a great deal if you will answer them simply and truthfully to the best of your knowledge. After that we'll certainly let you go right back to your Sunday morning recreation."

"Provided I get the facts I want," Mr. Conway said, and Boucher sensed that the tension in the room was even greater now. He could see it in the faces which had all swung toward him expectantly like so many weather vanes in a gale. Mr. Conway was looking at him, too.

"Did you climb the mountain with my son yesterday?"

"Yes, sir. Well—part way."

"Why only part way?"

"Me and Beckett and some of the other guys decided to go off together."

"Off where?"

"In the bushes. We wanted to go up a different way."

"Why didn't you take Tommy with you?"

"He wouldn't have wanted to go."

"Why not?"

Boucher tugged at his collar. He could not bring himself to look directly at Mr. Conway. "Well, Tommy wasn't very popular, sir."

Boucher risked a glance then and saw that a nerve or something was twitching in Mr. Conway's cheek right near that terrible scar he had.

"I see," said Mr. Conway. "Weren't you all supposed to stay on the same trail?"

Boucher glanced over at Mr. Kendrick. "Yes, sir."

"There was no one around to stop you from going off by yourselves?"

"Not just at the moment."

"No supervision of any kind?"

"Well, Mr. Follensbee—"

"I mean, right there with you?"

"No, sir."

Mr. Conway stopped and turned to the headmaster. "Point number one," he said. Then he looked back at Boucher.

"How did you and Tommy get along?"

"Pretty good, sir."

"Only pretty good? Why?"

Boucher tugged at his collar again. There were some things you just couldn't tell about a guy, no matter how much of a creep he might have been. With the toe of his shoe Boucher traced one of the designs in the Oriental rug. "I don't know why," he said.

"But you were roommates?"

"That doesn't mean the guy is your best friend or anything."

"I know," Mr. Conway said. He smiled grimly and this time he looked at Mr. Kendrick. "I remember."

For the first time since his arrival Boucher caught sight of Mr. Follensbee sitting alone at the back of the room. Whether this was by choice or arrangement, he certainly did look lonely and tired and sad. His face, normally so pink and healthy-looking, now had a sickly, grayish pallor. Boucher was profoundly shocked, and staring now at this man who was so terribly altered from the inimitable "Stinger" they all knew, he experienced a feeling of compassion that was utterly strange to him. He was actually sorry for Mr. Follensbee, a turn of affairs that he would not have thought possible. It was almost a relief to have Mr. Conway's harsh voice capture his attention again.

"Wouldn't you have preferred a different roommate?"

"Yes, sir." There was no doubt about that in Boucher's mind.

"And how about Tommy?"

Boucher shrugged. "I guess it was mutual."

"Then why didn't you make an effort to change?"

Boucher looked at Mr. Kendrick again. These questions were going to put somebody on the spot for sure, but he had been told to tell the truth.

"We did ask to change but they said to try it together for a while."

"Did you get along any better after that?"

"No, sir."

"Did you tell them?"

"Well, I spoke to Mr. Richards once."

"What did he say?"

"He said maybe we could both learn something by rooming together."

"Then, in spite of the fact that you were both unhappy, the school did nothing to improve the situation?"

"No, sir."

"Point number two," said Mr. Conway.

"That isn't true!"

Boucher saw that Mr. Richards had suddenly leaned forward in his chair and at the same time the headmaster had turned to look at him.

"What do you mean, Mr. Richards?"

"He acts as though we cared nothing about the welfare of these boys, sir, and that's not true. We care a great deal. In this case I didn't break up the combination because Tommy needed to be drawn into the group and Jim here, in spite of his faults, is a gregarious soul. If it hadn't worked out any better by the Christmas holidays, I was going to recommend a change, sir."

Mr. Richards sat back, and the headmaster looked up at Mr. Conway.

"We certainly do consider the best interests of each boy. You don't question that, do you?"

"Yes, I do." Mr. Conway was leaning forward now and thrusting his big chin down toward the headmaster. "Tommy was unhappy, and you and your masters did nothing about it. You weren't looking out for the boy at all. That's a lot of crap and you know it."

Boucher flushed at the sound of the word he had never expected to hear in the presence of masters. Instinctively he looked to the headmaster for a stern and instant reprimand, but Mr. Pettengill was looking down at his hand, and his lips were pressed tightly together in an expression that seemed to be more of pain than of anger.

"Yes," he said softly. "We have been wrong here, Mr. Conway, to some extent, and believe me we are fully aware of it."

"Well, that's more like it," Mr. Conway said. He straightened and looked around at the masters. "Now we can get on to the final point."

Boucher saw that Mr. Richards was twisting in his chair

and he looked as though he was going to say something any minute now. Mr. Tingue looked kind of scared as usual and Mr. Rogers had that same big-kid expression that was always on his face at the football games. Mr. Kendrick was just sitting back and watching everything. To Boucher he looked like a man who knew exactly what was going to happen and, come to think of it, Mr. Kendrick usually did know.

"What did you do when you got to the top yesterday?"

Boucher turned, aware that Mr. Conway was firing the questions again. He hoped that these would be the last ones or else he wouldn't have any time at all to hack around before chapel.

"We climbed up on the parapet." He had spoken the truth before he realized it.

"You did what?"

Boucher gulped. "Climbed up on the parapet, sir." Out of the corner of his eye he saw Mr. Follensbee's head come up.

"What did you do a damn fool thing like that for?"

"It's a kind of tradition, sir."

"You mean, you all climb up there together?"

"No, sir. One at a time."

"Then what?"

Boucher's voice had dropped to a whisper. "You're supposed to look straight down before you come back off there."

He could see the horrified stares on all of the faces now and he was suddenly convinced that this business of telling the truth was for the birds. What the masters didn't know hadn't hurt them any, but now, even though it was all over with, everybody was going to get in some sort of trouble.

"I see," said Mr. Conway. He looked oddly pleased. "A very nice little game for a bunch of kids to be playing on their own." He took a step toward Boucher. "Now, where was Tommy at this time?"

"He wasn't there. He came up later."

"Did he know about this—tradition?"

Boucher felt himself being pushed remorselessly back against some sort of wall. "I don't know," he said.

"But he climbed up there?"

"Yes, sir."

"And what were you doing?"

"Just sitting around—uh, looking at some rock formations." There was no point in going on with this stupid business of telling everything. They would not be climbing the Rock again but they did want to go on looking at Lindstrom's cards and the other things they had stashed away.

"Tommy didn't like high places, did he?"

"No, sir."

"Then why did he get up on that parapet?"

Wordlessly, Boucher shook his head. It seemed the safest thing to do.

"I'll tell you why." Mr. Conway was shouting as he swung toward the others. "Tommy got up there to prove he had as much foolish guts as the rest of those kids. I know my boy was scared of high places but that wasn't going to stop him. Nothing is going to stop a kid who isn't yellow from proving himself at a time like that, even though he is likely to get dizzy and fall."

The big man stopped and glared at the faces for a moment. That thing was twitching in his own face again, and his voice was low and sort of shaking in a way that made Boucher feel funny in his stomach.

"Nothing could have stopped my son except someone who was older than he was and who had more sense than to let him risk his life that way. But no master was there who could have stopped him. NOBODY!" He jabbed a finger at Boucher. "Where was Mr. Follensbee?"

Before Boucher could reply, the headmaster said, "We've already been over this privately, Conway. I don't see any need to further humiliate the man concerned or any of us."

Conway whirled on him. "Do you think I give a God-damn about that? Do you think I care a God-damn about your snob manners at a time like this?"

"It's not simply a matter of good manners. And I must ask you to moderate your language, sir."

"Never mind my language. You're not talking to one of your boys now."

Mr. Pettengill's face looked very white all of a sudden. "I will not tolerate cheapness from you or anyone else connected with my school. I see no reason to prolong this meeting and suggest—"

"I'm almost through with this meeting," Conway said, "and with your school, Pettengill, which I want nothing more to do with, incidentally. But I have a couple of things to say first, and all of you are going to hear them."

Boucher's mouth felt dry and he couldn't seem to swallow. He sensed instinctively that he was in the presence of a potential violence greater than his knowing and flowing from some deeper source than he could understand. It was an adult violence, and because its consequences could topple the very world itself, it was terribly wrong and should not be permitted to exist. He wondered why Mr. Kendrick didn't stop it, for he was the one master at Carver who could always stop anything and control everything. But Mr. Kendrick was just sitting there and it was awful to think that maybe even *he* was powerless now. Boucher wanted to run but he could only go on staring big-eyed at Mr. Conway and trying in vain to clear his mouth of the mucus of fear.

"I know we've been over this, Pettengill," Mr. Conway

went on. "We know that the master in charge fell asleep by
his own admission and neither he nor any other master was
at the top to supervise those young kids in a very dangerous
spot. We know that the master is very sorry and the school
is very sorry, but that's not enough. In my business when a
man or a company slips up like that, they have to pay with
something more than sweet talk. And so, by God, Pettengill, I demand that this school make some sort of public acknowledgment of your negligence in the death of my son!"

"What about *your* negligence?" Mr. Richards was on his
feet, hands on his hips, shoulders hunched.

Mr. Conway took a step toward him, but suddenly Mr.
Kendrick was there between the two men.

"Sit down, Alan!" he said sharply. And then more gently
and putting his hand on the big man's arm, "All right now,
Roger."

"You call *him* a housemaster!"

"Gentlemen?" Mr. Follensbee's voice was just loud enough
to be heard.

There was an absolute silence in the room all at once as
though the pounding waves of sound had suddenly with-
drawn, leaving an emptiness in which the other masters sat
motionless and expectant in their chairs. The headmaster
had turned sideways on the couch, and Mr. Conway had
backed up slowly to the fireplace with Mr. Kendrick still
beside him, all of them looking now at the little, white-
haired man who was standing at the back of the room.

"Mr. Conway, I have been teaching here at Carver nearly
forty-two years. I remember you when you were a boy here,
although I didn't have you in class—remember you especially out there on the football field." He smiled and then
a shadow came down over his face. "I think I can understand your feelings now, because I know what it is to have
lost a son."

Mr. Follensbee paused and for a moment he seemed to be looking out beyond the room. Then he went on again in his halting, quiet way.

"I've taken that field trip many times and in my younger days I was always the first to reach the top. Lately I have had to content myself with giving the boys specific instructions as to their conduct up there. In spite of my warnings, I have never felt that they were in any real danger unless they deliberately invited it. And although I know that Third Formers are of an age to do such things, I have observed that they rarely overtax themselves in any way. It is possible that Tommy wished to prove himself yesterday as you have suggested, but from my knowledge of the boy I don't think it was like him to do anything so thoughtless. However, that is not my point.

"I am a professional, Mr. Conway, and over the years I have developed the greatest respect for the standards which the real professionals set for themselves in every walk of life. Ever since this terrible thing happened, I have been aware of how I failed to meet those standards yesterday. For me there is only one inescapable course of action now." Follensbee paused and his gaze swept over the unbelieving faces.

"I hope, sir, that you will absolve the Carver School in general which did its best for your son. I hope, too, that you will accept this as the payment you referred to for an inexcusable mistake and as the public acknowledgment which you have demanded."

Later in his life Boucher would recall that moment as one of his first real glimpses into the adult world and he would see again Mr. Follensbee coming forward to hand the white envelope to the headmaster.

"What is this, Hugh?"

"My resignation, sir."

19

IT WAS fortunate, Kendrick thought, that the minister could not stay for lunch. Right after the service and before the last boy had fully awakened, Kendrick had hustled the elderly gentleman to the railroad station and sent him smiling off to conduct a vesper service at another school. Kendrick returned immediately to his apartment and called the headmaster.

"Is Conway with you, Ken?"

"No, Justin. I don't know where he is. Can't say I care. I've been talking to Hugh for the past hour. He can't do this after *forty-two years*."

"I know."

"But he insists that it's the only solution. What are we going to do?"

"Nothing at the moment. I have an idea that Conway may still be around."

"I hope not. I hope he goes as far away as' possible and takes his building with him." Pettengill made a whistling sound. "What a meeting that was! I don't ever want to go through that again. I hate to think of the lurid report that Boucher has probably given the boys."

"Something tells me that Jim won't have as much to say as usual. I looked at him a couple of times and I think he was rather sobered by the whole thing."

"Let's hope so, Justin. I wish you would talk to Hugh. I tried to tell him that, aside from the absurdity of his taking the whole blame for this thing, he would be leaving me in the lurch. I can't get another good science man this late in the year."

"Not these days," Kendrick said. "I'll see what I can do."

"I had another call from the *Gazette*. Told them 'no comment.'"

"Good. We'll just carry on now."

"Too bad about the dormitory, Justin, but we're well rid of that man."

Kendrick hesitated and his eyes narrowed. "That remains to be seen."

"Well, he'd have to change an awful lot before I'd even let him through the gate."

"He could change," Kendrick said.

He stood for a moment after he had put down the receiver, thinking over his next move. There were a number of places on the campus where Conway could be. On the other hand, he could have climbed into his car and departed. Kendrick was betting that he hadn't. From its hiding place in the strongbox he slipped the diary into his pocket. He had no present intention of showing it to Conway, but he was like a man who must go armed for any situation. There wasn't time for lunch, and after a little more deliberation and some hasty concocting in his kitchenette, he hurried out to his car. Several turns around the campus failed to disclose any sign of Roger Conway. Playing a hunch, Kendrick headed out into the country.

The meeting this morning had turned out just about as he had expected, although Follensbee's resignation had been distressingly melodramatic. Still, it was perfectly in keeping with the nature of the man. His deep sense of duty, his exacting standards, and his loyalty to the school had made the sacrifice obligatory in his eyes. Perhaps in the long run it would be a form of penance that would ease the burden of his guilt. But it was not in Kendrick's plans for Hugh Follensbee to exit this way in the vintage years of a fruitful life. It was not for this he had taken a calculated risk and was still taking it. He had wanted to make his intentions clear to Hugh, but right after the stunning moment of silence in which Follensbee had left the room, he had been required to deal with a chaotic reaction in which both the comic and the tragic had been inseparably mingled. Fortunately, Conway himself had walked out soon afterward.

Kendrick caught sight of Conway's car before he parked near the rusty chain that was still dangling between the rotting fence posts. "Parsons' Palace" had fallen into disrepair ever since the old man had retired. No one ever came here any more. In the springtime and in the summer the sagging cabin was hidden under shrouds of green, and now in autumn it stood unhappily revealed among the gaunt trees. Conway was leaning against the porch railing in a patch of warm sunlight. His back was turned and he was looking off into the dark caverns of the forest. As he approached, Kendrick deliberately stepped on a dried twig and Conway jerked around.

"What the devil do you want?"

"I thought you'd gone."

"How did you know I was out here?"

"Just a guess."

Conway watched with a sullen displeasure as Kendrick climbed the steps.

"Can't you stop meddling, Justin?" he said. "Can't you ever keep your God-damned nose out of other people's affairs?"

"This place," Kendrick said, looking at a broken window-pane, "is certainly falling to pieces. We ought to have some use for it."

"I suppose you came out here to tell me that I ruined Follensbee's life?"

"With a little carpentry and some regular care—"

"Listen," Conway said, taking Kendrick roughly by the arm, "don't try to be subtle, Justin. You're not very subtle, you know. You never were."

"What do you mean?"

"You know God-damned well what I mean."

Kendrick faced him, balanced heavily on his pudgy legs, his body slumped, his face suddenly old and weary of secrets.

"I could have ruined you, too," Conway said. "Every kid in school would have backed me up."

Kendrick said nothing, but his mouth was trembling and in his eyes, unmasked now, there was a kind of mute, helpless pain.

"Maybe you thought I was too young to know about things back there. Or too dumb. Well, I wasn't that dumb."

Kendrick continued to stand there silently. The color was flaming in his face but he was looking directly at Conway and it was his patient and deliberate acceptance of this lashing that seemed to sting the other man beyond endurance.

"We knew what you were!" He had begun to shout. "All of us. We talked about it. Compared notes. All the little signs." He leaned toward Kendrick and the livid scar was ugly in the sunlight. "Understand? We *knew*. You never fooled anybody and you still don't. Why don't you face up to yourself?"

"I have," Kendrick said quietly. Then, as Conway stared at him blankly, he walked off the porch.

When Kendrick returned a few minutes later, Conway was sitting hunched over on the steps, dragging on a cigarette. He looked up with a dull, uncomprehending stare as Kendrick unscrewed the cap of a thermos and placed two of the plastic cups on the railing. Kendrick saw that the first stage was over now. The terrible, blind, misdirected anger had spent itself. Now there was a kind of numbing shame. In a little while, perhaps, true awareness would come.

"Why did you have to come back?" Conway said. "Why make it any worse?"

"That's not my intention."

"Look, if that's hot cocoa or something, I don't want any."

"I don't usually mix my cocoas five to one," Kendrick said.

Conway stared at him in astonishment. "Wait a minute, Justin, don't you understand? I just insulted you. I—"

"I know."

"But I can't drink with a man I—"

"It's time you learned," Kendrick said. Then he added in a different tone, "I'm glad it's out, Roger. It's been on my mind for years that I might have upset you in some way."

"Oh God, no, Justin."

Kendrick looked down at the cat's-eye ring. "There are many different lives, Roger. I don't apologize for mine and I don't defend it. The important thing is for men to understand each other."

"I don't know what got into me," Conway said, his eyes averted. "I'm embarrassed as hell. To tell the truth, I hardly remember anything about my Carver days and as far as you were concerned—well, that was nothing much. You know how boys talk."

"We can forget it now," Kendrick said.

He refilled the cups. Off in the forest two crows signaled downwind to each other, and the north wind whispered to the trees of winter and the long sleep to come. Conway was still too embarrassed to look at Kendrick.

"Do you remember the first time we came here?" he asked.

"Yes."

"I was mad as hell that night, too."

"You certainly were."

Conway smiled grimly. "There was a dance down at the gym. I remember now." His face hardened. "Those snobs didn't think I belonged at the party."

"Neither did you."

"What?"

"I said, neither did you."

"That's ridiculous. You know yourself that a lot of those guys, like my roommate, Harvey Blanton, were awful snobs."

"You were a worse one."

"The hell I was."

"They looked down on you, but you looked down on yourself."

"That's a lot of psychiatric baloney, Justin. I remember during the war a corporal in our company went psycho on us. They finally took him to some twenty-five-bucks-an-hour couch specialist who said he was punishing himself because he felt guilty about running off and leaving his mother in the States. You can shove that stuff!"

"You're getting sore again," Kendrick said, "and you're getting vulgar. You think it bolsters your ego but it doesn't really."

Conway laughed. "You're an awful old maid in some ways, Justin. But don't let me interrupt the sermon."

"I don't like sermons," Kendrick said. "A man has to learn some other way within himself."

"And I haven't learned. Is that it?"

"Yes."

Conway smiled the good-humored smile of a man who can afford to listen to personal criticism that is patently absurd. His ruddy face looked more relaxed now; he had unbuttoned his coat and he was sitting back with his elbows resting comfortably on the top step. To Kendrick, leaning against the opposite railing, it was apparent that all of Roger Conway's defenses were still intact.

"All right," Conway said. "Go ahead. Tell me."

"You can't tell anybody this sort of thing."

Conway frowned. "I don't know what you're driving at, Justin. Where do we begin?"

"With your father."

"What about him?"

"Were you ashamed of him?"

Conway jerked erect. "I don't like that crack at all. My father was a miner. He worked in the pits. Every night he came home dirty and took a bath in a tin tub in the kitchen. To the day he died he had coal dust under his fingernails, but he was as good as the next man and so was I, even if the little snob bastards here at Carver didn't believe it."

"Did you?"

"Of course I did, but I had to prove it to them."

"Why?"

Conway stopped and stared at Kendrick. Then he laughed uneasily. "Hell, Justin, a man's got to have some pride. You can't let people walk all over you. I made up my mind right away to show 'em they couldn't do that. I figured I could do it in sports at Carver and then when I got out I'd really show 'em. And I guess I did, too. How many of them have got what I got now? Two million dollars in the bank—"

Conway stopped again. There was a sudden bleakness in his face. His big hands twisted together restlessly, and as Kendrick watched intently, the words seemed to be wrenched from him.

"All right, damn it! Maybe I did think they were better than me. Why shouldn't I have? They had all the money and the pretty girls and the fancy homes. I wanted what they had, but I wanted even more to know that I *could* have it."

"At any price?"

"Yes, I didn't think about that. I knew what I wanted and I started after it in college. I worked like a dog. Sometimes I'd get discouraged but then I'd remember that shack we lived in and I'd start working again. Once in a while I'd get drunk and end up with some whore." Conway laughed harshly. "They talk about the best years of your life. Not for me they weren't. But I got that diploma and nothing could have stopped me then. I was still working twelve, sixteen hours a day even after I met Louise." He turned away. "Louise," he said softly, "Louise. . . ."

The thermos was empty. Kendrick gathered in the cups and replaced the cap. Conway, head down, was pacing back and forth across the creaking planks of the porch.

"She loved to run around in the garden and have me catch her. Sometimes I couldn't. She was like quicksilver. She loved horses and early morning rides and dancing and just talking to people. I didn't have much time for those things. I was busy making money, but it wasn't the money that really mattered. It was—the power, I guess. It was beat-

ing the other guy to the punch, knocking him down, ending up on top. Do you understand, Justin?"

"Yes," Kendrick said. "You were proving something to everybody but yourself."

"But I got interrupted, Justin. The war came and I was overseas for quite a while. Tommy was born then, and I didn't even see him until he was nearly two years old. He and Louise had a private understanding already. I went back to my business."

Conway stopped his pacing and slumped against the railing. "No point in telling you all this. It's all over now." He shook his head. "I've wished to God so many times that I could have it over again. I don't think there are many cases where two people really love each other. One loves, but the other is too busy or too tired or too careless or just too damned stupid. And so one goes on loving and hoping for a change but there is no change, only this awful, one-sided love all over the world until maybe one night the other one gets liquored up and drives too fast and learns all this afterward when it is too late. . . ."

Conway straightened suddenly and turned to Kendrick. His bravado was all gone now and when he spoke again, his voice had a quiet urgency.

"Now—about my boy, Justin. I'm taking him back to Charleston tonight to be buried beside his mother. I know she would want that. I had a few hours to wait for the train, so I came out here. I guess I wanted to think things over a bit. I've been wondering about Tommy. I did everything I could for him, and I know he appreciated it even though he didn't say much. Kids his age don't say much, do they?"

"Some of them don't."

"Sure. Tommy was like that. You could give him a whole store full of presents and from the way he acted you'd think

every kid in the world was that lucky. But I guess that's a perfectly normal reaction, eh?"

"To some extent," Kendrick said, aware that Conway was watching him closely.

"Of course, I may have pushed him a little too much at times. Proud father, you know. Ambitious for his son. Guess you get a lot of those."

"Yes," Kendrick said.

"Wouldn't you say he was a perfectly normal boy?"

"He was a very fine youngster, Roger."

"You're darn right he was! That's why I was wondering— well, to tell the truth, we weren't as close as some fathers and sons. Tommy never told me how he really felt about a lot of things. I just wondered if maybe he talked to you?"

"No, Roger."

Conway plucked at something on his sleeve. He did not look at Kendrick. "Didn't he ever say anything to you about me or give any indication of how he felt?"

Kendrick's fingers strayed to the bulge in his pocket and came away again. Conway would not be able to survive that blow. Were he to see the diary now and perceive the truth in that way, he would not have a vestige of self-respect left. He was coming slowly on his own to an awareness of the central fallacy of his whole life. Even if he never brushed aside the last veil, there was something deeply pragmatic in Kendrick which insisted that a salvaged life built upon a little self-deception was better than a shambles resting squarely on the truth. The fact that Conway was not looking at him just then made it easier for Kendrick to reply.

"I don't recall his saying anything specific, Roger."

Conway waved his hand. "I'll have to admit that was a pretty damn fool question. Sounds as though I was fishing for a compliment or something. Hell, I'm not worried about that. I don't have to be told that my own kid liked

me." He laughed. "Guess there wasn't any doubt about that, was there?"

Kendrick's face was impassive. "Did you have any doubt?"

"Good Lord, no." Conway lit a cigarette, and Kendrick saw that his hand was shaking.

"I just meant," Conway said, "well—I know Richards is only a young pup and I'm not going to waste any time over his opinions, but I wonder where he got the crazy idea that Tommy committed suicide?"

When Kendrick did not answer at once, Conway rushed on. "Of course, it *is* a possibility. Anyone could go out of his mind for an instant, I suppose, but you don't think it was anything like that, do you?"

"The school has no positive evidence, Roger."

Conway's laugh was a little forced. "I'm sure you haven't. I don't know why I even brought it up."

There was a silence. Kendrick waited. He was aware of the struggle going on inside of Roger Conway. Tommy's father was not far from the truth now, but he would not want Kendrick or anyone else to know that.

"Just the same," Conway went on as though there had been no break in the conversation, "I wish I had talked to him recently or had a letter."

Suddenly, Conway turned away and covered his face with his hands.

"My wife and now my son, Justin! I ask myself what's it all been for, what good can come of it now?"

Kendrick's voice was very gentle. "That's what you've got to think about and discover for yourself, Roger."

Conway's head had sunk lower and his big shoulders were shaking underneath the heavy coat. Kendrick picked up the thermos and walked quickly down the path and this time he did not come back.

20

THE BEAUTIFUL day had brought an unusually large number of parents and visitors to the campus. They strolled along the paths, talking to their sons, or gathered in family clusters in the lingering patches of sunlight on the lawns and in the bleachers. Some of the boys had retired to their rooms to study, but the majority were still out on the playing fields which rang with an assortment of exuberant cries and good-natured Sunday arguments.

Immediately upon his return Kendrick was tagged by a fat, officious man and his blond doll of a wife who wanted first of all to praise their son and secondly to enter him in Carver the following year. Kendrick met many delightful parents in the course of his work, but with this pair he had to listen patiently and endure until he could escape to his office where he jotted down a memo for the director of admissions. The telephone operator who took Mrs. Henry's place on Sunday poked her head through the door.

"There was an accident on the soccer field a little while ago, Mr. Kendrick, but they said it was only a sprained ankle."

"They" would be the infirmary, Kendrick knew. "Who was it?" he asked.

"Timothy Mahoney. And the top-floor toilet in Darrow overflowed."

"Did you call the plumber?"

"He's away for the weekend, but I got somebody from town."

"Good," Kendrick said. He smiled to himself. In some ways it was still a typical Sunday afternoon. As for Tim Mahoney, his curiosity would be hobbled for a week or two.

He had not yet had his lunch and it was after three o'clock when he got back to his apartment. Alan Richards was waiting outside the door. From his grim expression and agitated manner it was obvious to Kendrick that another crisis was impending. He wished that he might have been allowed to have his lunch first.

"Sorry to bother you at this time," Richards said stiffly.

He was probably still angry about last night, Kendrick reasoned, and today he must have thought a great injustice had been done which had further angered and dismayed him. He had the appearance now of a man about to throw himself upon a funeral pyre.

"Come in, Alan," Kendrick said, trying to keep the weariness out of his voice. "Please sit down. I'll just make myself a sandwich and be right with you."

"Oh, haven't you had lunch yet?" Richards said absently. He sat down on the couch, clasped his hands together, and stared at the carpet.

Kendrick watched him from the kitchenette. Just as Roger Conway was at the crossroads now, so Alan Richards was approaching a critical moment. Like Conway, Richards could be salvaged through an inner understanding of himself and his fellow men, but here again Kendrick could only indicate the way. Each man had to find the road for himself.

"I've got a couple of things to say," Alan announced bluntly when Kendrick came in with a sandwich and a glass of milk.

Kendrick pulled up a chair. "All right," he said, "go ahead."

"First, aren't you shocked about Hugh?"

"By his resignation?"

"Yes."

"Not shocked, Alan, because I think you could expect something like that from him under the circumstances."

"But it was absolutely unnecessary."

"Not in his mind."

"He wouldn't have done it if Conway hadn't blamed the whole thing on him."

"I think," Kendrick said, "in fact, I'm sure that Hugh has standards of his own which have nothing to do with Mr. Conway's judgments."

"Well, are we just going to sit here and let him go after all these years?"

"No," Kendrick said.

Alan's head snapped up. "What are we going to do?"

"Nothing at the moment."

"But at this rate he'll be gone by tomorrow?"

"I wouldn't be too sure of that."

"You're not really going to do anything about this, are you?" Alan said in a hopeless voice. "I can see that now. Well, I've had enough of your methods." He pulled a sheet of paper from his pocket.

"What's that?" Kendrick said.

"My resignation."

Kendrick looked at him for a moment in silence. Then he said, "What's the matter, Alan?"

Alan laughed harshly. "What's the matter?" he echoed, looking at Kendrick as though he were unbelievably dense.

"It's very simple. I don't want to work in a place that cares more for a building than a human being."

"Are you referring to Tommy Con—?"

"I'm referring to him and to Hugh Follensbee and to anybody else who gets pushed around in the interests of power and money."

"And you think it would help anybody for you to resign?"

"Maybe not, but it will make me feel better."

"I see," Kendrick said. "And what do you think would help?"

Alan did not expect the question. "Well—I think we ought to make it clear to everyone that Tommy Conway's death was very likely a deliberate suicide. The way it looks now, the school is taking the rap."

"You mean we should publish some sort of official statement in the newspapers *after* the death has already been listed as an accident?"

"Yes."

"But what good would that do? Is it going to help the school's reputation?"

"Never mind that. Can't we think of people ahead of buildings once in a while?"

"We have to think of both."

"Then what about Hugh? Doesn't he deserve some backing from the school, some official support?"

"Do you think any sort of newspaper article could make it easier for him now?"

"Yes."

Kendrick fitted a cigarette into the amber holder. "You're wrong, Alan. That isn't what Hugh needs. He must find a way to forgive himself before he can carry on here."

"But supposing he can't find a way to forgive himself? Do we just say 'that's too bad' to a man who's been working here for over forty years?"

"No, Alan, we don't say that. There are times and situations when we can't say anything or do anything."

Alan waved his hand. "I've heard that before, but I don't believe it. I believe there are always answers if one cares enough and is determined to find them. Why can't we all sign a protest, for example, and send it to the headmaster?"

"You mean the whole faculty?"

"Yes."

Kendrick was so appalled at the naïveté of this proposal that his first impulse was to laugh, his second to scorn. He gave in to neither.

"You can't get twenty-five teachers to sign anything like that, Alan," he said gently. "As a matter of fact, I don't think you could get twenty-five teachers to sign anything."

Richards saw no humor in this remark. "I knew you wouldn't sign it," he said bitterly. "You don't want to get at the truth. You have your eye on that new building and to hell with everything and everybody else!"

"Let us say," Kendrick continued calmly, ignoring this outburst, "that I want the truth to be inwardly perceived by the people involved."

"Well anyway, I told Conway," Alan rushed on, "told him exactly what I thought and straight to his face early this morning." He stopped and looked at Kendrick as though expecting a violent reaction.

Kendrick stood up. "Did it make any difference?" he said calmly.

Apparently unaware of Richards' anger and confusion, he returned the dishes to the kitchen. Outside the sky was overcast. The parents had all gone home now, and dusk was falling. There were dark clouds over the mountains and soon the soft white flakes would come mushing down and these Indian summer days would flash from time to time upon the long memory of winter.

Back in the living room Kendrick turned on the table lamps and then struck a match to the kindling in the fireplace. He saw that Richards had crumpled the sheet of paper into a wad which he was pressing furiously between his palms. His jaw muscles had hardened and there were almost tears in his eyes.

"All right," he said, in a low, trembling voice, "maybe it didn't make any difference. Maybe nothing makes any difference. Maybe this so-called unselfish profession is just a cover up for another lie and another deal. I don't know, but I'm getting out of it as soon as possible!" He stood up and rushed toward the door.

"Wait a minute, Alan!" Kendrick's voice cut sharply.

Richards halted and looked back.

"You might like to see this before you go," Kendrick said. He tossed the diary onto the couch.

For a long moment Richards simply stared at the green leather cover with its gold clasp. Then, giving Kendrick a look of disbelief, he sat down and began to read the neatly written pages.

Kendrick watched him closely, his green eyes cool and thoughtful behind the thin spirals of smoke from his cigarette. Presently he rose and began to sprinkle fish food into the tanks from a small, round tin, noting with satisfaction the swirl of interest beneath his hand. When he heard Richards close the diary, he turned, seeing in the younger man's face the stunning impact of the truth.

"He killed himself," Alan said in a leaden tone.

"Yes."

"There's no doubt about it."

"Not now," Kendrick said. He came over and stood by the couch.

"How long have you had this?"

"Since early this morning."

"Where did you get it?"

"Boucher brought it to me."

"Boucher? But I asked him—"

"I don't want any mention made of this to Boucher, Alan. This is entirely between ourselves."

"You mean you had this all the time and didn't bring it up at the meeting?"

"That's right."

"Hasn't the headmaster seen it?"

"No."

"Or Conway?"

"No."

"But—"

"No one else has seen it," Kendrick said, "and no one will." With a quick motion he seized the diary and tossed it into the fire.

"Why, you—!" Alan gasped and leaped to his feet. "That's evidence. You've destroyed the evidence!"

"No one is on trial here," Kendrick said evenly.

For a moment he thought that Richards might strike him, but as the younger man stared at the curling black shreds of the diary, his fists slowly unclenched. All at once he slumped down on the couch, looking up at Kendrick with dazed, still angry eyes.

"What did you do that for?"

Kendrick drew on his cigarette and again he was watching Richards intently. "We don't need the diary any more."

"Why did you show it to me?"

"I thought it would help you to understand the situation."

"I don't get it."

"I know you don't."

"As a matter of fact," Alan said, "I don't get you at all, Justin, or what you are trying to do, or whose side you're on."

Kendrick smiled faintly. "I'm on your side."

"My side?"

"Yes."

"The devil you are."

"But I am."

"How am I supposed to know that? You've handled everything connected with this affair exactly the opposite to the way I would have. You must have expected opposite results."

Kendrick crushed out his cigarette. "No, I didn't. It isn't over yet. Right now is the crucial time. Everything is going to depend on what's happening right now."

"I can't see that anything is happening."

"It's not on the surface, Alan."

"Okay," Alan said, "I'm going to put it right on the line. What about that new building? Hasn't that really been your major concern all along?"

Kendrick smiled again. "A lot of people have thought so. They're a long way from the truth. On the other hand, I don't want to destroy our chances of getting it. Only a fool or a madman cuts his own throat."

"I still don't think you had any right to destroy that diary."

"No right in your sense of the word, perhaps, but I am perfectly certain it was the sensible thing to do when everything is considered."

"To hide the truth?"

"Yes, in this particular case. But that certainly doesn't mean I want it to remain hidden."

"I don't follow you."

"Look at it this way," Kendrick said. "If Roger Conway had seen that diary, it would have left him a shattered man. I doubt if he could have taken what was in there. At the same time, he is coming slowly from within to the truth about himself. In destroying the diary we permit him to keep one illusion: we let him think that we and the rest of the world don't know what a dreadful failure he was as a father. Thus, having some protection for himself, he can pick up the pieces and try to go on again."

"But he'll just put on another mask of self-deception!"

"No," Kendrick said quickly. "He was deceiving himself before. I think he really believed he was being a good father to Tommy. He can no longer deceive himself, but for a while it will be necessary for him to deceive others. Can't you see why?"

Alan stared into the fire for a moment. "Yes, I suppose I can see that much of it at least. But weren't you being rather presumptuous to take matters into your own hands this way?"

"I had to be."

Richards was clearly not convinced. In the warmth of the fire Kendrick wanted more than ever to rest, but he could not let go yet.

"Let me try to clarify this," he said. "From the moment I heard of Tommy's death yesterday morning I had to make a number of firm decisions, hoping to God they would be the right ones but knowing that no one can be sure at such times. You think I should have hit Conway with the truth in that diary, but hitting people with the blunt truth, Alan, when they are too blind, or too ill-equipped to see it, is not the answer and teaches nothing. You know that. You know that you can't *tell* your students the hardest things they have to learn, or at least you don't if you are any kind of a teacher. You have to resist the temptation to take the short cut and instead go the long way around, leading your boys to as much of the truth as can be determined, opening vistas for them, indicating routes for the journey but never simply throwing the answer in their faces even though it is such an old, familiar answer to you. That's all I've been trying to do with Conway, but he's had a long road to travel."

Alan was leaning forward in his chair and there was a new eagerness in his face. "I like that," he said. "You're right about not telling the boys the answers. But there's another side. In trying to help some people, haven't you been unfair to others, like Hugh Follensbee, for instance?"

"In what way?"

"He might not have resigned if he had known about that diary."

Kendrick shook his head. "No, I don't agree with you there. Hugh, as I told you, is struggling with something quite apart from the causes of Tommy's death."

"How about the headmaster? Should you keep information from him?"

Kendrick did not reply at once. He wore a quizzical expression as he turned the cat's-eye ring slowly, and for the first time Alan noticed how tired he looked.

"I can't answer that," Kendrick said quietly. "It was another of those decisions I had to make. I only know that I've done what I thought was best for the school. There's nothing more to say."

Alan stood up. For a moment he stared at the crumpled wad of paper in his hand. Then he walked over and tossed it into the fire. "I'd better get back to work," he said.

Kendrick got to his feet with a feeling of immeasurable relief. He saw that Richards had his hands in his pockets and was kicking absently at the edge of the carpet, very much as an embarrassed boy would have done.

"I'm glad we talked, Justin," he said. "I was ready to toss in the sponge a little while ago."

"I hope you've changed your mind," Kendrick said.

"Yes, but it's not all clear to me yet," Alan continued earnestly. "I mean, I'm not sure exactly what I want to do with my life. I'm not quite ready yet to commit myself fully to teaching, but I'm beginning to understand myself better."

Kendrick could not bring himself to look at the earnest young face a moment longer. It was part of youth, he knew, not to recognize the oldness of things and to regard each quite ordinary bit of revelation as being of supreme importance. Soul searching was necessary, but he had always believed that it should be personal and unobserved, like going to the bathroom.

Alan had reached the door. He turned. "Is there still a chance that Hugh may not have to resign?"

"Yes," Kendrick said. "There's a chance."

Alan nodded. "Well, see you later. I hope my house is still standing. Incidentally, Boucher has seemed a lot quieter since this morning. I hope it lasts."

"It probably won't," Kendrick said.

Alan grinned. "You know, Justin, someday I might even think you were right about all this."

Kendrick closed the door. It had been a long week end and his need for the refreshment of solitude was great. He walked slowly into his bedroom, thinking that for Richards, at least, it was going to turn out all right. But when he stretched out on the bed, his thoughts went back to the ravaged face of Roger Conway just before he had covered it with his hands there on the porch. He would be leaving in about an hour now, leaving Carver with the body of his son. Kendrick was gambling that something else would happen first.

21

FOLLENSBEE was sitting in his favorite chair by the fire, having a cup of tea. The tea was a Chinese blend of which he was extremely fond and which he drank only on special occasions of one sort or another. This time Emmy had added a touch of brandy without telling him about it. He had pretended not to notice.

It was typical of Emmy that she should undertake the reconstruction of their lives in a practical manner. Already she had made a list of alternatives for the next few months, although a decision would have to be postponed until he had seen how his resignation was going to affect their financial setup. Meanwhile, he had been amazed at Emmy's philosophical acceptance of the situation, and he was grateful for her calm support. At the same time he knew his wife too well to be fooled by her apparent cheerfulness. She had an ingrained sense of tradition which rejected any abrupt departure from a recognizable pattern, and he knew that she was secretly appalled by what had happened to them. For years she had looked forward to his retirement with full honors as being the only fitting climax to his teaching career. His going this way would be very painful for her and counter to all her expectations.

He leaned back against the worn leather of the chair, an old Morris which had been abandoned years ago by one of the boys and which had served him faithfully ever since. It was getting dark outside. The dusk came so quickly these days. He closed his eyes, hearing Emmy fussing around in the kitchen, thinking to himself that it was only thirty hours since he had closed his eyes out there in the sunshine and Tommy Conway had climbed the parapet. It was the brandy that was making him drowsy now, that and the fire which sang as something simmered at the core of the hard wood, the good wood from the tall trees which had stood against the frosts and the winds of so many autumns.

He liked the names of autumn: Baldwin, McIntosh; and the colors: russet, vermilion; and the sounds: rustling leaves driven by the wind, the raucous caw-cawing of the crows in the treetops, the cry of the gulls by the sea. Springtime was for youth and the lusts of the body, the thrusting, searching, yearning of hands and lips and breasts and thighs in the darkness beneath an eternal cheesecake moon. In summer cicadas drummed through drowsy hours, morning skies were halcyon and there was a wonderful vigor in all things. But in the autumn the heart knew that there was an end to lusts and vigor. It was this very knowledge of its own mortality that made the autumn far more precious than an everlasting summer. If a man were lucky, he might have his full share of the days of living in the springtime and the summer and so come to the autumn with his mind and spirit honed to their keenest limits. Then he could begin to know God. God was man's only worthwhile preoccupation; there was no other subject of any importance.

Follensbee had told this to one of his older classes re-

cently, and they had been shocked by his lack of sophisti-
cation. An older man should have had more sense. Follensbee smiled at the memory of their incredulous faces. They
were a conservative lot, this present generation, with a de-
plorable respect for conformity. Maybe it was because they
lacked the humor to be amused by their own sheeplike wor-
ship of security, but then this generation did not have the
bedrock under them, the deep-down certainties which had
made other generations want to laugh and take a chance.

"Hugh?"

Follensbee opened his eyes. Emmy was standing beside
his chair. He hadn't even heard her come in.

"I didn't know you were asleep, dear."

"I wasn't really," Follensbee said. "Just dozing and thinking."

"I've been thinking, too," Emmy said. "Couldn't we get
the trailer out right away and just keep going until we find
some place we like?"

"Yes, I suppose so, but I would much rather start out in
the summertime."

"So would I," Emmy said. "Oh, well." She touched his
arm. "Are you going to class tomorrow morning?"

"I'm not planning to. Best to make the break quickly."

Emmy looked away. "I know you had to do this, Hugh. I
know your conscience and your integrity forced it on you,
but sometimes I wish you didn't have so many good quali-
ties." She smiled. "No, I don't really, dear."

Follensbee reached out and patted her arm. He didn't
quite trust himself to speak just then. A moment later they
both heard the knock on the door.

"Damn," Follensbee muttered.

"I'll see to it," Emmy said. "You're not going to talk to
the boys tonight."

But the voice in the hall was not youthful. It was deep and rather gruff and it was saying, "I'm Roger Conway, Mrs. Follensbee."

Follensbee got up from his chair with a feeling of disbelief, and he saw his own astonishment mirrored in Emmy's face when she returned with their visitor.

"I apologize for coming in on you this way," Conway said. "I have an hour before my train and I, uh—"

"Won't you have a cup of tea?" Emmy said.

Conway's face relaxed a little. "I would like one very much, thank you."

"I'll have another cup," Follensbee said. "Just tea," he added.

Conway sat down, and it seemed to Follensbee that he had never seen a man appear so tired and completely washed out. The big, muscular frame had a spent look, but it also had a dignity that had been missing this morning.

"Good fire you have there," Conway said.

"Yes, it draws well."

"You must have good dry wood."

"That's cherry," Follensbee said. "Brought it down from my place in New Hampshire."

"New Hampshire, eh?"

"Yes."

"Didn't know you had a place up there."

"Only a small place."

"That's beautiful country up there."

"Yes," Follensbee said.

"Must be freezing up there tonight."

"I guess it is," Follensbee said.

There was an awkward silence. Conway, obviously ill at ease, rubbed his chin and stared into the fire. When Emmy came back with the tea tray, he started to get up. "Here, let me help you with that."

"You stay right where you are," Emmy said firmly but with a smile that had put many a boy at ease. She put the tray on a small table from which Follensbee had hastily swept some of his books and papers.

"How do you like your tea, Mr. Conway?"

"Plain with a little sugar, thanks."

Emmy followed instructions and then refilled her husband's cup. "Just tea," she said, her eyes twinkling.

When she passed around some cookies a moment later, Follensbee observed how quickly Conway's hand shot out toward the plate. Emmy saw it, too, and she fixed him with a practiced eye.

"Mr. Conway," she said in the same tone of disapproval that she might have used with one of the boys, "have you had any lunch?"

Conway looked absurdly guilty. "No, ma'am."

"I'll make you a sandwich."

"Please. I—"

"You've got to have something to eat," Emmy said severely. "What would you like?"

Conway gave Follensbee a helpless look. Then a smile relaxed the corners of his mouth. "Do you have any peanut butter?"

Emmy laughed. "Of course we do. Every house on the campus is stuffed with it."

"That would be fine," Conway said. He looked over at Follensbee again and his smile widened. "I remember the peanut butter. The masters' wives always had some on hand. We got a lot of handouts."

"I know," Follensbee said dryly. "When the boys come over here for help in the evenings, they always look first to see if Mrs. Follensbee is in the kitchen. Between their stomachs and their heads, there's no doubt as to which is in command."

Emmy came back with an enormous sandwich and from somewhere a chicken leg had materialized along with a large helping of potato salad.

Conway's eyes widened. "Good Lord, that looks good!"

Emmy perched on the arm of Follensbee's chair. "I remember you now," she said, looking at Conway. "You were thirty-eight."

Conway lowered the chicken leg. "Thirty-eight?" he said with a puzzled frown.

"Yes. That was the number on your football jersey. Remember, Hugh?"

"Yes," Follensbee said.

"I couldn't recognize you with your helmet on," Emmy continued. "When you made all those touchdowns, you were just number thirty-eight to me. And then I'd say to myself, 'That must be Roger Conway.'"

Conway's face had been slowly filling with delighted amazement. "You're right about that number, Mrs. Follensbee. I'd forgotten that. Never thought you'd remember a little thing like that."

"We remember lots of things," Emmy said. She stood up. "It's nice to have seen you, Mr. Conway, without your helmet on."

Conway laughed. "Thank you again."

"Not at all," Emmy said. "But you shouldn't go without your regular meals. It's not good for you."

On her way out she gave Follensbee a questioning look. He made a gesture with his eyebrows to indicate that he was equally in the dark as to the real purpose of Conway's visit. He finished his tea and then waited patiently until Conway put aside the empty plate.

"That was nice of your wife. I feel much better," Conway said. He leaned back and lit a cigarette. "As a matter of fact, I remember both of you, although to be honest I didn't really know you at all." He snapped his fingers as though his memory had suddenly yielded up a clear-cut fact. "We called you 'Stinger.' "

"They still do," Follensbee said.

"We had names for all the masters," Conway continued, looking back through the tobacco smoke, "except Justin Kendrick. I don't think we could ever agree on one for him. We couldn't seem to type him. He was always different and yet the same, like a chameleon. You'd think to look at him that he was just a big, pudgy—well, you wouldn't think he had much on the ball, but by God he was always a jump ahead of us, and one night I remember he made us feel about two feet high."

Conway broke off and chuckled softly. "Justin was housemaster of Darrow my year. I guess we were feeling pretty mean that night. We took a wastebasket and went around collecting wads of chewing gum and apple cores and anything messy we could find. We even dumped all the wood shavings from a pencil sharpener in there. Then we made a racket, and when he started upstairs, somebody let him have it. Dumped the whole basket right square on his head.

"He came into our room first. Just came in and asked if he might sit down for a minute. The stuff was all over his head, matted in his hair and spilling down his face and onto his shoulders. He never said a word about it. Not a word! Simply talked to us about some routine matter in a perfectly normal voice. Sat there for maybe ten minutes with that stuff all over him while we got redder and redder. Finally when we could scarcely stand it any longer, he got up to go. He stopped at the door, looked slowly around, and complimented us on the neatness of our room. That was the crowning touch. We would gladly have sunk through the floor. We couldn't even look at each other when he left. That night he went through the same procedure in each of the rooms." Conway shook his head. "I'll never forget that. He had the best house on the campus for the rest of the year."

Follensbee smiled. "Yes, that would be Justin's way of handling a thing like that."

Conway turned to crush out his cigarette in the ash tray on the table beside him. Abruptly his hand paused and he bent to look closely at the silver-framed picture of a young naval officer.

"Your son, Mr. Follensbee?"

"Yes."

"Mind telling me what happened?"

"There isn't much to tell. He was assistant communications officer on a cruiser in the Pacific. His first ship. They were torpedoed one night in the Coral Sea. Almost everyone was lost—including Pete."

Conway sat back grimly. His big hands twisted together in his lap and suddenly his voice was much too loud.

"Mr. Follensbee, I don't know how to put this, but I'm asking you to withdraw your resignation."

A log broke in the fireplace and a shower of sparks fluttered down on the hearth, but Follensbee took no notice of them. He was staring blankly at Conway. "I, uh—don't understand," he said.

"Don't blame you," Conway said with a rueful smile. "You see, I was pretty teed off at the school this morning. Guess I threw my weight around and I'm sorry about that now. This afternoon I had a long talk with Justin. He's still several jumps ahead of me." Conway looked down at his hands, opening and closing his fingers slowly. "I honestly don't believe it was your fault, Mr. Follensbee."

"It was my job to be up there with the boys," Follensbee said stubbornly.

"Sure it was. You made a mistake and you've got to live with it. I've made a few mistakes myself, Mr. Follensbee.

To tell you the truth, you'd be doing me a favor to keep on here."

Follensbee was about to ask why when he saw all at once exactly what Conway meant. He knows, Follensbee thought, what really happened to his son yesterday morning. He knows within himself but he is not yet strong enough to face the harsh reality of it openly, any more than I could face that telegram from the navy. If I keep on teaching here, I give him back a little of his self-esteem because he can feel with some justification that he is being magnanimous. I will always be somewhat beholden to him as a consequence, but perhaps that is really my punishment.

"I told Pettengill I'd ask you," Conway said.

"You saw him?"

"No. I had to make arrangements with a garage downtown to return the car I rented. I phoned him from down there and apologized for some of the things I said at the meeting this morning. I even told him I wanted to go ahead with the plans for the new dormitory. I'll give it in Tommy's memory. I think he would like that."

Follensbee had a vivid picture of an expensive camera dangling unheeded and unwanted from its pigskin strap as a desperate little boy walked alone for the last time. It was on the tip of his tongue to take Roger Conway a little further along toward the full truth about himself and his son, but he resisted the impulse.

Conway was looking at his watch. In some subtle way he had changed in the past few moments so that he was no longer the embarrassed, grown-up boy who had been sitting there awkwardly a few minutes ago. He was once again the successful man in whose voice there was a trace of condescension when he said, "Well, Mr. Follensbee, will you stay?"

Follensbee pulled himself out of the Morris. Very deliberately he took a broom and brushed a few stray embers back into the fire where they belonged.

"I guess it's best that I do," he said. Then, with more effort than he had thought it would take, he added, "Thank you very much."

"That's all right," Conway said. His handshake was vigorous. "I'll be back in the spring to have a look at things."

Follensbee followed him to the door. Conway got into his coat and then hesitated, twisting his hat brim, suddenly unsure of himself again.

"I guess I had to learn the hard way, Mr. Follensbee. Good intentions aren't enough, are they?"

"I'm afraid not," Follensbee said.

A few minutes later after Conway had gone, Emmy came into the room and found her husband standing with his hands clasped behind his back, staring into the fire.

"I heard him, dear," she said softly, "and I know how hard it was for you to let him think that he could give it all back to you that way. But I'm so happy you did."

"He's facing it all alone," Follensbee said. "At least I don't have to do that." He put his arm around his wife and then suddenly he began to chuckle.

"I was just thinking," he said, "how unhappy those little boys of mine are going to be when I show up for class tomorrow."

22

Coffee?"

Alan looked up from the tests he was correcting. "Thanks." He smiled. "I really need it tonight."

Nancy put the tray on the edge of the cluttered desk. The minute she had come into the study she had seen the mound of papers. There were no office hours in her husband's job. All over the campus now there would be other patient faces peering at the papers under the long night lamps.

"How are you doing?" she asked.

"Not bad. Digging my way through."

"Boys all in bed?"

"Yes."

"The house seems quieter than usual."

Nancy poured a cup for each of them. "You know," she said, "I've been trying to read but I keep thinking of Mr. Conway."

"I do, too," Alan said.

"I hope he won't always be alone. I hope there'll be something left for him."

"I know," Alan said. "I guess there will be. I never

thought I would feel sorry for that man, but I do." He looked up at her. "Nancy, I've thought about a lot of things tonight. A little while ago I tore up that offer from Hall & Crandon."

Nancy smiled. "I'm glad."

"There go mink coats, honey, Cadillacs, penthouse parties—"

"And Lord knows how many hang-overs," Nancy said.

Alan got up quickly and took her into his arms. His hands moved lovingly across her shoulders and down her back. "It sounds corny," he said, "but I love you very much."

"It doesn't sound corny to me," Nancy said.

They drew apart slowly. Alan said, "I came to another conclusion tonight. I think Justin Kendrick had us all figured—me, Follensbee, Conway, even the headmaster. Justin knew all the time how each of us was going to take this thing."

Nancy smiled and said nothing.

"Justin took a chance that Conway would go to Hugh in the end," Alan continued. "He took a lot of chances, he made deals, he shaded the truth—all the things I would have said were wrong yesterday. I guess I need a new set of bearings."

Nancy straightened his tie. "You're getting them, Mr. Richards."

They both heard it a moment after that, a faint, hesitant knock on the door that led into the corridor.

"That must be one of the boys," Nancy said. "You're getting popular in your old age. I'm going to check on Bill. The last time I looked in, he was snoring."

"Babies don't snore, Nancy."

"Ours does," Nancy said. She started for the living room and then turned impulsively and came back to Alan. With an infinitely feminine gesture she put her arms around his neck and reached up to kiss him. "Just for the record, darling," she said softly, "I love you, too."

The knock sounded faintly again. When Nancy had gone, Alan walked over and turned the knob. A moment later he found himself looking down into the anxious face of Larry Connors.

"Sorry to bother you, sir, but Mr. Rogers said I could have late lights to talk to you."

Out of all the masters, Alan was thinking, this boy had chosen to confide in him. There was absolutely no reason for it that he could see. Larry was beginning to inch toward the hall.

"Maybe some other time, sir?"

"No," Alan said. "This is a good time. Come in, Larry."

Before he sat down at his desk, Alan glanced out the window. Dark clouds veiled the moon, and out there in the night the buildings of Carver were anchored like a friendly fleet. It came to him now with more certainty than ever that these buildings were his home and the men who lived in them were his neighbors—men as far apart in their personal lives as Rogers and Tingue, Kendrick and Follensbee. They had their differences but they worked together.

"Sit down, Larry," he said.

"This isn't anything to do with school, sir."

Alan smiled. It was good to know at last where he belonged and who really needed his help at Carver. The job sometimes was not so much to fill the heads of these boys as to empty their hearts.

"I don't care what it's about, Larry," he said gently, seeing some of the tenseness fading already from the boy's face. "Just tell me what's on your mind."

The clouds had drifted off the moon, and now the shadowy outlines of the maple tree beneath Tommy Conway's window were very distinct and very beautiful.